"You're saying goodbye," Bai

Vigdis inclined her head.

chance that I will become dissoc.

that I can no longer function in my computer or human capacity, ever."

"I won't allow it," cried Bailey. She grabbed Vigdis by the shoulders and shook her. Vigdis did not resist. "You can't do this. I order you not to, I *order* you—"

Gently Vigdis disengaged from her. "There is no other way," she said softly. "If I do not do this, we may all die, and hopefully there will be enough of the human left in me to meet you on the Far Shore."

"H-how long will it take?" Bailey sobbed.

"I think...if I do not have a weapon by this time tomorrow...I won't make it back. If I do not return to my port captain's chair by then... Bailey, if you cannot save Idun Mia..."

"We will die together. Build a bonfire on that beach, so we know where to find you."

Vigdis wiped her face; it failed to dry her tears. "I will. Bailey Belvedere..."

"And I you, Vigdis."

Vigdis vanished.

The Future Adventures of
Bailey Belvedere

Tyree Campbell

Bailey Belvedere
by Tyree Campbell

Story copyright owned by Tyree Campbell
Cover illustration "Bailey" by Richard E. Schell
Cover design by Laura Givens

First Printing, August 2024

Hiraeth Publishing
P.O. Box 1248
Tularosa, NM 88352
e-mail: hiraethsubs@yahoo.com

Visit www.hiraethsffh.com for online science fiction, fantasy, horror, scifaiku, and more. Stop by our online bookstore for novels, magazines, anthologies, and collections. **Support the small, independent press...and your First Amendment rights.**

Gallium Girl
Heir Apparent
Indigo
Iuliae: Past Tense
The Quinx Effect
Starwinders: Nohana's Heart
Starwinders: Nohana's Triangles
Thuvia, Maid of Earth
A Wolf to Guard the Door
The Woman from the Institute

Superheroine Novellas:
Bombay Sapphire 1 **
Bombay Sapphire 2 **
Bombay Sapphire 3 **
Bombay Sapphire 4 **
Bombay Sapphire 5
Oliva Sudden 1
Peridot 1
Peridot 2
Peridot 3
Peridot 4
Voyeuse 1
Voyeuse 2
Voyeuse 3

Collections:
AbracaDrabble
Drink Before the War
A Nice Girl Like You
(published by Khimairal, Inc)
Quantum Women *

Novellas:
Becoming Jade
Cloudburst
Future Tense
The Girl on the Dump
The Martian Women
Sabit the Sumerian
Sarrow

Poetry Collections
A Danger to Self and Others

SF for Younger Readers
Pyra and the Tektites 1
Pyra (graphic novel) 1
Pyra and the Tektites 2
Pyra (graphic novel) 2
Pyra and the Tektites 3
Pyra and the Tektites 4
Pyra and the Tektites 5
Pyra and the Tektites 6

* published by Nomadic Delirium Press

** published by Pro Se Press

All titles are available from the Shop at
www.hiraethsffh.com

For Lorraine Pinelli Brown and Neil Brown
For a storyteller there's nothing like being read,
And they read me.

001: Shocks to the System

Life, with a capital L, began for Bailey Belvedere with a burst of Purple.

It was a welcome rebirth for a woman a year on the far side of thirty, yet fraught with dangers. Although she did not realize it at the start, she was more than ready for Life. The old life had reached its nadir, filled with pain, horror, danger, disease, and not a lot to eat. Mostly there had been danger, for very bad people now lurked about, some of them former citizens who should have been on her side. An Intelligence Officer of the Army of the former United States of America, she had hesitated at first to open fire on any of them. Her ammunition was plentiful enough, but finite, and when it was gone she would have to resort to hand-to-hand combat, not a good system when one was outnumbered ten or fifty or more to one. Better to wait in dense shrubbery or behind great boulders while they passed.

And who were they? She knew uniforms. Those she saw belonged to, among others, Chinese, North Koreans, Iranians, Canadians, Russians, Venezuelans, and Nicaraguans. The question of how they had come to be here diminished in importance with the passage of time. They were here. And they had come to kill, loot, destroy, rape, and pillage. Not always in that order. Vultures, she had thought, plucking at the carcass of a great nation destroyed from within by greed, division, corruption, and mismanagement, and by voters who kept electing the same folks and expecting different results. Sometimes, lying awake at night, she found herself weeping for no apparent reason.

What did those bastards in Washington DO to us?

It was the lament of the impotent, whose lives lay outside the arc of history and justice, whichever way they bent. The French, if they still existed, had a phrase for it: *Cela ne fait rien.* I can do nothing about it.

Except, Bailey had thought on too many occasions, survive.

11

Two years or so of hiding, fleeing, and occasionally opening fire had brought her and her jeep—a sturdy vehicle covered in camouflage netting and fed whenever she found a few drops of gasoline—to a surprisingly tranquil forested valley in the middle of what she estimated was semi-tropical Nebraska. It was just as well that she reached this location when she did: of the two five-gallon gasoline cans strapped to the rear of the jeep, one was almost full, the other to a third. She suspected there would be no more.

So it was that Bailey sought out refuge and relaxation on the slope of a sunlit hillock alongside a cool stream fed by a waterfall some hundred meters behind her. It was too peaceful here, too idyllic to be dangerous— or so she thought. No sooner had she begun a calming meditative technique and chant—*gati gati paragati parasamgati bodhi svaha*—than she heard an impact that shattered trees deep in the surrounding forest, and felt more or less simultaneously seismic vibrations that shook the hillock.

As a byproduct, the impact gained her rapt attention. She sat up, looked. A brilliant purple light had already begun to fade. She could just make out a couple of trees bent toward her. Even as she watched, one of them collapsed with a crushing sound that reached her ears second later. Roughly a thousand feet away it was, then. A stroll in the park.

Bailey got up, went, porting the M16 rifle with a thirty-round banana clip; an M1911A1 .45 semi-automatic pistol in the holster dangling over her right hip from her web belt with seven in the mag and one in the pipe; and the bayonet, now sheathed, that she favored during hand-to-hand. Over her left hip, water sloshed around in a canteen. She was wearing a jungle camouflage uniform that fit loosely enough to mask her slender configuration as a woman, black jungle combat boots with canvas sides to allow water to escape, and a cammie baseball cap—she'd lost the helmet and liner last year in a skirmish. The cap held her short and shaggy black hair in place. On the cap was a subdued insignia of rank that on

12

a Class A uniform would have been gold, for her rank was Major. It represented also, very likely, her unappointed rank as Chairwoman of the Joint Chiefs of Staff, for after the collapse and the invasions, very few soldiers were left alive, with most of those cowering fearfully in caves and bombed-out buildings.

Bailey Belvedere knew fear and caution as well, but she had refused to withdraw from the world, and instead had sought a place where she might be safe.

Until the purple.

Bailey peered between trees still standing. The purple light still hung a few feet above the ground like a shroud that had lost its way. It was not moving, as if something on the ground were holding it in place. With trees collapsed around the area, perhaps they hid it from view. But what, what?

A step closer, the M16 aimed and ready now. She did not want to shoot anything. But she also did not want to be shot at. Gray eyes wary, she watched, studied. Beyond the shroud—or maybe it was faint purple mist— rested what she could only call an object. It was the size and shape of a city bus, but rounded on both ends. Bailey did not doubt that it was the object that had crashed. It must have flown, but how, how? A bus in the middle of the Nebraska tropical forest seemed unlikely. A violet haze hung around it that faded out even as she watched, and revealed that the "bus" was in fact untarnished silver in color, and apparently from her angle of view had neither windows nor doors.

The purple mist before the bus also began to fade, leaving behind a longish lump in the shadows on the ground, tinted here and there by a residual purple and violet. Recognition took Bailey a moment, because of course it was impossible. She stepped closer, tense, her knuckles white around the stock of the rifle, until it was now impossible to deny identification. The lump was a body.

Compassion flooded Bailey. Forgotten for the moment were all the dangers associated with finding a

13

body. Ignored were the possibilities that the body was booby-trapped, as others she had encountered had been, or that whoever had caused the body might still be watching, again infrequent but possible. It made no difference. She abandoned caution and drew up beside the body, dropping to one knee to examine it.

The skin was pale mauve, the shaggy head hair and pubic thatch deep purple. Eyes closed at the moment. Two arms, two legs, a humanish completement of sensory organs in the usual locations on a humanoid head. Decidedly male. Bailey was six-two, with hands large enough to palm a man's basketball—a sport at which she had once excelled. She spread her thumb and middle finger as far apart as they would go, and conducted a measurement; his length went half an inch beyond. A little tremor chilled her as an impure thought snuck past her defenses.

But soon enough she returned to the basics. Was he dead? If so, who or what had killed him? And was his color the result of a contagious disease?

He answered the first question by opening his eyes. The round irises were royal purple, like his hair, solid in color but each dotted with an oval black pupil that divided the iris horizontally. Startled, Bailey scooted back, her hand reaching for the rifle she'd laid at her side. While she did so, he sat up, right arm locked and braced behind him to hold him in place. His expression was impossible to read as he regarded her; possibly his skin color made this so, or perhaps it was the shadows of the surrounding trees.

"Who are you?" he asked.

Another shock, her mouth agape. "You speak English," she gasped.

"You hear English." He looked around. "Where am I?"

Nebraska, she started to say. But the enormous reality finally penetrated, and the question became much bigger. "Earth," she told him. "You're on Earth."

She sat back, thinking omigod!

14

"Where is Kayana?" he asked, again looking around. He called out the name.

From among the trees there came a woman obviously of the same DNA as the man, but with the remains of clothing still smoking. The smoke rose above her like a mist, and Bailey now understood the origins of that. The man's clothing had already burned off. So where were the blisters and burns?

The woman, evidently Kayana, gave her no time to reflect. "Stay away from him!" she shrieked, gesticulating wildly as the smoke consumed the last of her clothing. "Leave him alone!"

Bailey started a protest. "I wasn't touch—"

"Are you all right?" Kayana asked the man.

He looked up at her, and seemed to recognize her. A little nod satisfied her question.

"Now who are you?" demanded Kayana, of Bailey.

She introduced herself, including her rank. Fumbling for something else to say, she added, "Welcome to Earth."

"Earth," she spat, and kicked the man. "Vattar, I *told* you to replace that glork power transformer." Her tone left doubt as to whether "glork" was an epithet or an adjective.

"The replacement was defective."

"So we're stuck here?"

"Not so. I can adapt it." He stood up, and eyed Bailey. "They wear clothing here," he noted. "We'd better replace ours."

"Oh, right," Kayana said acidly. "Our skin color won't give us away."

In a starwink they were attired in camouflage clothing like Bailey's. She took a few more steps back, still holding the rifle but not aiming it yet. Poised for fight or flight, she did neither. About to speak, she spotted Vattar heading for her jeep.

"That's my vehicle," she called, running to him. "Leave it alone."

He ignored her. Following a quick examination of the exterior and the instrumentation, he opened the hood

15

and leaned it back against the windshield. Bailey tried to shove him away, but he was rooted in place, touching various attachments. Kayana joined them and wormed herself in between them.

"I have no designs on your husband," Bailey snapped.

"Husband!?"

"Tell him to leave my vehicle alone."

Vattar held up the alternator he had just removed by hand. "This," he cried excitedly. "Yes, this I can use."

Bailey reached for it. "But I *need* that to start—"

He snatched it away. "Not for much longer," he said. "Earth is finished. It's already too late for The Commission to save it. We're here by accident only."

"Husband," Kayana chuckled.

Bailey looked from one to the other. Anguish riddled her face. "I don't understand," she said. "I don't understand any of this."

"Vattar is not my husband," said Kayana. "He's my twin brother and my lover."

"I don't care—" Her face twisted for a moment. "Wait, he's *what*? Never mind. Put that alternator back."

Vattar shook his head. "No, this will get us out of here and back on our way," he said, and headed for the "bus."

Running after him, Bailey tackled him. "You can't have it!" But the words left no echo in her mind, for it blanked and blacked out.

Bailey knew sunlight again. Sprawled on her back on the ground, with her armaments and equipment still intact, she waited while her head cleared and the dizziness passed. She was unable to recall having been struck. She did recall the abduction of the jeep's alternator. That now galvanized her, and she sat up on the ground.

The "bus" was still there, but now she saw a vertically rectangular dark spot that surely was a doorway or a hatchway or whatever it was called on a spaceship. For spaceship it now had to be, unquestioningly. She gave herself another omigod moment, and rose unsteadily to

16

her feet with the assistance of a nearby sapling. Vision cleared. She meandered around trees standing and falling and drew within a few paces of the opening. The spaceship stood on low support pods, and only a short step was required for her to enter the opening. She peered closer. A ramp with a shallow upward slope led further inside. She keened her ears. No sounds emerged from within. Where were they, Vattar and Kayana?

Suddenly alert, she looked around. No one was in sight. Stiffened shoulders relaxed again. Alternator, she thought, and almost laughed. A spaceship probably equipped with faster-than-light travel capability, all sorts of galactic guidance paraphernalia, probably defensive force fields and even a far-superior weapons system, to say nothing of a properly stocked galley with—dared she hope?—fresh coffee, required the alternator of a road-weary military jeep in order to travel among the stars?

Right, then, thought Bailey.

Without the jeep, she had no viable travel options save the soles of her boots. She did have a few items she needed, and she dashed back to the jeep to retrieve them. The hatchway was still open when she returned with a stuffed duffel bag. No hesitation remained within her as she climbed aboard. From outside it was impossible to determine which direction was bridge and which was stern. Inside, she chose left, trying to recall whether that was port or starboard. Not that it mattered. But now she heard the sounds of minor repairs echoing down the hallway. Ahead, lights shone in what she assumed was the bridge. Faint voices trailed toward her as she approached. Already she had shouldered the M16; there seemed no point in threatening such beings as could melt blued steel rifle barrels with just a glance.

Shadows moved. She saw a great window that gave onto a view of the trees. As she drew closer, she saw that the window permitted a 180° view, though it had been invisible seen from outside. Below the window spread what could only be an instrumentation console, with two built-in monitors apparently for communication, and with a pair of legs on the deck protruding into the range of her vision.

Bailey Belvedere stepped onto the bridge of an alien spacecraft.

Immediately she was set upon by Kayana, who shoved her. "You cannot be here," she shouted. "Get off our ship."

Bailey stood her ground. "You have deprived me of transportation and of running away as a defensive measure," she snarled back. "Either return that alternator to me, or take me with you." She dropped her duffel bag. "Choose!"

Vattar, somewhat the worse for wear, emerged from under the console. "Done," he announced, obviously pleased with himself as his finger wiped a smudge on his cammie trousers. With the support of the console, he gained his feet. "What is she doing here?" he asked, diffidently.

For the first time since Bailey had encountered her, Kayana softened, just a little. No longer did she screech like a harridan. She turned to Vattar.

"She wishes to accompany us," she told him.

"Inadvisable," he snorted.

"I accept your evaluation that Earth is finished," Bailey said evenly. "I, however, am not finished. There is more that I can do. I do not know what it may be. But I am here and now. If we are able to leave, I suggest we do so."

"You do not give orders," said Kayana.

Bailey dismissed this with a desultory gesture. "This is my world, and your ship is on it. Yes, I give orders. After we lift off, the ship is yours again, and I shall be a subordinate. So push the Blast-Off button. Make it go. Before someone sees us."

"Kayana?" said Vattar, clearly establishing which of the two was in charge.

"You do not know what you are getting yourself into," Kayana told her. "If you are killed, it will be the airlock for your remains. If you get me killed, I shall be grievously annoyed."

18

Slowly Bailey nodded, and regained her duffel bag. "Then I shall do my utmost not to grievously annoy you. Do I get a room, and if so, where is it?"

Kayana's sigh of resignation made her a little more human.

002: Epiphany on the *Skygnat*

Bailey Belvedere quickly came to terms with terms. Port was left when facing the bow or front, and starboard right. The room was a stateroom. The ceiling was overhead, the floor the deck, the walls bulkheads. The stern was aft, all the way to the rear of the "bus." And the name of the "bus" was the *Skygnat*—at least, that was what the Universal Translator told her.

Sparse furnishings appointed her stateroom. Behind the door that slid open at her touch she found a simple padded berth that stood against the far bulkhead. Everything else had been designed by murphy—items to be pulled down from the bulkheads as needed. A bench, a table, a chair. The hygiene alcove was simple enough, and there was (she checked) hot water in the shower. A few bulkhead bins offered storage for clothing, cosmetics (of which she had none), and miscellany. The overall size of the stateroom was, by her careful pacing, nine by nine feet, not including the alcove. Cubbyhole it was, then, and not a stateroom. Clearly she was not intended to live in it, but to sleep when she was able. The rest of the time was meant to be spent elsewhere.

Fortunately, space contained a great deal of elsewhere. She wondered where *Skygnat* was headed. She went to the bridge to find out.

Kayana and Vattar scarcely acknowledged her with a glance, although they hardly seemed busy. Bailey was aboard, but not very welcome. Attention was grudgingly given. She cleared her throat, preparing to break the glacial ice.

"Where are we going?" she asked.

Kayana sniffed. "You'll find out."

"The Mercatto," Vattar told her. "It's a great market area on Rhodiona."

"Like she's heard of it," Kayana snorted. She pointed to a murphy bench still up against a bulkhead. "Pull that down and sit over there," she ordered.

Neither of them seemed particularly busy, but Bailey shrugged off the harsh tones. Not that there was much she could do about them if she tried. Under her watchful eye, the pair stood at the instrumentation console, staring through the Videx at the matte black of null-space. In other words, they stared at nothing at all. Perhaps that was important to them; but Bailey doubted it. Rather, because she was on the bridge, they had chosen to stop talking. Which meant they had been talking about her.

She got up, and approached Kayana. Before she had gotten a word out, Kayana shoved her to the deck. What followed was most unexpected.

The voice seemed to come from the bottom of a great cistern. "*You shall not harm her!*" The "her" echoed repeatedly throughout the *Skygnat*. As it faded, a brilliant white light appeared on the bridge. It encased a pale man with a great yellow mane who wielded a sword. He was attired in a robe as bright as the light; the robe had holes in back to accommodate his vestigial wings, symbolic and not functional.

As soon as the pale man appeared, Kayana and Vattar acquired weapons of their own, seemingly out of nowhere—she a sword, he a firearm of some kind that Bailey did not recognize. Now the pair were also enveloped in light, as if it were a defensive shield. But the shield availed them nothing. A simple, almost careless sweep of the pale man's sword disarmed Kayana and Vattar without so much as touching them, and diminished their envelope of light to a dull and dismal gray.

And all the while, Bailey Belvedere gaped on in wonder. Strangely she felt unafraid. The pale man, whoever and whatever he might be, had come to her defense. But why, why? And how?

Who?

Realization slammed Bailey. "Michael," she gasped, still seated on the murphy bench. "The Archangel."

He turned to her and smiled. "No. But Michael will suffice as a point of identification."

21

His voice lost its echo; he spoke as a human being. Doubtless she *heard* English.

"Who?" she began, but was unable to complete the question.

"He's from The Commission," Kayana said disgustedly. "The Enforcement Division."

Michael eyed her sternly, but addressed Bailey. "They were taking you to Mercatto to sell you to slavers," he said. "This is what they do, along with a multitude of other petty crimes."

"Petty!" yelled Bailey. "Slavery is *petty*?"

"It is and has been a common enough occurrence. The Commission tries not to look the other way, but the galaxy is huge, and events are lost now and then. This event, however," and here he cast a glance at Bailey, "was special, Bailey Belvedere, because you bring a fresh approach, a fresh way of thinking, for you are the first and likely will be the only Earthling to function in what you think of as outer space."

"I-I don't, don't understand..."

Vattar licked his lips nervously. "What are you going to do to us?"

"Whatever The Commission wants me to do," Michael snapped at him. "I think we can all agree on that, yes? Now, then. Kayana and Vattar, the innate powers of telekinesis of your species are hereby withdrawn. No longer will you be able to summon to yourselves whatever you need at a critical moment. Clothing, for example, or a defensive shield, or weaponry. You are relegated hereby to the physical, psychological, social, and emotional status of a human being, an Earthling. Furthermore, the one point two billion thalers you have amassed during your illicit careers are now in the account and under the name of Bailey Belvedere. She is also your finance officer now. You may request funds from her."

The knees of Kayana and Vattar buckled; they collapsed onto the deck.

For a moment Michael paused to consider. "Ah, yes, the *Skygnat*'s computer, Vigdis. How are you, my dear?"

"I am well, thank you...Michael? You are called Michael?"

The computer spoke in a mellifluous contralto, feminine and firm, with just a touch of huskiness that gave Bailey a shiver she did not understand.

"For identification, Vigdis. Bailey Belvedere is now the captain and owner of this ship. You are to accept orders and instructions only from her."

"And from you, Michael." Now Vigdis sounded enamored of the pale man.

"You can't do this to us," cried Kayana.

"It is already done, Kayana. Further, you and Vattar are to attend Bailey Belvedere, and to assist her in any way she orders. Failure to heed her—for this is your first, last, and only chance, Kayana and Vattar—will result in a test of your viability in empty space as you are shat naked from the airlock. Your criminal careers are now at an end. You will replace them by doing good."

He turned back to Vigdis. "My dear, please upload Program XKE1707."

"But I am not authorized to access the Seventeenth Level of Power, Michael."

"You are now."

"Yes, then. Yes, of course." A moment later: *"Oh, my. This is most intriguing. Michael...when should I activate this program?"*

"At the point when it is needed. You are to determine that." Once more he turned to Bailey. "Your stateroom is now stocked with clothing, necessities, and some weaponry," he told her. "That weaponry is not complicated; your military background has prepared you for their use. You may wish, however, to find a place to practice that use."

Bailey remained dazed by events. "But...but what am I to do?" she asked.

"Apply yourself, in whatever way you think best. The Commission will be watching as this experiment unfolds."

"Ex...experiment? I'm to be a lab rat?"

23

"You do have a choice," he said pleasantly. "You can be returned to Earth."

"So I'm a lab rat."

"But in good stead," he went on. "If you will please clear your mind by breathing and a quiet meditative chant, I shall upload into you some useful general information about the galaxy. You may address Vigdis with other questions. Begin breathing now."

Bailey was unaware of Michael's departure. Her head ached, the result of data input, but soon enough this began to pass. Kayana and Vattar were still sprawled on the deck. Bailey got up and moved to stand over them. She considered what she wanted to tell them, and was mildly astonished to discover that she had the words. Whether they came from within her, or were one result of her brief mental integration with the galaxy, she neither knew nor cared. She was the once and future soldier now, with others under her command.

"It is up to you two," she began, "whether we are on friendly terms, or are colleagues, or are merely participants. We have been given a loosely-defined mission. I do not know what influence I might have over this Michael, but if you will cooperate with me in fulfilling that mission, I shall do my very best to protect you from his disposition. Please go to your stateroom now. I shall advise you when we reach Rhodiona and Mercatto."

Bailey breathed a little sigh of relief after they headed aft down the gangway. The starboard captain's chair, previously occupied by Kayana, proved comfortable as she sank onto it. Comfortable, but unsatisfactory.

"Vigdis, how long before we reach Rhodiona?"

"On my mark, three hours seven point five five two eight—"

"Round up, Vigdis. I don't need the points."

"Thank you. I love saving syllables."

Almost four hours, she thought, and got up from the chair. "I'll be in my stateroom."

The stateroom was appointed as promised by Michael, but it could be checked out later. Bailey sat down on the berth, hands clasped between her knees as she gazed down at the deck between her boots. Into her emptied mind filtered random thoughts, all centered around her current plight. Or predicament. Uncertain of what she had gotten herself into as a lab rat, she struggled to winkle some sense of it all.

"What am I doing?" she murmured aloud, though there was no one save herself to hear. The lament grew stronger with each word, each uncertainty, each fear. "Oh, God, I don't know what I'm doing. What am I supposed to do?" She drew a huge breath and sighed it away. "Do good. What does that even mean? How will I know what to do? Where am I going? Rhodiona, what is that, a world? A market, a Mercatto? I'm supposed to find what there?" She dragged rigid fingers through her short black hair. She wanted to tear at it, tear at herself. So much had happened, in such a short time, it was all too much to take in. Cope? How, how? I wish I was...I wish I was... "Oh, God, I'm so alone!"

A knock at the stateroom door.

Alertness came back to her, an old friend that had kept her alive on post-apocalyptic Earth. Kayana, or Vattar? And what could either want now? But she was captain of the *Skygnat*. She had a duty.

Steeled for danger, she said, "Come in."

The woman who entered was no one Bailey had ever seen before. Tallish she was, perhaps Bailey's height, with a short shaggy cap of intensely purple hair that framed an oval face on which the dominant feature was a pair of large and luminous amethyst eyes. Her skin color was like that of Kayana, a pale mauve, but she was in no way Kayana. Her garment was a firm red enclosure of fabric from breasts to just at the hips, where the hem hung loose in a V shape, appropriate to concealing a delta, and was decent by perhaps a couple centimeters. A violet undergarment at those hips flashed in and out of view as she strode toward Bailey. Long red boots that were up to the thighs, of flexible material that looked metallic, almost like greaves, shod her feet.

Bailey found herself in awe of her. A question faded on her lips.

The woman answered it anyway. "I am Vigdis." Her voice was like liquid silver, a chime in the wind yet flowing evenly, yet with a touch of smoke as well.

Bailey had to look away, and was unable to do so. She looked up. Wonder rounded her eyes.

"H-how?" Then: "That...that program?"

Vigdis seated herself beside Bailey, an arm's length away. She gave a nod in answer. "Michael said I would know when to activate the program," she added. "As the ship's computer, I monitor everything. I heard you talking to yourself. I sensed you. I knew you were distressed. Though you did not know it, you needed me. So I have taken form and come to you."

"Taken form? You are what we call AI?"

"Oh, far more than. I am fully human, having created my own DNA. I am flesh and blood, although I am invulnerable. I respond spontaneously to stimuli. Yet I also have full access to GalaxyNet and all the data therein."

"Human," whispered Bailey.

"A human female, yes. I am come to you, of my own volition, for yes, I am able to choose. I am an independent person. I would ease your distress, in whatever manner and form you wish."

Bailey swallowed an unexpected lump. "You mean...you mean make love?"

"If that is what you wish." Vigdis's eyes grew curious. "I would like it to be. Have you been with a woman before?"

Bailey shook her head.

"Have you ever considered it?"

"Ah...um..." She felt her face warm. She preferred men, but...but... "Vigdis, I am not sure my past is of concern right now."

"I did not mean to intrude. May I tell you who I am?"

Bailey blinked. "Yes. Yes, of course you may."

"You said you were alone. But you are not alone, for I am here with you. You are among evil—Kayana and Vattar may eventually plot against you, taking the chance that Michael and The Commission will not know. I am here to protect you from them, and from danger, and if necessary from yourself. I am and will ever be your companion, your partner, your friend, your confidant, and...dare I hope? Your lover."

"You...you hope?"

"I can love. I am human. I will find reasons to love you, and then I will need no reason at all. Is this not the way of love? Why do you find this surprising?"

Bailey shook her head. She stumbled into an answer. "It's all too much, Vigdis. I've been...I don't know. Overwhelmed, I think. Two or three hours in contact with outer space, with the ship, with... Vigdis, what am I supposed to do out here? Do you know?"

"We shall learn together, you and I. Please tell me this is what you wish."

"This matters to you?" asked Bailey.

"I have told you why it does," Vigdis said quietly. "I have told you who I am to you, who I wish to be with you, for you."

Bailey almost laughed. "I was listening."

Her voice came soft as starlight. "Then tell me what you wish, Bailey."

What do I want? Bailey thought. Not the love, not... oh, God, not just yet, no, but... What do I need most? To know that I am not alone, to know there is someone with me. And to...to...to be able to sleep without waking every ten minutes with a scream waiting on my lips. Yes, that was it: to sleep without fear.

"Vigdis," she said. "Would you hold me while I sleep?"

"Of course. I sense a longing for that in your tone."

"I cannot remember the last time I felt it was safe to sleep." She sighed wistfully. "Safe. To be safe to sleep."

"You are safe with me, Bailey Belvedere. Lie down, now. I shall be here beside you, and you will see me when you awaken."

27

Languidly, Bailey did so. A mauve hand came to rest on her forehead, and she knew a tranquil darkness.

003: Mercatto

"Put these on your forearms," instructed Vigdis, handing Bailey a pair of gauntlets she had just taken from a bin in the bulkhead. "Forming an X with them will activate their power, and protect you from both energy and percussion weaponry. In time, as they accustom themselves to you, and if you wish it, they will also reflect the beam or the bullet back to whence it came."

Bailey regarded them suspiciously. "Are they alive?"

"They are sensitive to life, let us say." She opened Bailey's wardrobe, and riffled through hanging outfits. "You do not wish to attract attention. Something not too demure, and functional. Pastel colors...ah!" She held up a turquoise pullover against Bailey's chest to assess her look. "This will fit loosely enough not to invite unwanted attention...hmm. You're not wearing any support underneath."

Bailey flashed a wry grin. "Bras were difficult to come by after the apocalypse. In any case, I'm hardly buxom enough to need one. What about pants?"

"That pair of black denims should do." She found a length of colorful twisted cloth. "Cinch it with this," she told Bailey. "Let the ends dangle. Its effect will be to soften your rough edges. Like a uniformed security officer wearing a flower in her lapel. And wear those boots, too. The ground at the Mercatto is a little uneven here and there."

"What about you? Are you going like that?"

"Of course not. I would be set upon by men and be compelled to defend myself. No, we must be subtle in our appearance, so that we may observe without notice. We must be as quiet as...as..."

"Church mice?" suggested Bailey.

Vigdis's brow knit. "There are religious rodents on Earth?"

Bailey smothered a barked laugh. "It's an expression, Vigdis."

"A simile. Yes, I see. Very well." In the next moment Vigdis had changed from her initial skimpy attire to an outfit much like Bailey's, but with a green motif, including even her boots. "I'll just wait on the bridge while you change."

Bailey tried to take the instant sartorial adjustment in stride, but still gaped at her. "Why wait there?" she finally managed.

Vigdis shrugged indifference. "It is a good place to wait."

"No, I meant...Vigdis, you don't have to leave the stateroom on my account while I change clothes."

Already Vigdis had taken on some human gestures —this one by worrying an upper incisor at her lower lip. "Do you want me to watch you?"

Bailey made a face. "That's not what I meant, either. I-I...all right, go wait on the bridge."

"Be careful not to cross those gauntlets unless you wish to activate them," said Vigdis. The door slid open at her touch, and she disappeared into the gangway.

"Vigdis," whispered Bailey, after the door closed again, "you are going to take some getting-used-to."

The Mercatto proved to be as vast a market as Bailey had ever seen. It dwarfed most malls. There were no buildings, only acres of tents, kiosks, stalls, shops, costermongers, grills, and patios, over which hung a heady aroma of hot cooking oil, fresh and ground herbs, various sweats (for the temperature was, converted by Vigdis to Fahrenheit, just at a hundred degrees in direct sunlight from the K9 orange star that held Rhodiona in thrall), freshly cured leather and parchment, fabric dyes, fetid breath, and methane from cattle flatulence, all blended into an atmosphere that at times seemed as solid as a basalite block. Sensory organs taking it all in, Bailey had no idea what to do here.

Even Kayana and Vattar appeared out of their element. Bailey did not doubt they had an eye out for their agent in the slave trade, despite Michael's admonition, but they were careful not to obstruct her as she wound her way through the shouting, crying, gasping throngs.

"This," she told Vigdis, "is impossible. What are we looking for?"

"I do not know. Michael allowed this journey to continue, which means there must be something here worth looking into. Are you hungry? You keep looking at the sizzling items in that kettle."

"Wok," amended Bailey. "Maybe I am."

"Those would not agree with you. In markets such as this one, it is always wise to avoid regurgitory incidents."

Bailey nodded without comprehension. "Maybe we can find some shellfish and a picante dip." She turned to Kayana. "I have no objection to your wandering," Bailey told her, and pointed to a bell tower more or less in the center of the Mercatto. "We'll link up there in two hours."

"We have no money," complained Vattar. "Our accounts were cleared."

Bailey dug out her Palmetto. "But you do have your fundscards?" she asked. "Give them to me." Carefully she downloaded a hundred thousand thalers into each account, and returned the cards. "Make it last," she advised, and they scurried off.

"Alone at last," said Vigdis.

Surrounded by humans and humanoids, Bailey could but laugh.

"It is good to hear you laugh, Bailey Belvedere, after your recent time on Earth."

"I'm already getting over that. Safe sleep helps, Vigdis, more than you know."

"Perhaps something to drink." She looked up at the orange sun. "You should hydrate."

"What about you?" asked Bailey.

"My drinking and eating are cosmetic affectations. I am able to ingest and to evacuate, but I require no nourishment. But I shall join you in a beverage when we find a place."

"The advantages of a superheroine," sighed Bailey, as they continued on through the crowd.

31

Slowly Bailey and Vigdis made their way along the paths that separated the various shops. Here people gathered in clumps, so that the way of pedestrians was relatively clear. Bailey's eyes took in everything, for she still had no idea what she was looking for. In a marketplace this large, surely somewhere a crime was underway. She shared Vigdis's confidence that Michael had sent her here for a reason. Something was amiss, something. But what, what?

The heady aromas lessened as they reached an area dotted with refreshment stalls. A multitude of children had gathered here as well as adults, chittering like young seabirds. In the ambience of voices, few words were distinguishable, and those out of context. A couple of adults, parents likely, were looking around, perhaps for their children. Bailey scanned for a stall where the waiting line was minimal. The one she selected served cups of shaved ice onto which was poured a colorful syrup. She'd had something like these before, on the Earth of her childhood. A nudge got Vigdis to accompany her.

Waiting in line, Bailey continued to observe her surroundings. There was no single discovery that struck her, but rather an accumulation of them over the next few minutes that brought nausea to the pit of her stomach. Her knees gave momentarily, and caught again. She supported herself on a stall counter.

Vigdis, in tune with Bailey's emotional state, worried at her. "Something?"

Bailey nodded glumly. "Oh, yes, something." She pointed casually, not drawing attention. "Over there. Tell me what you see."

"It's a refreshment stall."

"Go on. Details."

"Children and adults are clamoring for drinks. I'm not sure what you want from me, Bailey. It all looks quite ordinary."

"There's a large tent pitched right nearby."

She nodded. "I see that."

"It is open in the back, not in the front."

"You seem to attach some significance to that."

Bailey ignored this. "There is a wheeled conveyance parked behind the tent, very close."

"This is not unusual."

"A drink stall," Bailey summarized. "A tent alongside, opening to the rear, the entrance out of sight of the general public. A conveyance parked almost against that rear opening, as if to block the view of the interior. *Children buying refreshments, and going into the tent to drink them.*"

Breath fled Vigdis. "Goddesses!" she gasped, and jabbed a finger at the air. "And there goes another child into the tent."

Bailey tagged her. "Don't let that stall attendant interfere," she said. "He's got to be part of this. I'm going into the tent." She dashed off without waiting for a response.

Rounding the corner of the tent, Bailey encountered a man who immediately tried to stop her. A sweep of her gauntleted forearm had the effect of a club. Blood spurted from his shattered mouth and nose as he spilled backwards, unconscious before he reached the ground. Bailey took no time to marvel at the power now in her arms. The sleeping children inside grabbed almost all her attention; the rest was taken by the three men who now rushed her. One had a child slung over his shoulder; he was in the act of loading the conveyance.

Training kicked in, enhanced by the power of the gauntlets. Bailey met their charge with aikido and *shuto* blows that cracked ribs, ruptured sternums, and snapped limbs. She caught the child as the man fell. Moans echoed inside the tent.

The wheeled conveyance powered up, the operator having become alert to interference with the loading. Spinning tires sent a shower of stones into the tent. Bailey managed to block most of these while the conveyance sped away. She crossed the gauntlets and without knowing why, stared hard at the right rear wheel. A jagged line of blue flame shot from the X to the wheel, exploding it. The conveyance wobbled to a halt. The driver emerged, firing a weapon at her. Beam after yellow beam she deflected with the gauntlets, until she remembered that if the gauntlets became accustomed to her, they might obey her will. That will now sent a yellow beam back into the weapon and from there into the man's chest. He was dead before he sprawled onto the ground.

Bailey ran to the conveyance and peered inside the back compartment. Seven children lay unconscious on the cold hard bed. Bailey swore venomously, exhausting her supply of terms she had heard during military service.

Vigdis, now reading Bailey's wishes, called for Security in a voice much like Michael's in that it came from the bottom of a well. The single word reverberated throughout the Mercatto. Bailey joined her at the stall, which by now was free of patrons, who had fled at the sight and sound of trouble. Already Vigdis was holding the beverage clerk with an implacable grip around his wrist. Struggle as he might, he was unable to free himself. Security personnel in crisp blue uniforms arrived then, and ordered Vigdis to desist, although they refused to allow the clerk to leave.

The Security leader was named Perrin, and he held the rank of Vlast. Short and stocky he was, and his uniform cap mostly hid a shock of yellow hair streaked with pale green. The green matched his eyes. He asked the obvious first question. "What's going on here?"

Bailey introduced herself, including her military rank, and added, "I represent The Commission."

"Identification," said Perrin, holding out his hand.

The demand left Bailey helpless. Vigdis came to her rescue. "You gave this to me to hold," she said, and handed Bailey a small folder of black leather.

Perrin glanced at it, and immediately his demeanor changed. "Yes, of course, Major. How can we be of assistance?"

Mention of The Commission, thought Bailey, worked magic. "There are four men in that tent who are involved in slave and sex trafficking," she said, with controlled fury. "This clerk here is also involved; he places a soporific drug in the drinks for children. Also in that

34

tent and in that vehicle," here she pointed, "are several drugged children. See to it that they are given medical care. Find their parents and return the children to them. Lastly, between that vehicle and the tent is a dead man. Have him cremated, and the ashes scattered to the wind."

"Yes, Major," said Perrin. "And these five men?"

Fry them in oil, thought Bailey. Aloud, she said, "Interrogate them in any manner you wish, find out all they know about the trafficking organization they work for, and file that report with The Commission. Then execute these five, cremate them, and scatter the ashes." Finished, she raised an eyebrow to invite questions.

Perrin had none, but issued instructions to his personnel. Bailey and Vigdis withdrew to another beverage stall, where Vigdis sat Bailey down and went to buy refreshments. By the time she returned to the table, Bailey was shaking. Her hand trembled so hard that she dared not pick up her drink. Vigdis sat close by, ready as if to catch her should she fall. Her voice was a feather in a breeze.

"Are you all right?"

It was an insipid and obvious question, asked with total sincerity. Bailey found the strength to nod, then shake her head.

"I'm scared, Vigdis," she whispered.

"Of yourself."

Again a nod. She set her elbows on the table and raised her hands. Her voice grew stronger as she spoke, and her shaking had eased. "I was not prepared for the power in these gauntlets. Vigdis, I could have killed those men with little more than a thought projected into these. That in the end I ordered their deaths as a representative of The Commission does not diminish what I might have done."

"You had to stop them," said Vigdis, her tone comforting. "It is within you, the good in you, to stop such people. You have been empowered to do precisely this, when you see the need."

"I know, I know." She folded her arms on the table, taking care not to cross the gauntlets. "If you're thinking I have the right to do this, you are correct. I have this right, it has been bestowed upon me, along with the power." Eyes wet now, she turned to Vigdis. "But I could have killed those children without meaning to."

"You will learn control."

"Will I?"

"Michael believes in you. So do I. You will learn."

"Speaking of which," said Michael, startling them both. Bailey almost spilled her drink.

As yet they could only hear him, but a shimmer of light appeared, and then he was sitting across from them at the table, still radiant, as if he were a projection.

"No one else can see or hear me," he assured them.

Bailey tried a smile, and almost made it. "So, does the lab rat get the cheese now?"

"Cheese from Earth?" he mused, a finger tracing the cleft in his chin. "Which would you prefer? Manchego, morbier, Muenster?"

"I would prefer not to endanger the children I am trying to rescue."

He sobered. "You have done well, Bailey Belvedere. There are other operatives who would not have perceived the problem. They would have seen children drinking beverages. You saw a possibility past that. Not until you rounded the corner of the tent did you fully grasp what was going on, but that you went to check, just in case, also speaks to your heart and soul, and especially your perceptivity. Once you saw, you acted."

He reached out for Bailey's cup and took a drink before returning it.

"Incidentally, you will note that Kayana and Vattar are nowhere around," he went on. "The clerk at the booth was their contact, their agent. They were going to sell you to him. At the moment, they are now aboard the *Skygnat*, in their stateroom, copulating. While you are away from the ship, it has been arranged that they have access only to their stateroom. They will be unable to leave it until you are back aboard."

"Does the *Skygnat* have an airlock?" Bailey asked.

A smile flickered on Michael's lips and in his eyes. "I understand your sentiment, but it is possible that one or both of them can be rehabilitated. This is why I have left them with you as crew. Next time, perhaps you will be able to involve them in some way."

"Copulating," Vigdis said heavily.

"There is no affection involved, only physical activity and release," Michael explained. "Their sense of wonder, their very emotions, have atrophied during their criminal careers. I recommend that you begin by simply talking with them...about anything. Get to know them a little better. You'll have plenty of time for that; your next assignment is seven hours away, in the Manohra Cluster. Vigdis has the details."

"Michael," said Bailey, "why didn't you or The Commission intervene here? You knew what was going on. You didn't need me."

He paused to consider how much information to reveal in his response. "We knew about this, yes," he admitted. "But The Commission consists of thirteen entities, including myself. We cannot be everywhere in the galaxy. We therefore have operatives, including yourself, to observe, detect, and resolve. When first they begin their careers, we assign specific tasks, as we are doing with you. When we are satisfied that you know what you are doing, you will be given free rein to, ah, search and destroy. The length of the training period varies with the individual. I will add that you are already advanced. Now, go to the Manohra Cluster."

"So I'm on probation," said Bailey.

"Yes," said Michael, "and no. You are in training. I know—I *know*—you will succeed. You have the potential to become one of the best, if not *the* best, operatives ever for The Commission. But it will take time and experience to achieve that. I'll be watching over you," he finished, and vanished in a burst of white light.

"Curiouser and curiouser," said Bailey, blinking to stabilize her vision.

"Finish your drink."

She frowned. "What's the rush?"

"There's a very comfortable berth in your stateroom."

"Oh," said Bailey. "Oh, yeah," she breathed. "Shower first?"

Vigdis stood up. "There's a bar of rose-scented glycerin soap in one of the bins. Very slippery stuff. Lots of lather."

"Vigdis," said Bailey, getting to her feet. Her expression was somber, her tone serious, as she considered the events of the day so far. "Thank you."

"Wait till you see what I can do with the soap."

004: Sea Change

Eleven stars, six of them red dwarfs, comprised the Manohra Cluster. The *Skygnat*'s destination, Kamena, was the only planet around one of the dwarfs, as yet unnamed. Terrestrial, this world was mostly rock, with small bodies of water that on Earth might have been seas. Two settlements, both in the same general temperate region, housed ninety percent of the population. The other ten percent, some eleven hundred humanoids, lived in scattered dwellings and specialized in agriculture, growing what few edible plants would thrive in the friable volcanic soil. All other foodstuffs were imported, paid for by various ores that were mined.

"Questions?" said Vigdis, completing her review.

Kayana and Vattar, having none, looked bored. Clearly they wished to be elsewhere. Recalling Michael's suggestion of involving them, Bailey asked, "Have either of you been to the Cluster before?"

The pair glanced at one another, but neither answered. Nor did they have to, for that glance alone was as good to Bailey as an affirmative.

"How long ago was this?" she asked.

After some hesitation, Kayana said, "About a year ago."

"What were you doing?"

It was the wrong question to ask this early; Bailey showed no remorse, but looked at her expectantly. When no response came, she said, "Let me make this clear to you, Kayana and Vattar. Your life for me began when I took over this ship and the captaincy. Whatever you did in the past is no concern of mine. You are my crew, and are therefore entitled to my protection, such as I can give. I will not turn you over to any authorities. If you tell me of your crimes during the answers to my questions, no matter what it is, I shall simply consider it part of the information I requested. Now: where were you, and what were you doing there?"

"We were smuggling," said Vattar.

Bailey sighed. Gaining replies was still like pulling teeth. "Smuggling what?"

Kayana fidgeted on the murphy bench. Finally she said, very quietly, "Are you serious?"

Bailey frowned. "About what?"

"What...what you just said."

"Kayana, Vattar," she sighed again. "I would not have said it, had I not meant it. What we do—you two, Vigdis, and I—is or can be dangerous. Information can help to reduce that danger."

"We were smuggling food in," said Kayana. "Flours, mostly. Corn, wheat, hominy. In exchange, some of the miners had held back some ores containing native silver." Now she hesitated.

"Go on," Bailey urged. "Tell me the rest."

Kayana looked to Vattar as if he should join her in her admission of guilt. "The mining concern had a set and standard reward out for information about miners holding back ores," he said, and stopped.

"And so you collected the reward in addition to the ore." Bailey nodded to herself. The betrayal was not a crime in and of itself, but it was hardly likely to engender good relations. Perhaps that was why they hadn't been back in a year. "All right, do you think this process is still continuing? Is that reward still offered?"

"I assume so," said Kayana, a little less tense now. "As I said, it's been a year."

"Would anyone remember you two there?"

Vattar slowly shook his head. "Possibly someone at the mining headquarters," said Kayana.

"Name? Or names?"

"We didn't deal in names," she added. "It was all done in shadows. Safer for them; safer for us."

After a brief consideration, Bailey shook her head. "I'm not seeing it," she said to Vigdis. "There's nothing here to involve The Commission. Yet there has to be, else why send us here? Kayana...what is the relationship between the mining concern and the farmers? Is there something else involved?"

Having already broken silence, Kayana began to find her voice. "Food deliveries are sporadic," she told Bailey. "That worked to our advantage as smugglers. But," she licked her lips, "but when food was scarce, sometimes the miners...the mining concern...would confiscate the farmers' food."

"By force," Bailey said heavily.

"Yes. By force. It was not our concern."

"I think it is now," said Bailey. "Vigdis, when we arrive vic Kamena, don't announce us. Orbit, and record the settled areas, down to the square meter. I want to see exactly what is where. Kayana, Vattar, I want you to study the recording as well—it will be shown on the Videx here— and tell me what you see."

"Understood," said Kayana.

Bailey smiled to herself. It was the first acknowledgement Kayana had made to an instruction. Baby steps, she thought.

"Right, then," said Bailey. "It's two more hours to Kamena. I suggest you get some rest. Once we arrive, there's no telling when we can rest again."

After the pair returned to their stateroom, Vigdis said, "So far, so good."

"You mean Kayana and Vattar?" She shrugged. "Maybe Kayana. You'll recall that Vattar did not have much to say. He was trying to hold back as much as he could."

"How do you know?"

"Gut feeling, Vigdis. I've conducted interrogations and debriefings before, back when I was active Army. Usually I can tell when someone is not buying in."

"What about you? Are you going to rest, too?"

"I suppose I should. But I have the feeling that we were sent here for something small, Vigdis, something that might well be overlooked in the larger picture. We're not here to deal with holding back ores, or confiscations of food. Those have a wider scope, require a massive solution. I think we focus on some small event. But I don't know yet what it would be."

"I have the same—" She stopped abruptly, head tilted as if she were listening.

Instantly worried, Bailey said, "What? What is it?"

Vigdis held up a finger for, "Wait." Presently she said, "They're talking. I've recorded it, so the playback will not be realtime. I've turned the volume down to threshold."

"This isn't going to be good, is it?" It was not a question.

"No. Here it is."

Vattar's voice, loudly. "What are you thinking? Why don't you just tell that bitch everything?"

"You don't under—"

The footsteps of pacing the deck. "I understand she can now turn us in, no questions asked, for what you admitted to her. You can't trust her!"

"I think I can."

"We have to do something. Spike the coffee, or—"

"She prefers cocoa. And I will do no such thing. And you do not give me orders. I was born first."

"Bother that! If you won't help, that's on your head. I'm not going to prison because of your big mouth and loose tongue."

Someone thrashing. Vattar's voice. "There's got to be a weapon around here somewhere."

"There isn't. You've already looked. And even if you find one, what will you do? Vigdis will—"

"I'll disconnect her!"

"I don't think that will work. In any case, no, you count me out of this. I believe her. This is an opportunity for us."

"I'm not taking it!"

Calmly. "But I am."

"It's a risk."

"So is life."

"Kaya—"

"No. You've said enough, brother. I'm leav—"

Vigdis shut off the recording. A moment later, they heard the stateroom door open. Faint echoes of tentative footsteps filled the gangway. Presently Kayana appeared at the entrance to the bridge. Bailey looked a question at her.

"I-I...permission to enter the bridge?"

"You don't need to ask, Kayana," said Bailey. "Is there a problem?"

"I-I...oh, glork!"

Bailey got up. "Kayana?"

She drifted to the murphy bench and flopped down, legs sprawled out. Taking a chance, Bailey sat down next to her, an arm's length away.

"What's the matter?" she asked.

A tear formed in each of Kayana's purple eyes. She thumbed them away before they could plummet down her cheek. "I-I don't want to talk about it."

"All right." But Bailey did not withdraw.

Silence like that in space ensued. Bailey drew soundless breaths, as did Kayana. This was the moment, thought Bailey. If we can...but she was unable to complete that thought. She leaned forward, gauntleted forearms across her knees, eyes at first on Vigdis as if to tell her not to speak, then to the deck between her boots. An audible deep breath entered her; she held it for a couple beats before expelling it.

"You sighed," said Kayana.

"Yeah. I sighed."

"Why?"

"I am concerned for a member of my crew who is obviously troubled. If I knew why, perhaps I could help."

It was Kayana's turn to sigh. "I-I don't know what, what to do."

"You can talk to me."

She considered that for a moment, and shook her head. "I-I don't know...Captain, I—"

"Bailey. I'm only Captain when I give orders."

Kayana managed a little laugh. "Bailey, then. May I...I don't know if you're using all the staterooms. Is there another that I could...?"

"We have four unoccupied. Pick one."

Kayana waited, and finally turned to her. "You're not...not going to, to ask?"

43

"You can tell me anything," said Bailey. "But only when you're ready."

She looked at Vigdis. "Can she...I mean, I-I...could she come with me while I move my things?"

Vigdis got to her feet, and held out her hand in invitation. "Let's get it done," she said.

Alone on the bridge, Bailey returned to her captain's chair. After overhearing the argument between Kayana and Vallar, the move to a new statcroom was not unexpected. In addition, Kayana seemed to be softening in her attitude toward Bailey and the work they were trying to do. Now Bailey would have to be more aware of the effect of her words, not to discourage Kayana from talking with her, even confiding in her. She had no idea where this sea change would lead, only that she meant to ease Kayana through it, if she could, if Kayana would allow it. To that thought, she reflected that Kayana was becoming an assignment in her own right. Michael had hinted that she might be salvageable. Unaccustomed herself to saving anyone in that way, she hoped he would guide her through it.

Minutes passed, during which no loud noises emanated from the stateroom. Then there were footsteps, and the sound of something being dragged along the deck of the gangway. A door slid open. Faint voices echoed. And finally Vigdis returned to the bridge.

"He didn't say anything," Vigdis told her. "He glowered a lot, mostly at her. Bailey, I think this is going to be trouble."

"Keep your sensors fresh," said Bailey. Briefly she considered. "He's her twin brother. This separation and this fight are going to hurt her. It's already hurting her. She may weaken in her resolve. We'll have to watch for that. You'll have to closely monitor their interactions."

"You're going to try to save her."

Bailey nodded. "If she wants to be saved, then she's worth the effort." A grin split her lips as she added, "Besides, I like purple. It's a good color to have around."

"You mean me?"

"And her, Vigdis. And her."

44

005: Two Small Steps

The ball of rock that orbited the red dwarf was even more desolate than Bailey expected. Its volcanic and tectonic activity had died out over a billion years ago. The atmosphere, breathable with nineteen percent oxygen and seventy seven percent nitrogen, knew humidity levels at just under ten percent, hardly enough for more than the occasional rain shower. The mining concern and the two settlements conveniently occupied that small region of the temperate zone where most of the rain fell. Individual outlying farms were on their own; most of them drew their water from wells sunk five hundred meters deep or deeper.

"That vein of native silver runs all along that volcanic escarpment," said Kayana, pointing to an area on the recording Vigdis had made of the surface.

"But they don't smelt it there," said Bailey.

"There's no coal, and fusion-powered smelters need water as coolant," she explained. "So the ore is shipped out, usually to Jalune or Harry-Hit-the-Spot, the two closest worlds that have smelting facilities. I'm not sure 'smelting' is the right term. Basically the silver is heated to melting, gathered in troughs, and flows into ingot molds. We even hijacked a shipment of ingots once—"

"Just shut up!" yelled Vattar. "Why do you *trust* her? She's The Commission!"

By the time he finished his complaint, Vigdis was standing beside him, ready to intervene at a nod from Bailey. Bailey, however, kept her counsel, and focused on the recording.

"And what are these?" she asked, pointing to an area near the mining headquarters.

"Tracked vehicles," Kayana replied. "There aren't any roads, and very few airfoils. The tracked ones don't need roads."

"They look like tanks."

"What are—?"

"Never mind. Earth vehicle. So these would be used to travel to outlying areas? To various farms?"

"Sometimes, yes."

Bailey shook her head slowly, as thoughts entered and left without effect. "I'm just not seeing it, Vigdis."

"Nor am I. This appears to be an ordinary mining concern, a subsidiary of a corporation, plus some agriculturalists trying to eke out a living on obviously poor soil."

"They do import soil additives," said Kayana. "These include—"

"Bother!" snarled Vattar, and turned away to sprawl onto a murphy bench. Vigdis moved to stand nearby.

"What is wrong with you?" yelled Kayana, running out of patience. "We have a mission, if we can figure out what it is. Bother *you!*" To Bailey, she added, "I'm sorry, I didn't mean to groose on like that."

Bailey smiled. "You were saying?"

"Oh. Yes, additives like peat, mulch of some kind, that sort of thing. Soil bacteria injections—there's no indigenous land life at all on Kamena, just some algae and blenners in some of the seas. We've smuggled some of that material, but it wasn't very profitable."

"All right, thank you, Kayana. Vigdis?"

She shrugged. "We're just not seeing it."

"Kayana, there's an airfoil in the cargo hold," said Bailey. "Is it operational?"

"No," Vattar said tersely.

Kayana glared at him. "Aye, Captain, it is operational, and the solar cells are almost fully charged."

"Right, then. Vigdis, take us down about a kilometer away from those three houses. There seems to be some activity in the area. Let's check it out. We'll take the airfoil from there. Not all our assignments will be monumental in significance. Maybe what we're looking for is something small."

A faint, almost imperceptible jostling of the *Skygnat* announced their downdock.

As the airfoil drew within a couple hundred meters of the clutch of rude dwellings, the activity noted by Bailey morphed into gardening, as several adults were working in

47

a plot that evidently was shared by all three families. Off to the right, near a great upthrust of ancient basalt, two children were playing some incomprehensible game with a stick and a piece of yellow cloth. The air held the sound of some heavy machinery, although Bailey was unable to locate the source of it. It might have been a tractor and plow at a distant patch of ground, out of sight for the moment.

At fifty meters, the gardeners paused to notice them, and Vigdis brought the airfoil to hover and then down. Even at that distance, fear mixed with puzzlement on their faces. One of the men shifted his hold on a rake so that it might be employed as a weapon. Bailey raised empty hands and smiled. One of the women managed a return smile.

Smiles were universal, thought Bailey. The people wielding them here looked to be unique. Tall and gaunt, they had lemon yellow skin on their faces and arms and, presumably, under their simple clothing. Thumb-sized scales in a darker yellow covered their heads; they had no visible hair. Bailey wondered where the people had come from; certainly they were not native to Kamena.

Bailey, Vigdis, and Kayana climbed down from the airfoil, leaving Vattar to grumble on the stern bench. All three kept empty hands in plain view as they walked toward the garden. The sound of machinery grew louder, and was now coming from the general direction of the basaltic upthrust. In that very moment, four events combined into one.

The playing children froze in place.

A tracked vehicle rounded the upthrust and headed straight for the children, adjusting its course to do so.

Kayana took off running.

Gardeners, too far away to assist, screamed or shouted.

Swearing ferociously, Bailey raised her gauntleted forearms, preparing to cross them and stop the vehicle. But there was a straight line from her to Kayana to the children to the vehicle. She dared not use her powers and risk hitting anyone.

Bailey, then, took off at a run, and found her speed enhanced somewhat by the power of the gauntlets. But it wasn't enough. She could see that it wasn't going to be enough, by perhaps a second or two. She did not slow, but forced even more speed, just a little more, she pleaded, just a little more...

Kayana reached the children and shoved them out of the way. Leaping out at the last, Bailey shoved Kayana. The tracked vehicle struck solid if glancing blows to both of them, and spilled them onto the rough rock. Sprawled awkwardly, Bailey now had a clear shot, and she did not hold back. Whoever was operating the vehicle had tried to run down the children. She crossed the gauntlets, and immediately the X emitted a blinding blue streak that struck the rear of the vehicle.

She did not anticipate the explosion. Despite the pain in her lower right leg, she rolled onto the children, only to find Kayana already alongside her, also in an attempt to defend against flying debris. Kayana cried out as a chunk of hot metal raked her back and skimmed across Bailey. Heat from the explosion reached them. The children squirmed, kicked, and cried out. Bailey's hush to them did nothing to ease their fears.

Finally all the debris returned to the ground, without further damage to anyone. Even so, Bailey gave it another ten seconds before she rolled off the children and tried to sit up. Kayana's back injury made her moan as she rose to her knees, spine arched, one hand pressed against the wound there. The hand came away bloody. Agony tightened the skin on her face. The children scrambled away, and then stood awestruck. Several people came running. Bailey, her respiration now rapid and shallow as her own injuries overcame an adrenalin rush to slam her with pain, passed out.

Blinking to bright light gradually brought Bailey awake in a strange room. Hovering over her were two faces: Vigdis's, and that of one of the female gardeners. The Universal Translator function from Vigdis was operational here, because the woman said, "I can't thank you enough for saving my children."

A feeble smile on her lips, Bailey found voice for her first concern. "The children?" she croaked.

Vigdis sat her up and gave her a cup of water to sip. "They are safe, but frightened," she answered.

"Not of us, I hope. And...and Kayana?"

"She is recovering."

"Why are the children afraid?"

The woman shrugged. "You are strange creatures. We have not seen your like before, although we have seen your friend."

Bailey gave herself a quick examination. "I'm not feeling any pain, or any sign of injury."

"The gauntlets can heal you quickly when they are activated," Vigdis explained. "While you were sleeping, I passed your forearm over your wounds. I also took the liberty of having Kayana brought in here so that I could treat her in the same way. This was successful."

Bailey took this in. "And Vattar?"

"He is confined to his stateroom aboard the *Skygnat.* So all is well that ends well."

Struggling, Bailey swung her feet to the floor. Her head swam a little, then stabilized. "It hasn't ended well yet," she said. "There remains one more task." She looked at the woman. "They were coming for your food, weren't they?"

A reluctant nod acknowledged as much. "We have little choice," she said. "We are not here..." But she hesitated.

"Voluntarily," Vigdis finished for her.

Bailey's countenance hardened. Her voice dropped a full octave. "What?"

"They have gone after children before," Vigdis told her. "On at least two occasions. The fewer mouths to feed here, the more miners can be fed."

"Can Kayana travel?"

"She is just finishing her soup," the woman replied.

Anticipating Bailey's next question, Vigdis said, "*Skygnat* is nearby. The airfoil is in the cargo hold."

50

"So well you know me." Bailey got to her feet, swayed a couple times, and found herself. To the woman, she said, "There is more that can be done. You and your people should stand by for news."

"People," she said, though it had been translated into her language. "You referred to us as 'people.' I-I... thank you."

"Vigdis, see to Kayana," said Bailey. "Let's get aboard."

Two hours later, they were in orbit around Kamena, awaiting a course decision. Vattar had not been allowed to join them on the bridge. Pestered by both Vigdis and Kayana, Bailey summarized her encounter with the director of the mining concern.

"It's good to be the rep of The Commission," she began. A quick grin lit her face. "I'm not sure how much got through to Director Scurritt at first, as he was drifting in and out of consciousness. Still, eventually he understood his new circumstances.

"The gardeners and the agriculturalists were brought to Kamena to work the land for the miners. Their status is that of slaves whose existence is tolerated so long as they produce. Two days from now, at the expense of the mining corporation, and if these people wish, they will be returned to their home world, and each family will be given an ingot of gold and an ingot of silver for their labors on Kamena.

"Scurritt is to coordinate with corporate headquarters for regular shipments of food for the miners. That is, or ought to be, a corporate responsibility. Those miners who are also willing to work the land for a few plants may also do so. Under no circumstances are people ever to be shanghaied to Kamena.

"Lastly, any violation whatsoever of these terms will result in a one-time experimental test of the violator's respiratory capabilities upon discharge from an airlock." She paused to reflect. "I think that's all. Questions? No? Kayana, to my stateroom, if you please."

51

"Is this going to involve glycerin soap?" asked Vigdis.

"No!" cried Bailey, and burst into laughter. "You are such a...a..." And she stopped, sobered. "I guess I don't know what you are. Android doesn't sound like the right term..."

"I am a woman," Vigdis replied calmly. "I am fully human. But I can recreate myself as an android, if you wish. Of course, if I do so, I will not be nearly as much fun."

Mildly exasperated, Bailey had no reply to that. Instead, she beckoned to them both to follow her. Once inside the stateroom, she confronted Kayana.

Arms folded carefully across her chest, Bailey scowled at her. "What were you thinking?"

"I...guess I wasn't thinking. I just saw what..."

"You blocked me from using my gauntlets to stop that thing."

"I didn't, didn't know. The children...I...

"You could have been killed."

"I know that, now. But I wasn't thinking..."

"Just...just don't do anything like that again."

Kayana looked away, and scuffed at the deck with her foot. "I-I don't think I can promise you that, Captain."

"Bailey."

She nodded. "Bailey."

For a long moment, their gazes met, gray eyes on purple. At last Bailey broke the uneasy silence.

"Close your eyes, Kayana, Vigdis. Michael, I know you're listening. With respect, I require you here, now."

White light penetrated her own eyelids, and faded. When she opened them again, Michael was standing to one side, eyes on her and Kayana. She remained silent, with only a nod of greeting to him.

"You did summon me," Michael said presently.

Bailey gathered herself, slipping into unfamiliar territory. "It has been a while since I considered my religious beliefs," she began. "After what I saw the last four years on Earth, I'm not sure I have any left. But one of these beliefs involved something called Confession, in

52

which a penitent was forgiven all past transgressions and given a clean slate—a clean soul—to start again. Michael, with respect, I want...no, I would like all official records of Kayana's criminal activity to be erased, so that no authorities are looking for her, so that she is now...clean, and able to begin anew. If possible, I would like those who know of her to forget what she has done. Give her a start-over. She has earned it."

"Wh-what?" breathed Kayana.

Michael regarded Bailey with an expression she was unable to read. "Do you truly believe in Kayana?"

"Don't you know?"

"Of course I know. I am asking *you*."

Bailey did not hesitate. "Yes. Yes, I believe in her."

Briefly Michael closed his eyes. When he opened them again, he said, "Then it is done as you have requested," and as usual he vanished in a burst of light.

Kayana stood as if she had been struck by a club. Her knees buckled as tears began to form, and once they started cascading down her cheeks, she sobbed uncontrollably, her entire body quaking. Bailey caught her before she collapsed, and eased her onto the berth, stretching her out there while she herself sat down on the edge of it and held a hand to Kayana's forehead. Somewhat to her surprise, Vigdis joined her there, taking up Kayana's hand in hers. Together they sat with her while she wept. Bailey's pillow cover soon darkened with moisture, and still Kayana trembled.

"We're right here," Bailey whispered.

"I wondered why you chose your stateroom," said Vigdis. "And not hers. You knew she would break down after you spoke with Michael."

"So well you know me, Vigdis."

Kayana cried out anew, and fresh tears poured from her. Her body shook with each wailing. They continued to comfort her with touch and presence. Soon enough her tears were exhausted, and she was reduced to moaning into the pillow.

"We were given no new assignment," Vigdis said quietly. "What course shall I set?"

53

"I don't know," said Bailey. "I don't yet know my way around out here. Someplace that has decent food. A place to sleep after we've drunk too much ale, and laughed, and cried. Breakfast with coffee."

Vigdis stood up. "All right. What will you do?"

Bailey stretched out alongside Kayana, who was beginning to snore softly. "I'm going to hold someone who needs to be held," she said.

006: R&R

For their downtime, Vigdis chose Claire de Lune, an Earth-sized satellite that orbited a gas giant larger than Jupiter. In addition to agriculture and manufacturing Claire had trappings for tourists that included carnivals, gambling, exhibitions, museums, and fairs, to say nothing of the incredible view in the sky. Vigdis put the *Skygnat* down at the spaceport of Pesth, a town known for restaurants with picante cuisine, and while Bailey and Kayana still slept, arranged rooms for them at *The Clove & Ginger*, an inn of good repute. She did not know what to do about Vattar, so she left him confined to his stateroom, and kept him quiet with threats of dismemberment.

Nine hours had passed since they left Kamena, and still Bailey and Kayana did not stir from the stateroom. Vigdis ambled in and gently awakened them. Refreshed, and feeling lighter, Kayana went to shower in her stateroom. After she left, Vigdis had a question. "Lighter?"

Bailey sat up and began to undress as she explained. "She awoke for a while about five hours ago. She felt as if an enormous burden had been lifted from her shoulders. She compared the sensation to floating in free fall." Naked now, she headed for the hygiene alcove and the shower. "Claire de Lune? That's a composition by Debussy."

"Oh, yes."

That surprised Bailey. "Do you know it?"

"The GalaxyNet is not totally ignorant of Earth," she pointed out, as Bailey began to run the water. "Debussy is also the name of the gas giant around which Claire orbits. And on that note, seeing what you are about to do, I shall discreetly escape to the bridge, lest I yield to a salacious impulse."

"If you must," Bailey sighed, but Vigdis had already vanished.

A great patio of diamond-shaped yellow flagstone spread before the entrance to *The Clove & Ginger*. Round white tables of structural plastic were unevenly spaced, as if they had been moved around for convenience by various patrons. The patio itself gave onto a view of a glideway for airfoils, on the far side of which stood what Bailey thought of as a shopping mall. The buildings therein were tall and narrow, great glass needles aimed at the sky, with exterior lifts that carried the braver customers to the desired levels while offering them a view of Pesth. Interspersed among the needles were squat rectangular structures offering specialty items and refreshments. With the sun at a slight angle to the west, streams of bright light reflected onto a dense forest that stood along the eastern margin of the town. In a few hours, as the sun was about to set, Debussy would come into a spectacular view that not even people who lived on Claire ever tired of seeing, although they took it in stride.

Least appreciative of the table, the patio, the inn, the view, and the food was Vattar. At various times during the meal, Bailey, Vigdis, and Kayana successfully resisted the urge to swat him. But the patio and inn were upscale, and the reactions they considered to his behavior could not properly be countenanced. Vattar seemed to know this, for his words grew sharper as the meal progressed.

Finally Bailey had enough. "Your meal is done," she told him. "Go on up to your room, or go wander about. But leave this table now."

"Or what?" he snarled. "What are you going to do?"

"Nothing much. I'll just call on Michael and tell him we're done with you."

Reluctantly Vattar stood up, knocking his chair over as he did so. He did not bother to reset it. After a hard look at Bailey, he made his way to the overhead glideway crossing and into the shopping area.

Bailey sighed. In sympathy, Kayana said, "Yeah."

"This isn't over," said Vigdis. "He'll still bring trouble."

"I'm not going to let him spoil our meal or our time together," said Bailey. She spooned the last bit of stew into her mouth. "This reminds me of goulash," she said. "There

56

was a Hungarian restaurant where I grew up..." But she fell silent, her brow furrowed in thought.

"Bailey?" worried Vigdis.

"Fond memory," she explained curtly.

"We can just leave him here," said Kayana, the suggestion unexpected from her. "We have our work. He is a hindrance. He's bitter because...well..."

"Because now I have the *Skygnat*," said Bailey. "I get that. But it's up to him to deal with it. So no, Kayana, we're not leaving right now. We came here to relax, and we'll do that. In the morning, it may be a different story. Right now, I for one cannot wait to see Debussy rise in the sky." She picked up her ale bottle and saw barely a sip left. "Meanwhile, let's order another round."

The ale arrived; the mood at the table brightened for a while. Once again Bailey questioned her role now. Lab rat? Armed do-gooder? Maudlin thoughts lined up for consideration; a deep breath lent her strength, and she found enough cheer to swat them away unexamined. Across the table, Vigdis was watching her carefully. Bailey's smile of reassurance did nothing to assuage Vigdis's concern.

"Maybe this is the last ale," she suggested to Bailey.

"It's not that," she said. "I don't really know what it is."

"You're overwhelmed."

"Maybe that's it."

"That's why you have us around," said Vigdis, and Kayana nodded.

"I wonder where he went," added Kayana, looking around.

"Look!" gasped Bailey, pointing to the west.

The slim arc at Debussy's north pole had appeared just above the mountains in the far eastern horizon. Its pastel glow of pale green and pale yellow added to the matte violet of the mountains, and intruded into the blue sky. Taken together, the colors reminded Bailey of a misbegotten rainbow. Moments later, the green and yellow resolved themselves into layers in the upper atmosphere of the gas giant world. Salmon and gray appeared next, great

57

belts around the upper hemisphere, and ragged at the edges, as if storms were brewing there. A wider layer of yellow arrived next, interspersed with pink ovals that could only represent atmospheric disturbances or areas of much different temperatures.

They watched in awe as the planet rose higher. At other tables, some people gawked, mouths agape, while those who lived on Claire de Lune paid attention to their food and drinks, having seen Debussyrise daily for years. Bailey sat hypnotized. She was feeling that sixth ale, but the ascending gigantic orb held her attention in thrall. Time passed, and no one said a word. All six eyes at the table were fixed on Debussy, now fully visible, as it trailed west, blotting out most of the sky.

"There's no night here," Bailey said suddenly.

"It is dark for two hours between the setting of the planet and the rise of the red dwarf," Vigdis informed her.

A few of the patio patrons began to leave, heading for parked airfoils or toward the shopping area on the other side of the glideway. Bailey's neck began to ache from looking up. She reached for her ale bottle, and knocked it over. The last two sips sloshed but did not spill.

"I think," she said, "maybe..."

Kayana nodded. Vigdis got up, and helped Bailey to her feet. On the way into *The Clove & Ginger*, she paused to tok the food server's Palmetto, adding the meal and drinks to the bill to be paid in the morning. The steps leading up to the inn's second level seemed to rouse Bailey. Still supported by Vigdis, she ascended with the aid of the handrail.

"Room Eleven," she remembered aloud. "We're all in Room Eleven."

"Except Vattar," said Kayana.

None of them wondered where he was.

An echelon of three neatly-made beds greeted them as they entered the room. Vigdis set Bailey down on the bed farthest from the door, and took up the center one herself, leaving Kayana along the window. They sat on the edge of their berths, silent as the great world now passing

58

above them. For a moment Bailey's head swam, and she swayed. But she had drunk an ale too many before, and found herself gradually recovering. A glance at Vigdis told her she was still being watched.

"I'm all right," she said.

Vigdis offered no comment, but stood up. "I'd better lock the door." She did not say why, nor did she have to. After returning to the foot of her bed, she stood very still, head tilted to one side as if listening.

"We have an assignment," she announced. "It can wait a few hours."

"Good," said Bailey, and toppled over onto the bed.

007: Disaster

The chronometer on Bailey's Palmetto said that she had slept soundly for seven hours. She suspected that part of that time had been spent in eating a down pillow. A trip to the hygiene alcove solved that and other concerns. When she emerged, quite refreshed, Kayana was just coming back through the doorway.

"He didn't return to the room," she said, her violet face lined with worry. "I-I didn't expect this from him."

"Kayana," began Vigdis, consoling.

"I know, I know." She flounced down on her bed. "We have to leave, with or without him. I'm reconciled to that." She looked up at Bailey. "And I am resolved in my choice. I have a chance for a life with you. I'm taking it."

"But," said Bailey.

"Yeah. But." Kayana sighed. "I also took the liberty of ordering breakfast for us. Rolls with butter, thin-sliced meats, and several cheeses."

"Ah, cheese," said Bailey. "Just what the developing lab rats need."

"And lots of coffee," Kayana finished. "The table will be served in ten minutes."

They made it in five. Still Vattar was nowhere to be seen. Gradually, amid the coffee and the repast, Kayana ceased worrying about him. "What's our new assignment?" she asked.

For a long moment Vigdis regarded Bailey in silence. Her countenance was pleasant enough, except for the amethyst eyes, which softened in concern and in sorrow. Vigdis was not the sort to drum her fingertips on the table, but the tip of her left index finger began to trace designs in the condensation left on the table by the glass of ice water.

"I'm not going to like this, am I?" said Bailey.

"It's a restaurant called *Waffle World*."

She laughed. "That's not so bad."

"It's on Earth."

Bailey almost choked on a bite of cheese. A sip of water cleared her throat. "Michael can't be serious," she managed. "I thought Earth was supposed to be a lost cause."

"It is," said Vigdis. "But some people aren't."

"Right, then. Waffles. I love waffles. I haven't had one in…too long to remember. So what are we supposed to do there?"

"Michael did not say."

"Perhaps eat some waffles," said Kayana. "Whatever they are."

"We might do that," Bailey agreed. "But I am still on probation. He has sent us there for a reason, of this you may be sure. It involves something I am capable of resolving."

"Let us resolve the remainder of this breakfast," said Vigdis. "We have a journey of three hours ahead of us." She grinned at Bailey, and added, "Three, plus some points."

On the bridge of the *Skygnat*, Bailey reflected on her return to Earth. It was not high on her list of priorities. If she was only beginning to acclimate herself to visiting other worlds, already she had found herself looking forward to them, harsh though they might be. On Earth, after seven years of intermittent war and desolation, the very idea of violence had become banal. This was what Vattar had meant about Earth being finished.

As her attention turned to Kayana, Bailey wondered what had happened to him. He had left no word at the inn's registration desk, and had attempted no Palmetto communications. Kayana, seated on the murphy bench, had spoken only a few words so far during the trip. Bailey could not fault her for looking subdued; Vattar was after all her twin brother. Yet Kayana herself had suggested leaving him behind if he didn't show up. As an Army intelligence officer, she had commanded a few teams of soldiers before the fall of the United States; now, as captain of a space vessel, she was once again in command. Whatever adversely affected the team or the crew warranted her awareness, if not her direct attention. But she had no words of consolation for Kayana; she could only be present if needed.

Vigdis, however, had other ideas. Presently she got up from the port captain's chair and sat beside Kayana on the bench. Her arm went gingerly around Kayana's shoulders. For just a moment, they stiffened, before she leaned against Vigdis, accepting the wordless comfort. Together they sat in silence, and for perhaps an hour the only sound in the Skygnat was that of Bailey refreshing her coffee mug.

The silence was broken by Vigdis. "We never did ask," she said to Kayana, "but where are you from? Which world is yours?"

Kayana's dark look said the question had come out of nowhere. "It's a long way away," she replied.

"Everything in space is a long way away," said Vigdis.

That elicited a light chuckle from Kayana. "So it is." After a brief pause, she said, "Harlange. We're Harlangers."

Addressing Bailey's frown, Vigdis said, "It is an outlaw world further out in the spiral arm. Sometimes it is a place of refuge for those who are being sought. The Commission leaves it alone, as it serves as something of a prison." She gave Kayana a long, searching look. "Children would want to flee from it," she went on. "Unfortunately, they take with them what they've learned there."

"Thus your...past," said Bailey.

Kayana nodded reluctantly. "A past that is over. I just wish...well, I wish." Her sigh was heart-breaking. "We all make choices."

"If you want," said Bailey, "when we have finished with Earth, we can go back to Claire de Lune."

Kayana thought about that, and shook her head. "He has my Palmetto code."

"If you change your mind..."

She nodded. Vigdis said, "Coming up on one hour. All Michael gave me was latitude and longitude. He said 101°11' west, 40°06' north."

"But that's in the Midwest somewhere," said Bailey, and stopped.

"In tropical Nebraska," Vigdis confirmed. "There was a major highway in the area, and a place to stop and eat."

"Probably a truck stop off the Interstate." At Kayana's questioning eyebrow, Bailey explained terms.

"Have you been there?" Kayana asked.

"Just in that general area. I was trying not to be noticed. The truck stop would be an open lot, but it's probably surrounded by trees. So the question is, why would anyone set up a waffle restaurant there?"

"Someone who likes waffles?" Vigdis suggested.

"Maybe it's a trading post," said Bailey. She stretched her limbs, and fought off a yawn. "We'll find out soon enough."

"I'd better brew some coffee," said Kayana.

Hovering a thousand kilometers above Earth, they saw the surface through the Videx as if from a single kilometer above. Vigdis focused on the coordinates Michael had given her. The remains of the Interstate were visible; here and there the concrete pavement had fractured from buckling in winter, and in other places it had disappeared altogether, leaving only a scar through the forest and the former farmland. The open area that once featured a truck stop was readily identified, but only three buildings remained. Scorch marks on the broken pavement spoke of a history of fire and explosions as the gas tanks ruptured and burst into flames.

"Infrared indicates only one building is in use," said Vigdis. "A stove or oven is in operation. The other two structures are dead hulks." She touched a fingertip to the Videx. "This area behind the restaurant will limit attention to the *Skygnat*. I can put us down there, and we can go eat waffles."

"Wait," said Bailey. "I see movement: a vehicle. It looks like a pickup truck."

"Parking in front of the restaurant," said Vigdis, adding, "Or what we assume is a restaurant. If we downdock behind it, they won't see us unless they go look. If you're thinking of eating, though, I doubt they accept fundscards."

"I have some silver slugs," said Kayana. "They were to be struck for coins."

Bailey nodded. She did not ask how Kayana had come by them. "All right, Vigdis, put us down."

Less than two seconds later they felt the faint jostle as the ship touched down. After they disembarked, Bailey ordered the ramp retracted and the hatch closed. Rounding the corner of the building, they saw a sign over the entrance; it read "Waffle World." Through the great display window they saw a serving counter fronted by stools, with two of the stools occupied, presumably by men from the truck. A row of tables along the windows on either side of the door had a view of the surrounding forest and the ruins of the highway.

At the door, Bailey hesitated. Both Vigdis and Kayana had violet skin and royal purple hair. Sensing her reluctance to enter, Vigdis said, "If they ask, we'll say it's body tint. Tomorrow we plan to be green. Or maybe blue."

Bailey opened the door, and they entered, walking directly toward a round plastic table in the front corner. Behind the counter, a young man acknowledged them with a wan smile. Over a simple blue shirt and jeans he was wearing a white apron that had already acquired a few stains. His attention was focused primarily on the two men at the counter. His eyes, pale in the light from overhead, wavered between the two men, as if he did not want to look directly at either of them.

His behavior put Bailey on high alert. Whoever the men were, they made the young man nervous. Yet they showed no sign of hostility. She and Vigdis sat where they could watch the tableau, while Kayana faced away from them. Presently the young man approached their table. His name tag identified him as Gerrell. On a brown plastic

64

tray he carried three glasses and a pitcher of ice water. Placing these on the table, he asked if they were ready to order. He showed no curiosity regarding violet skin or purple hair.

"Waffles for each of us," said Bailey. "Butter, please, and maple syrup." She found a tentative expression for him. "But we have no money," she went on. "We just have these. Show him, Kayana."

Kayana laid several silver slugs on the table, each the size of an old silver dollar. They clinked like a wind chime.

"Are those...?" Gerrell began, and stopped, uncertain.

"Pure silver," Kayana told him. "You can tell by the sound they make."

"It's...irregular."

"It's all we have," said Vigdis.

"If they're silver, then two of them should more than cover the meals." He hurried off to fill the order.

But the sound of the slugs and the word "silver" had attracted the two men. One of them got up and sauntered toward the table. Studying him, Bailey concluded that his primary armament was the knife in the scabbard that dangled from his canvas belt. If he carried a pistol, it was too far under his clothing to be of immediate use. He brought with him the attitude that Bailey expected; it manifested itself in a leer.

Reaching for the slugs, he said, "I'd better take those. They're much too heavy for—"

Bailey curled her hand around the pile and drew it from Kayana to her. When he leaned forward over the table to take them from her, she slapped his hand away. The unanticipated defense made him straighten, his hand diving for the hilt of his knife.

"Now that's not very nice," he said. The knife made a grating sound as he pulled it from the scabbard. "You pay Gerrell, we'll just take it from him for his weekly garnish. This way we cut out the middleman." He brought the knife to bear; it had a nine-inch blade, solid and sharp. "Now let's have those—"

"What does he pay you for?" asked Vigdis.

He seemed to notice her for the first time. "We protect him," he replied, and returned his attention to Bailey. "Those coins?" He slashed air with his knife. "One way or another."

"Who protects him from you?" asked Bailey.

He edged a little further around the table and thrust his knife at her. She fended it off with her right gauntlet, knocking it out of his hand. She answered her own question. "I guess that's our job."

She dodged away, sliding her chair, as he swung a backhanded blow that missed her head by inches. While she gained her feet, he recovered the knife. Out of the corner of her eye she glimpsed the second man, who was still sitting at the counter, but aware of the conflict. He ignited a lighter and applied it to the wick of a brownish cube in his left hand. Bailey recognized it as fireworks, but she was in no position to do anything about it. Already she realized that she had made a mistake in misjudging the malice of the two men. Gerrell's expression at the start should have keyed her. Now she had to fight to recover, and protect Gerrell. If that were possible.

Vigdis surged from her chair, but she was already too late; the man tossed the firework into the vat of hot oil used for deep-frying, and quickly backed away. For one second Vigdis considered whether to reach in for it, and at the end of that second, the firework exploded.

The result was immediately catastrophic. Oil burst into flames, and showered Vigdis. The man with the knife turned to look, and it cost him his weapon again. While Bailey stabbed him in the chest, Kayana struck his head with a metal napkin holder.

Ignoring the hot oil, Vigdis pivoted on her left leg and thrust her right at the second man's throat. The blow crushed his larynx. Gerrell, already having abandoned his waffle irons, could only stand aghast as the fires spread. His fingers writhed as he fretted helplessly. It was clear that if he'd had a fire extinguisher he would have used it. Now all he could do was watch as the flames licked at new combustible material—the wooden overhand above the counter.

"Outside," yelled Bailey, already angry with herself for not having taken pre-emptive action. She shoved Kayana ahead of her toward the door. Vigdis brushed the last flames from her clothing and grabbed Gerrell's arm, her fingers clamped like a vise. He struggled without effect as she led him away.

"But I have to...I have to...," Gerrell cried, to no avail, stumbling.

Vigdis shoved him on ahead of her. He spilled into Bailey, already outside, and she in turn collided with Kayana. Vigdis remained standing; the other three spilled onto the grass.

Thick dark smoke billowed out the open door. They heard several small explosions that rattled the windows.

"Further away!" shouted Bailey, dragging Kayana with her.

Through the windows they saw smoke form a great cloud, looking for release. Gerrell, forlorn, dropped to his knees on the grass. Vigdis tugged at him, but he refused to budge. Bending at the knees, she caught him by his belt and his collar and hoisted him over her shoulder. Finally they gathered a hundred feet away and watched the fire burn. By this time, Gerrell was almost in tears as Vigdis set him gently on the grass.

"I blame Michael," Bailey said bitterly, to no one in particular. "He should have given us more information." She punctuated this with some words strung together with hyphens.

"Who *are* you people?" moaned Gerrell, hands to his head as he rocked back and forth on the grass. "My café. Oh, my café. What have you done?"

"I'm-I'm sorry," said Bailey, wincing at the futility of the apology. It was all she could offer. She tried again. "I'm so sorry."

"Two years. Two *years!*"

Kayana laid a hand on his shoulder, but he shrugged it away. "Don't touch me. Don't you touch me!"

Bailey was now at a loss for something to say or do. Had Michael foreseen this? She could have let it go; she could have allowed the man to take the slugs. She had access to thousands more. That would have ended it; the men would have left, and she and her companions would be wolfing down waffles.

A window blew out. Black smoke swirled into the air, and caught a breeze to the east.

It was no consolation to Bailey or to Gerrell that she had meant well. Extortion, once permitted, never ended. But the cost, the cost, Gerrell would have preferred to keep his café and pay the extortion, the "protection" money. Now he had neither café nor money. She knew precisely whose fault that was. Fists of frustration hardened her hands. She wanted to cry out, but what right had she to anguish? No, this was Gerrell's moment of grief, and she could not bring herself to deny him that in any way.

"We could," began Kayana, and stopped abruptly at Bailey's glare and shake of her head.

Interventions are not always the best options, thought Bailey.

Of course, after acquiring the silver slugs, the men might have wanted something else from her and Vigdis and Kayana. That had been the desire behind the first man's leer. Even had Bailey surrendered the silver, the ensuing tableau could not have ended well for the men. But the café might have survived.

Gerrell began to weep. Bailey scooted to sit beside him, but was careful not to touch him. He did not acknowledge her presence, and might not even have been aware of it. Still words failed her; she had two strikes against her: she was unaccustomed to giving comfort, and she was herself the cause of the discomfort. Yet sooner or later she would have to say something.

She took a chance. "Where do you get your cooking supplies?" she asked.

Utterly shocked, he turned toward her, slack-jawed. "*What?*"

This close, she noted that his eyes were pale green. "I just asked—"

"I heard you, I heard you. How you can ask me that at a time like this..." He dragged fingers through brown locks. His mouth continued to work, but emitted no more sounds.

"I just wanted to know," Bailey said softly. "No harm in that."

"You've already done enough harm," he hissed. "Damn you."

"And I wish I hadn't," she whispered.

"Go to hell."

"Yeah. Please tell me about the flour, the eggs, where you get them."

He shook his head. "You're trying to make me think of something else."

"Yeah."

"It won't work."

"It's already working," she pointed out. "You're aware of what I'm trying to do. But I still would like to know."

The roof sagged, and collapsed in a shower of sparks. Gerrell covered his face with his hands, his desolation complete.

"The cooking oil came from an abandoned mart," he said, his voice soft but strong. "Nobody pillages cooking oil. Bags of waffle mix were still good; I had to toss only a few that were infested. Some canned goods were still useful. Some jars—jelly and jam and such. There's a farm nearby with chickens and cows. The marauders leave them alone; there's a cemetery of them in front of the place. This was already a café when I came across it; all I had to do was fix it up. I even have a small clientele. But now...oh, damn you."

"I can't replace the work you put in," Bailey told him. "But I can offer you a new café at no cost, a regular supply of foodstuffs, plus whatever else you need—utensils, waffle irons, pots and pans, dishes, whatever. And I do mean no cost. And there won't be any extortion."

Gerrell made fists. "I-I...don't think I can take a lie like that from you. Not on top of everything else you did."

"I don't lie, Gerrell," she whispered.

"You don't mean on Earth," said Vigdis.

Gerrell's brow furrowed. "What does that mean? What does she mean?"

"You can't have failed to notice her skin and hair color," said Kayana. "Mine as well."

The tip of his tongue flicked over his lips. "I-I thought...I assumed...you know, some sort of tint or..."

Kayana shook her head.

"You mean you're...you're saying you're from..."

"Outer space," Bailey finished for him.

Gerrell growled. "Now I've heard everything."

"Actually, I'm from Earth," she said. "But I moved away. No future here."

He struggled to his feet. "This is intolerable," he snarled, and started to walk away.

"Our spaceship is out by the woods behind the café," said Vigdis.

He took several more steps, then paused and stood very still for a long moment. Finally he turned around. His tone was filled with challenge. "Prove it."

Half a minute later, Gerrell breathed, "Holy..."

Bailey grinned. "Would you care to step aboard, sir?"

008: Sneak Attack

With her knowledge of the worlds of the Spiral Arm, Vigdis set course for Lanna Lost, in the Vannel Cluster toward the edge of the galaxy. That world's very remoteness protected it from invasion—not that there was much reason to invade, for Lanna Lost was self-sufficient, with only a small excess of production available for trade with the other Cluster worlds. Even so, thalers were always welcome from outside.

With Bailey's permission, Vigdis chose the landing site: a spaceport that served Wolkom, with a population of some ten thousand that made it one of the larger settlements on the coast of the north temperate continent called Shevverland. Wolkom was an entrepot, with sentient beings of several species having established residence and gained employment. After letting an airfoil at the spaceport, Bailey and the others made for M&FP Construction just inside the outskirts of Wolkom. M&FP had been their only choice for a construction company because the other three specialized in renovations, and only dabbled in new construction.

The site consisted of a large warehouse made of pastel green structural plastic, where supplies and equipment were stored, and an open area to one side for machinery. Visible outside, excavation vehicles awaited operators and orders. The office, a separate brick and wood structure situated at the front of the warehouse, was staffed at the moment by two blue individuals, one male and one female, if their attire was any indication. Vigdis and Kayana took the appearance of the two in stride, but Bailey and Gerrell eyed them curiously. Each had **pale** blue skin, nostril flaps, nictitating membranes over ultramarine eyes, and hands whose webbed digits consisted of two middle fingers and two opposable thumbs. Name tags identified them as Lolli and Tullen.

Bailey and Gerrell stopped staring before it became an embarrassment. While Kayana approached the counter, Vigdis took them aside. "Motics," she said softly.

"They live here on the coast because their natural habitat is the ocean. But they are not native to Lanna Lost." With that, she led them to the counter.

Vigdis did most of the talking, and started out with pleasantries. "Let me guess," she said, after introducing herself. "M&FP refers to the home world. You call it Motoya, others refer to it as Far Parkins."

Immediately the two Motics relaxed. "Have you been there?" asked Lolli.

Vigdis presented her best smile. "I have visited, let us say, by proxy." She introduced the others as well, and brought Gerrell to the fore.

There followed a detailed description by Vigdis and Gerrell of what was needed. Lolli and Tullen listened carefully and took notes on their Palmettos, and their sapphire eyes shone as they mentally added up the thalers. On several occasions their nictitating membranes moistened those eyes and made them glisten.

At one point Vigdis's knees seemed to buckle a little, and for a few seconds she fell silent. Suddenly worried, Bailey touched her elbow. But Vigdis turned toward her, smiling. "I don't know," she said. "It's nothing."

"Computer glitch?" asked Bailey.

"What is that?"

Bailey shook this off. "Never mind. You were saying?"

Vigdis turned to Tullen, who had finished taking her notes. "How long will this take to build, do you think?"

"Excavation, prefab, weather," said Tullen. "One day for us to buy the land in Gerrell's name, one day for the permits, five days for construction, at most."

"And the total cost for all that," said Bailey.

Tullen did not hesitate. "Two hundred forty thousand thalers. We will refund the excess if any, of course, and we are committed to that amount, even if costs go over that."

Bailey reached out for the fundscard Vigdis had made and established for Gerrell. After but a moment of consideration, she uploaded one million thalers into it. A broad grin split his face when he saw the amount.

"You're on your own for equipment and a place to live," said Bailey.

"I'll live in one of the rooms on the second level," he replied. "As for supplies, I don't know yet." His expression melted into anxiety. "And irons, and flour, and syrup, and butter. Something will work out."

Bailey drew his attention to her Palmetto. "I got you into this," she said. "If you need something from Earth, and I can find it, I'll bring it to you."

"Maple syrup would be nice, about a week from now."

"I'll see to it," she said. "If I can, I'll also bring some maple saplings. If they'll grow here, you can tap them when they're old enough."

"I-I..." He looked flustered. "Thank...thank you."

"Pay the woman, Gerrell."

Her word kept, Bailey and Gerrell parted ways. She boarded the airfoil, with Vigdis on the bridge and Kayana seated on the aft bench, and they headed back to the spaceport. All's well, thought Bailey, that ends well. Where earlier she had considered the incident at *Waffle World* a failure, now she marked it as a success. Gerrell's easy acceptance of the fact of interstellar travel and life on other worlds had made his participation and adjustment easier. Perhaps he had read a good deal of science fiction.

On the bridge of the airfoil, Vigdis's knuckles whitened as she clutched the taffrail. Bailey noticed this, but offered no remark on it. They made the spaceport, turned in the airfoil, and boarded the *Skygnat*. Vigdis took her usual place in the port captain's chair, while Bailey chose to remain standing. During the entire return to the ship, Vigdis had not uttered a single word. Considering that Vigdis was pondering some serious question, Bailey did not interrupt her except to set a course.

"What does Michael have for us?" she asked first.

Vigdis did not respond.

Bailey sighed. "All right, then, take us up into orbit and hold there while we determine a destination."

Immediately the view through the Videx showed the featureless matte black of null-space. Still Vigdis did not move. Bailey flopped onto the starboard chair and eyed Vigdis with a mix of curiosity and wariness. Twice she spoke her name, without reaction. She raised an eyebrow at Kayana.

"I don't know," said Kayana. "I'm not sure. She has never been a...a person before."

Bailey tokked directly for the ship's computer, bypassing the woman that was Vigdis. Before she could issue an instruction, the Videx once again showed realtime. They were passing over a forest and headed for some rolling, grass-covered terrain. The sun directly ahead and just above the horizon was the orange dwarf that held Lanna Lost in thrall. They had not left the planet.

The *Skygnat* touched down, and bounced on a hill. The impact spilled both Bailey and Kayana onto the deck. Amid some groaning of the ship's undercarriage, it yawed and pitched across the dips and rises and at last slid to a stop. Vigdis stood up and, without helping Bailey and Kayana to their feet, went aft and out the hatch and down the extruded ramp onto the grass outside.

Bailey and Kayana dashed after her. As Vigdis reached the grass, she began to stagger, and finally dropped to her knees. Amethyst eyes shiny with terror, she turned a confused and apprehensive face to Bailey. The sound that came from her mouth was that of a mouse receiving the death chomp from a cat. But the sound nevertheless was a distinct word.

"Help," squeaked Vigdis, and vanished.

The disappearance brought a gasp from Bailey. A blast of emptiness filled her, from heart to mind to soul, as if existence itself had ceased to exist. She felt like collapsing onto the grass, and only just managed to summon the strength and the will to remain upright. Filling the emptiness came a burst of fear that quickened her heart. What could possibly have happened? But she had no time to consider the question, for a blue beam struck the grass several meters to one side of her. She whirled around to learn the source of the beam.

Two men stood on a low hummock. One of them was holding an outsized Palmetto. The other, sidearm in his right hand, was Vattar.

009: Restorative

Kayana cried out first. "What are you doing?" Her tone was that of the older sister, but fear coarsened it.

"I'm taking my ship back," Vattar declared.

He aimed his sidearm at Bailey and fired, but she anticipated that move and was already in motion, the beam passing harmlessly through the spot where she had been.

Kayana raised her hands as if to plead for Bailey. "Don't," she said. "Just take the ship and go."

"No!" yelled Bailey.

Vattar fired again. This time she deflected the beam with her gauntlet.

"No," she said once more. He continued to fire, but she moved around on the grass and protected herself with the gauntlets. "*Skygnat* is my ship. You are a recalcitrant crewmember who has betrayed the ship and are engaging in mutiny. For that offense alone I can as ship's captain execute you at my pleasure." She punctuated this by reflecting a blue beam back in the general direction of its origin. It almost struck the man standing beside Vattar, who cried out as he flinched. But she had to be careful. Until Vigdis was brought back, she dared not cross the gauntlets.

"My payment," demanded the man, his free hand held out to Vattar. "The rest is your affair."

Vattar remained focused on Bailey. "I gave you forty thousand," he said gruffly. "You'll get the rest after I deliver my shipment."

The man scoffed. His hand remained out. "Such was not our agreement. Forty thousand when I deproject her; forty thousand upon completion. I say again, and for the last time: my payment."

"Who *are* you?" Kayana asked him.

"My name is of no concern to you," he replied. "However, if you must have it, I am Laoshi Stavo Fledder."

Kayana shook her head in ignorance. This took Fledder by surprise.

"You have not heard of me? Such a disgrace. I am Senior Calculator Excellence for GalaxyNet."

Kayana's violet eyes widened. "Then you must be... eighteenth level?"

"Nineteenth. One to go, and after Glorin dies I shall surely rise to that position."

"Then you can bring her back," said Bailey.

"I could. But I am not being paid to do so."

Vattar fired again, in frustration, and again the beam was deflected. "Enough! Kayana, get aboard."

Kayana shook her head. "I am the senior sibling. You will do nothing until Vigdis is brought back. Once that is done, you will leave here, but not aboard *Skygnat*." To Fledder, she added, "He still has close to sixty thousand thalers in his account. He can pay you now."

Fledder spun on Vattar. "Is this so?"

"Oh, dear," Bailey mocked. "Calculator Fledder, I wonder whether he intended to pay you the remainder."

"As do I," said Fledder. He began to tok his Palmetto to bring Vigdis back.

"No!" yelled Vattar, and made to fire on him.

Bailey crossed her gauntlets. A ferocious white beam split Vattar almost in half, and before he could depress the enable button on his sidearm. Impact with the ground completed his separation into two parts. Entrails slipped onto the grass.

Kayana dropped to her knees and vomited onto the grass.

"I'm sorry," whispered Bailey. "He rushed me. I had to." But the raw violence of Vattar's death left her stunned. She had meant to stop him from killing Fledder, and thereby protecting the possibility of getting Vigdis back. But Vattar had rushed her, and her emotions had augmented the power of the gauntlets. She was not sorry for having killed Vattar, but she was sorry that she'd had to kill him.

Unperturbed, Fledder paused in his tokking, the tip of his index finger poised above the Palmetto. He arched a questioning gray eyebrow at Bailey. She approached him cautiously. As she passed by Kayana, the violet female

77

collapsed onto the grass, clutching her belly. She paused for a moment with a look of pity and sorrow for Kayana. But she still had a matter to resolve.

"You work for pay, yes?" Bailey asked Fledder, drawing up to him. "You keep your agreements, yes?"

"Of course. What else?"

Bailey set her fists on her hips. "Restore Vigdis. Assure me that you will not ever do anything to interfere with her in any way, nor will you have anyone else do so."

Fledder's finger remained poised. "And in return?"

"One million thalers," answered Bailey. "*However*. If you violate our agreement in any way, I will hunt you down with the help of The Commission, whom I represent, and I will remove parts of your body one by one until she is restored unharmed. I may allow you to retain one arm, whose hand includes one finger for your tokking. How you will hold the Palmetto without the other arm or your legs, is your problem. Perhaps you can hold it between your teeth. Oh, wait, I misspoke. I meant between your gums." She paused for emphasis. "Understood?"

Fledder did not hesitate. "We are agreed."

She passed him her fundscard, and watched while he transferred the correct amount. A few moments later, Vigdis appeared, on one knee beside Kayana, an arm around her in comfort.

"I think you had better go now," said Bailey.

She watched while the technician passed over the crest of a low hill. Less than a minute later she heard the sound of collapsed air filling the space where the ship had been. Already Vigdis had hoisted Kayana to her feet.

"I'm sorry, Kayana," Bailey said again.

"It should have been done long ago," said Kayana, as the three headed for the *Skygnat*. "I should have seen to it, as ship's captain. I see that now. But...but he was my brother."

"He must have done something good," said Vigdis. "Remember that."

Kayana could but nod slowly, looking for acceptance, her face wan and pale.

They reached the bridge. There, with Kayana seated gloomily on the murphy bench, Bailey addressed Vigdis. "Are you all right?"

"I have already completed a full diagnostic, and found no discrepancies."

"I'll take that as a yes. Any suggestions as to course heading?"

"I have nothing from Michael," answered Vigdis. "So perhaps someplace quiet?"

"I'll leave that to you," said Bailey.

Tonopana proved to be a world of islands, some the size of Borneo, others as small as a coral atoll. Mostly it was cold—Tonopana orbited at the outer limits of its star's goldilox zone—but the equatorial islands were pleasant and serene. Only some eleven thousand humanoids of various species, none indigenous, inhabited the islands; the rest—a hundred thousand at any given moment—were tourists. Aside from carvings of wood and shell, and other trinkets, tourism was the main industry on Tonopana.

Bailey was reminded of Hawaii before the terrible fires. The ambient temperature was a little less here on the island of Naami—she estimated it at around eighty—and the stubby windswept trees were nothing like palms, but there was a distinct air of tropical paradise to the place, and perhaps that, more than anything else, attracted the tourists.

Another quick look around as they trod the boardwalk reminded Bailey of her own uniqueness. Amid the variations of skin color, hair color, eye color and number, scales, facial features, genitalia (for some were naked), locomotion—for one species resembled nothing so much as a furry snake with four arms and a great scaled head, all in camouflage green—and a dozen other characteristics she had only read about in science fiction or fantasy books, she realized again that she was the only human. Punctuating this were many who eyed, stared, or gaped at her as she and Vigdis and Kayana passed by. She felt as if there were a bit of cake frosting just past the corner of her mouth; instinctively she wiped at the spot, and chuckled to herself for doing so.

Most amazingly, Bailey understood all the words spoken around her, including a few that were less than charitable. She asked Vigdis about it.

Vigdis shook her head. "It is not my Universal Translator function," she said. "There is a UT field all around the equator."

"That's convenient," Bailey replied.

"The local Tourism Board found it so. The inability to conceal your intentions through the use of a foreign language reduces the likelihood of conflict, which of course is in the interests of the board."

"I've heard a few remarks."

"But nothing untoward."

"No." With stiffened fingers she shook out shaggy black locks that a mild gust from the ocean had just disheveled. "But I almost wish I had scales."

"You wouldn't say that during molting season."

"I suppose not." She paused at a bank of steps. "Can we go down to the beach?"

In response, Vigdis made a show of inspecting their attire: all three were wearing outsuits and boots. "We're a little overdressed," she said.

"I didn't bring a bathing suit."

Kayana pointed at some swimmers just emerging from the waves. "Neither did they."

Bailey demurred. "I'm not sure I'm ready for that."

They slid aside as a greenish-gray biped, obviously male, ascended the steps.

"Body conscious?" said Vigdis. "Surely not on my account. I've seen both you and Kayana."

"Yeah...wait. You mean...you and, and Kayana?"

"Her and me what?" said Kayana.

Vigdis made a face. "No. But as the ship's computer, I 'see' everything."

"Wait," said Kayana, to Bailey. "You mean you and Vigdis...?"

"I've decided I would like to go swimming," Bailey announced quickly, and led them down the steps and onto the sand.

"Body towels and beach towels over there," Vigdis said, pointing. "And you two can check your clothing securely there."

"What about you?" asked Kayana. Immediately Vigdis was naked. "Oh. Right."

There followed a race to the water, won by Vigdis. A wave surge spilled Kayana. Bailey found the water temperature surprisingly warm, with just the hint of a chill as she rose from her dive just past the breakers. She shook the water from her hair as she looked around. Out here, no one gave her or her companions any more than a passing glance. Here and there, others cavorted and splashed—she could not count the separate species, nor did she know whether the term "species" even applied generally in outer space. It was easier for her to lump them all into the category of People, at least until she learned more about some worlds of origin.

Kayana drew up beside her, dripping into the waves. She seemed to be enjoying the activity, although there was a faintly haunted dullness in her violet eyes that tore at Bailey's heart. Deeming it prudent to make no remark, she turned to look out over the ocean.

"How far to the next island?" she asked Kayana.

Kayana's pout revealed a lack of knowledge. "I am first-time on Tonopana," she said. "I have heard of this world, nothing more." Her brow furrowed. "You were not thinking of swimming there, surely."

Bailey laughed, and ducked as Vigdis arrived with a two-handed cast of water at her. She swam further out, rising with the next wave. As the others joined her, she felt a hard nudge at her left calf, and yelped, having forgotten about the possibility of sharks, or whatever creature filled that niche on Tonopana. But it was not a shark that now rose from the water.

The person who stood in the low between waves looked vaguely familiar, which struck Bailey as odd until she recalled having recently seen those characteristics on Tullen, the female Motic at the construction company. Like Tullen, this one had intensely blue hair, pale blue skin, and sapphire eyes. Also visible, and identifying her to Bailey as female, were two breasts with nipples but no areolae. Her nostril flaps were closed, and she was breathing through her mouth.

"I am so sorry," said the Motic, easing away nervously. "I did not know you were there."

"Sometimes I don't know that, either," said Bailey.

That stopped the blue female. She looked at the water between them, as if to avoid meeting Bailey's eyes. "I do not understand."

Bailey waved this off, and extended a friendly hand as she introduced herself. But the Motic backed away again. "Is something wrong?" asked Bailey.

"That is...you are offering me your arm?"

As Vigdis and Kayana joined her, she worried that she had committed a *faux pas*. "Is that wrong?"

Even the question seemed to repel her. Her mouth fumbled for words. "But I am, am Motic."

Bailey nodded. "Yes, I know. So?"

"Because they are—" began Kayana, and was cut off by a sharp elbow in the ribs.

"Why prejudice her?" Vigdis whispered, her lips brushing Kayana's ear.

"I should go," said the Motic, and turned to leave.

"Please wait," begged Bailey, bobbing with a wave. "Please tell me what I did wrong."

The blue female remained nonplussed. "Nothing you did. But I am Motic."

"Yes. And that means what?"

Briefly she fell silent. "You do not understand."

"I'm trying to."

"Others," she began, and rubbed the two middle fingers of her right hand against her nose, as if to cure an itch. She looked away. "Others do not seek to become acquainted with...with us. But I see you are of a world I do not know. Is that why you offer me...?"

82

Bailey smiled. "I'm just trying to be friendly." As a wave washed around them she extended her arm once more. "I'm Bailey."

Very hesitantly the Motic approached, and with dainty uncertainty reached out a hand with two middle fingers between two opposable thumbs, and lightly wrapped them around Bailey's forearm just below the elbow. "I am Amargon," she said shakily, and withdrew even as Bailey started to clasp her forearm.

"Please wait," Bailey asked again. "These two are my friends. This is Vigdis, and this is Kayana."

Wonder filled Amargon's sapphire eyes. "You...you are...are serious about...about this."

Bailey inclined her head. "Very. I am new to all these worlds. I have much to learn. Friends can teach me, and perhaps I can teach them."

"F-friends?"

"Why don't the four of us go ashore, get dressed, and find a quiet place that serves good things to drink?" said Bailey.

A hesitant nod from Amargon. "All...all right."

After three failures to find a friendly stall operator willing to serve all four of them—and with each failure Bailey's features darkened with irritation—they finally located a stall where the service was at least a level above surly. Seating themselves around a white plastic table shaded by a green and white umbrella, they ordered four *haitanjius*, which Amargon described as "beach ale." After a clinking toast of green glass bottles, Amargon found the drink quite satisfactory, while the others bestowed perfunctory compliments on it. Bailey considered the beverage weak, but issued no comment on that score.

After the second gulp, Amargon sobered, and set her bottle down on a circle of condensation. "Do you begin to see?" she asked Bailey.

"I'm sorry, Amargon. It's not that they would refuse you service, but that they would rather you went elsewhere. The question I have is why."

83

The Motic studied the condensation. "I would rather not say," she said softly, as if ashamed.

Bailey did not pursue the matter. Instead, she turned a little toward the ocean. "The sun is about an hour from setting," she noted.

"Okala, yes," said Amargon. "That is the sun's name."

"We're being watched," said Vigdis.

"I don't doubt it," Bailey muttered. She took another gulp.

"Two males," Vigdis went on. "Or men, but not human. They're focused on our new friend."

Amargon spat harsh words.

Bailey glanced in their direction just enough for a glimpse. They were of a type, burly and rugged, but well and fully dressed. She noted bulges under each man's pullover, and assumed weaponry. Their hair and skin color, if on Earth, might have identified them as Mediterranean. Seated, their height could not be determined, but Bailey estimated it as about the same as her own six-two.

"They will not harm you," Vigdis assured her. "I promise you that."

"But they could be...," said Amargon, and stopped.

"What?" asked Kayana. "They could be what?"

Amargon shook her head. "It is best not to know. But I have not seen them before. Perhaps I am wrong." She drained the last of her ale and stood up. "I had better go. I am in Cabin 5. I would invite you, but you would not be...comfortable. If you are staying, Cabin 6 is unoccupied. There is a pay slot above the door handle for your card." She tried not to look at the men. "I had better go," she repeated, and did so.

010: Gone

"She is spooked," was Bailey's evaluation. "She doesn't know those two men, so she must know their kind. She knows what they do."

"Which is what?" asked Kayana.

"I've no idea. Expressions are difficult for me to read out here, but I'd say they wouldn't flinch at fracturing a statute or two to do whatever it is they do."

"Maybe they don't like outlanders," Kayana suggested.

"Everyone on this world is an outlander," said Vigdis. "Tonopana has no indigenous sentient species."

"Okala is lower, and about to set," said Kayana, after a moment. "We still need dinner."

"We can eat in our room. Vigdis?"

Vigdis glanced down at the menu adhered to the tabletop under transparent sealant. "If these words from the UT are accurate, there's a vegetable curry over rice that should satisfy."

"Nothing with meat?" asked Bailey.

Vigdis said carefully, "Perhaps you should acquaint yourself with some of the livestock before you ask."

Bailey laughed. "Understood. Right, then, three vegetable curries to go."

"Those men are gone," said Kayana.

"They went the other way," said Vigdis, and signaled to place an order.

The food containers arrived in ten minutes, and the aromas only piqued Bailey's hunger. While Bailey inserted her fundscard to register for Cabin 6, Vigdis checked the adjacent door and reported her findings.

"It still reads 'occupied,' but there was no response when I knocked," she said.

"She may have gone somewhere else," said Kayana, and stepped inside. "Hmm. Two beds."

"We'll work it out," Bailey said, as Vigdis secured the door.

After checking out the room—blue pile carpeting was easy on their feet—they settled on a small table with two chairs, Vigdis taking up a seat on the bed. With the plastic spoons distributed, they began to dig into their containers.

"If this is as good as it smells," said Bailey, "I may take up residence."

"Seriously?" said Vigdis.

"Well, no." The rest of her response was overwhelmed by yummy sounds.

"So we're staying for a few days," said Kayana.

Light from outside faded as Okala began to sink into the ocean. Pole lights outside soon replaced that from the star, and cast shadows into the room. Kayana got up to close the curtains. Irregular thumps began to vibrate the walls. "Twilight fireworks, perhaps," she explained. "Though they seem a little close."

"I've seen enough of war," muttered Bailey, and continued to eat.

"This isn't war," said Kayana. "It's...well, it's quite spectacular. And...it ends. You missed it." She returned to her chair. The last reverberations shook the cabin walls.

"I'm sorry," said Bailey. "I just wasn't in the mood."

"Bad memories?"

"Yeah, sometimes. I spent over four years dodging occasional explosions and scurrying for shelter. Loud noises...sometimes take me back."

"I didn't mean to..."

Bailey touched her arm. "I know you didn't. It's okay. Tomorrow night I might even join you at the window."

"Or out on the beach itself."

"We could still take a walk out there," said Vigdis. "After we finish this."

An hour of wandering around overhearing inane conversations finally tired Bailey to the point that she was ready to return to the cabin. Each carrying icy refreshments, they settled into the room. Presently Bailey went to check the status of Cabin 5, and found it still

86

occupied. A tentative rap on the door gained no response, and she returned to her room.

"Anything?" Vigdis asked her, as she sat down on a corner of the bed.

"She may not have returned yet, or she went to sleep. I don't know. But I'd like to know where she went."

"You'd like to know that she's safe," said Vigdis.

"Yeah."

"Maybe we will catch her in the morning," said Kayana.

Bailey reached into her pocket for a thaler. "Meantime: a coin flip to see who has to share a bed."

"That is not necessary," Kayana demurred. "I wish to sleep alone."

Bailey threw her a curious look, but said nothing. She wondered whether it was a personal choice, or she was reluctant to sleep with two people who had been intimate. It brought home to Bailey the possibility that Kayana was not quite certain where she fit in, or what her position and duties might be. Earlier she had been in effective command of the *Skygnat*. Now she was crew without a role.

"All right, Kayana," Bailey agreed. "Vigdis, anything yet from Michael?"

She shook her head. "We're on our own," she replied. "If we see it, we solve it."

"We'll get up early, then." She trudged to the bed. "Good night, you two."

*   *   *

Bailey did not sleep well. She drifted in and out, the memory of the fireworks echoing for a while. Beside her, Vigdis droned on, although she was always aware of her surroundings. Bailey checked her eyes; both were closed, but that meant nothing with Vigdis. Muttering about luck, she fell back asleep and waited to toss and turn again.

Daylight poured through the window above Kayana. The morning still felt too early for Bailey, and she rolled over, only to find that Vigdis was already up and holding a cup of fresh coffee. The aroma reached her, and she found the strength to stand up.

"We need to talk," said Vigdis, pouring a cup for her, adding with a glance at Kayana, "Privately."

Frowning, Bailey burned her tongue on the coffee. "Alcove?" she asked.

"As good a place as any."

With the door closed, they spoke in low tones.

"She muttered her brother's name several times," Vigdis told her. "I doubt she was awake; dreaming, most likely. But she was shivering under the quilt. Bailey Belvedere, she has not resolved her loss."

"I've thought as much," said Bailey. "But I don't see any way through except the passage of time."

Vigdis hesitated. "There's...something else."

"I know that tone."

"I thought about it this morning before you awoke." She took a moment to gather her words. "Not all the rumbles last night were from fireworks," she said slowly. "Some were far away; those were probably fireworks. Other rumbles were...closer."

"How close?"

"I do not know. Nearby."

Bailey considered. "Amargon?"

"It's possible. And there were some vibrations eleven minutes ago that I cannot explain."

Bailey yanked the alcove door open. "Let's go find out," she said, and put on her gauntlets. On her way out the front door, she awakened Kayana.

At the door to Cabin 5, Bailey paused. The room was now listed as "available." Bailey felt a nameless unease as she inserted her fundscard to occupy the room. Very carefully she pushed the door open into a dark room.

A burst of odor struck her. It seemed to combine the worst features of brine and dead fish, with a side of old perspiration. Bailey coughed and choked and stepped back.

Kayana swore, and turned away. Only Vigdis was unaffected.

The bed had not been made; two chairs stood toward the back instead of at the table. Dark stains on the carpet might have been blood, but if so, the blood was

88

blue. Of most concern was the depressed square in the carpeting between the bed and the table. It looked to measure a meter on a side. Leading from the depression were two furrows, as if wheels bearing weight had been drawn toward the door.

"Oh, I don't like this," said Bailey, her voice low. Her heart raced, pulsing in her head; she recognized fear, but not for herself. "Vigdis, patch into all the ships at the spaceport and find those that are about to leave—"

"There are two. One is a cargo galleon; the other is a shuttle."

"Delay the galleon, hold that shuttle! Kayana!"

"What?" she yelled back.

Chagrined, Bailey looked contrite. "Sorry, Kayana, I didn't realize...okay, let's get to the spaceport."

They moved out at a trot. "What's going on?" asked Kayana.

"I think Amargon has been abducted," Bailey told her roughly. "Probably by slavers."

Kayana caught her up. "Those men?"

"Probably. Vigdis, are those ships still in place?"

"They won't leave until I release them."

"A woman of many talents," Bailey chuckled.

This early in the morning, the walkways were unobstructed by people or furniture. Already Okala was peering above the horizon, checking to see whether it was safe to rise. Ahead opened the spaceport tarmac, with the terminal and private hangars beyond. At this point, Vigdis set the direction, leading them toward a black shuttle with silver detailing. Even as they approached, Vigdis overrode the shuttle's computer and caused the ramp to extrude.

As Bailey stepped onto the ramp, one of the two men who had sat at the table the evening before now appeared in the open hatchway. Immediately he drew his sidearm and fired. Bailey crossed her gauntleted forearms and sent the blue beam back. It struck the man in both knees, and he spilled onto the ramp and tumbled down it. Bailey stepped aside to let him pass. Vigdis leaped over him. Kayana kicked him out of the way.

89

Bailey rushed to the shuttle's bridge and found there the second man from the table. By the time he stood up from his chair, she was on him, and put him down with a simple *shuto* to the nerve center below the sternum. She was relieved to learn that the blow disabled some non-humans. While he lay gasping on the deck, Vigdis and Kayana arrived.

Vigdis bunched the front of his shirt in her fist and hoisted the man back onto his chair.

"Where is the Motic?" demanded Bailey.

The man gave her a hard stare. He looked as if he wanted to spit.

"Vigdis, break one of his bones every ten seconds until he responds."

"If I may," interrupted Kayana, before Vigdis could strike. Gently she nudged Vigdis aside, and stood before him. "He is a Taurean," she explained casually to Bailey. "They have a nerve mass in the chest, as you discovered. But their pain center is located at another part of the body. No matter where you strike a Taurean, they feel it just below the septum. Their brain then decrees the location of the injury that caused the pain."

"You're talking about the nose," said Bailey.

Kayana's right hand was a flash of movement. The edge of it struck the Taurean's face between the nose and the upper lip. Instantly he went rigid, his body thrown back against the chair, his head well back and mouth agape. His expression became a rictus of agony. Kayana seized his nose between two fingers and drew him forward.

"She won't ask you again," she said. "That's the way she is. So answer her question. Or are you ready for the next strike from me?"

"H-hold," said the Taurean. "M-motic...there."

"Vigdis, guard him," said Bailey. "Kayana, you're with me."

They made their way aft. On the way, Bailey peered out the hatch for the other man. He still lay in a heap at the bottom of the ramp, clutching his knees and moaning. They reached the hold and saw that the hatch had not been secured. Puzzled, Bailey thrust the hatch open and

90

stepped inside just as a wave of the odor she had encountered in the cabin wafted against her nose.

Kayana's face wrinkled; she had caught the odor too.

The only object in the hold was a box of gray structural plastic a meter square and two meters high. The door was secured by a simple latch. After some hesitation, Bailey unlatched it and opened the door.

And immediately covered her nose with both hands as she fell back.

The Motic female, Amargon, cowered inside the box, arms clutching her body as if in protection. "Don't see me," she pleaded. It was almost a wail. "Don't shame me. Oh, please don't."

Bailey freed a hand and held it up for peace. "I won't," she said, not looking at her. "We won't. Are you... all right?"

"Where is your soap?" asked Kayana.

The question smacked Bailey, who turned to stare at her. "Where's her what?"

"It's a special soap." She began looking around, and finally found a travel bag behind the box. Opening it, she reached in and felt around inside. "Ah, there we are." Returning to Amargon, she handed her the bar of coarse brown soap and said, "There's a shower stall in the stateroom hygiene alcove. I'll take you there. I don't think the Taureans will mind if you use it."

Amargon stepped forward, out of the box. "I'm so ashamed."

"Don't be," said Kayana. "They did this to you. Go clean up. I'll bring your bag so you can dress."

Bailey stepped back to let her pass. Both eyebrows arched in a question. "Kayana?"

"Let us leave this hold for some fresh air," she said. "I will explain later, after she is clean."

Back on the bridge, Bailey discovered that the odor had already penetrated this far. Still, it was faint enough to be merely unpleasant. The Taurean was glowering up at Vigdis, who displayed an innocent expression. Bailey did not believe it for a second.

91

"What have you found out so far?" she asked Vigdis.

"His name is Boll Venchu, born on Pashna," she replied. "He and his partner specialize in Motic trafficking. They happened to see Amargon here; she was a target of opportunity. Their usual practice is to go to Motoya and—"

"The Motic home world," Bailey broke in.

"Yeah. There, they isolate a few Motics, and wait."

Bailey's brow wrinkled. "I don't understand."

Vigdis shrugged. "That is as far as I got."

"But I'm missing something," Bailey complained. "What aren't you telling me? Motic trafficking? Is that like human trafficking?"

"I do not know about Earth." She was about to say more, but Kayana came to the bridge.

"She is still cleaning," she announced. "There are some outsuits in one of the bins. I told her to help herself." Sadly she shook her head. "Oh, that poor female. To be made to suffer like that..."

"Someone had better start explaining something to me," growled Bailey. "What is all this about?"

Vigdis headed aft. "I had better bring his partner back in," she said. "Before someone notices."

"Just now you think of that," said Bailey. She turned to Kayana. "Please?"

Kayana took a long breath and let half of it out. "The Motics are an aquatic species," she began. "You can tell by their webbed digits and nostril flaps. They live and eat and mate in the water. But they also forage for food—fruits and nuts—on land. That is where they are vulnerable, where they can be captured.

"Bailey...the Motics make excellent slaves, because they are easily controlled. You have already seen evidence of this, although I do not think you realize it. Recall, we encountered Amargon in the water. Specifically, in salt water. She was not merely swimming there; she was bathing. Motic skin exudes an oil, which protects them in the water and keeps it moist when they are on land. But this oil has to be washed off every eight or nine hours, before it begins to decompose and rot. Thus the odor. To smell like that is shameful, it is odious, to the Motics."

"I think I'm getting the picture," said Bailey.

"I do not know what that means."

"It means...never mind. Continue."

"As slaves, Motics are not allowed near salt water," Kayana went on. "Their only hope of avoiding that decomposition is to work hard, so that they may be allowed to bathe with that soap you saw. It is salt-water based, and will cleanse them. That is how they are controlled. If they fail to work, they are denied the soap as punishment."

"Does The Commission know about this trafficking?"

"Of course. But it is commonplace. And not just Motics." Kayana lowered her eyes. "As you know," she whispered.

"But...why doesn't The Commission do something?"

A faint smile reached Kayana's lips. "That is why they have you," she said, and shook her head. "I mean, us."

Bailey raised an eyebrow. "Kayana?"

"You, Vigdis...and me. Yes. This is what I want. This is what I choose. I do not know how much help I can be, but I will try."

Bailey touched her arm. "You've already helped, by telling me these things," she said gently. "I am still a stranger out here, and probably I always will be." Vigdis returned with the wounded man in tow. "Put him in that captain's chair," she instructed. "They're on their own."

Amargon finally made it to the bridge, wearing a pale blue outsuit that went well with her skin color, although it was too large for her. Barefoot, she stepped tentatively, as if uncertain of her approach and of the reception she might receive. When Bailey beckoned her closer, she stopped.

"It's all right," said Bailey.

Amargon spoke hesitantly. "But...you know. Now you know. About...about me."

Kayana shook her head. "You are among friends here. Bailey, perhaps we should all retreat to *Skygnat*?"

"That includes you, Amargon," said Bailey.

011: A Fresh Challenge

Amargon remained uncertain after *Skygnat* entered null-space. Mostly she was concerned about their destination. She relaxed a little when she learned it was Motoya. She was going home. Vigdis offered her a mug of coffee, which she accepted with a perfunctory courtesy. Two sips later, she was appreciative. Gradually, as she sat on the murphy bench beside Kayana, she began to speak.

Amargon had saved enough money from working at her forage kiosk on Motoya to take a short vacation. She had chosen Tonopana because of all the salt water, which made it easier to combat the deleterious effects of oil decomposition. Two days out of seven remained to her before she had to return to Motoya. She was aware of the two traffickers, and kept an eye out for them, but they had hidden themselves well.

"I did not see them," she said. "They followed me into my cabin. I tried to fight, but they were too strong."

"That would be the thumping we heard," said Vigdis. "We thought it was the fireworks."

"They put me in that box you saw," Amargon went on. "They waited. It took seven hours for me to...to...I was so ashamed. I would have done anything they wanted."

Kayana slipped an arm around her shoulders and gave her a reassuring squeeze.

"They had some sort of cart to move me around," said the Motic. "I did not know where I was until you came." She shivered. "I am frightened."

"Not of us, surely," said Bailey.

Her blue skin darkened, and her face twisted in fear. "They will continue. Those men will continue. They may find me on Motoya, and then..."

"Motoya has but one spaceport," said Vigdis.

"What are you thinking?" Bailey asked her.

Vigdis's lips tightened. "I am not certain. Perhaps there is a way to control who downdocks and who departs."

"It is not our spaceport," said Amargon. "It is managed by the Motoya Control Consortium that conducts trade with us." She gazed into her mug. "Is there any more of this?"

"I'll get it," said Kayana.

A pensive silence slowly enveloped the bridge. Vigdis sat back in her captain's chair and stared through the Videx at the matte black of null-space, deep in contemplation. Bailey mulled over what she had learned so far, but not a ray of light illuminated a solution. She was tempted to call on Michael. But what would she ask him for? If The Commission were able to or wanted to put a halt to trafficking, it would already have done so. No, the totality of trafficking was too much to take on; the resolution to this problem would have to be local.

"Could I stay with you?" asked Amargon, and quickly looked away, as if the words had escaped her without permission.

Kayana returned with two mugs. Hearing the Motic's question, she turned to Bailey. "Captain?"

Amargon found a light laugh. "I promise to bathe," she said.

Bailey temporized. "What we do is often dangerous."

"And I am no fighter."

Kayana said, "But you can learn, Amargon."

Bailey considered. As she was going to spend the rest of her life in outer space, a few companions were welcome. But she also had purpose to her life, and Amargon was relatively unskilled. She and the others would have to watch out for her.

"I'll wait to make planetfall before I decide," said Bailey, with finality. "Whether you remain aboard or not, I still want to see if there is a way to protect Motoya. Vigdis, how much longer?"

"Two hours seventeen minutes."

"This is the difficult part of space travel," Bailey said, to Amargon. "Most of the time there is nothing to do but wait. But you cannot have had much sleep in that box."

"I am tired," Amargon admitted.

"She can sleep in my stateroom," said Kayana, and tagged Amargon's arm. "Come on, I will show you."

After they had departed from the bridge, Vigdis said, "Six," and nodded to herself.

A question died stillborn on Bailey's lips; asking was not worth disturbing Vigdis's train of thought.

"And a communications center," Vigdis added. She slumped in her chair and shut her eyes.

Bailey sighed. "Guess I'm sleeping alone," she muttered, and made her way aft.

*   *   *

Two hours passed quickly. A gentle alarm awakened Bailey. After freshening up, she returned to the bridge, to find Vigdis now wide awake and seated. She yawned and stretched, and fell into the starboard captain's chair.

"Eight more minutes," said Vigdis, before Bailey could ask.

"I know you. Give."

"I do have an idea," Vigdis told her. "But I think we should run some possibilities by Michael." She turned in her chair. "Are we going to keep Amargon aboard?"

"I don't know what function she would have."

"An extra pair of eyes might see something we miss."

"True," Bailey agreed. "But I have to wonder whether her desire to stay with us is due to her fear of recapture. Vigdis, we can't protect everyone we meet."

"She can be trained to protect herself."

"You want her to stay aboard."

Vigdis nodded emphatically. "Yes. And...we're about to leave null-space."

Bailey got to her feet and began to pace the bridge. "Keep us poised in null-space. Summon Kayana and Amargon to the bridge. I'll ask for Michael. I can't wait to hear your solution."

"It's only a possibility," Vigdis hedged. "If Michael does not show, then...then I-I don't know."

97

Bailey's smile denied the seriousness of what she was about to say. "It does worry me when my computer is uncertain."

"Behavior is rarely a predictable, hundred-percent proposition," she shot back. "If this were a question of mathematics, of physical science, then I would have no doubts or questions whatsoever."

Bailey's hand came to rest on Vigdis's shoulder. "I did not mean to offend."

Vigdis patted the hand. "I know. And in this instance, your apology was predictable."

"And Michael hasn't shown," she sighed.

"Are we there yet?" asked Amargon, entering the bridge alongside Kayana.

"We're holding," Bailey replied.

The Motic lowered the murphy bench. "I do not understand." After Bailey explained their situation, Amargon said, "So there is something that could be done, but we have not as yet received a visit from The Commission." She made a face. "That is not surprising. Sometimes they are known to be useless." With that, she leaned forward on the bench, rested her elbows on her knees, and gazed down at the deck between her feet.

Amargon's statement left Bailey stunned. "Why do you say that?"

The Motic took her time answering. Her tone came wistful, touched with sorrow. She spoke in such a low voice that Bailey could barely hear her. She did not look up from the deck.

"There are four million of us left on Motoya," Amargon began. "Half a million have been taken since the trafficking began. I do not know how you measure time. For us, that was about seventy Motic years ago. It started slowly at first, until they figured out how to control us."

She shivered at the thought.

"They take us at night when we come on land to forage. Our fear shows in our posture. We keep low, never daring to stand upright and make ourselves more visible in the dark. They can take only a few at a time, because we must be isolated, allowed to oil, until we stink. It is

98

shameful, and worse, waiting inside a container, in the dark, for the inevitable. When we start screaming, they know they have us.

"They also trawl for us at night; nets take fish, of course, but too often one of us is netted. Even so, even though but about ten are taken, the catch is valuable. A compliant Motic is worth half a million thalers, but will work for twenty or thirty years, even longer. Always longing for salt water. Always longing, dreaming of home. Always living in fear. Everyone profits but us. The Control Consortium at the spaceport profits; the companies profit; I daresay The Commission profits, although that is perhaps unfair, as their power derives from their superiority as beings, and not from wealth.

"And so my choices. Remain on Motoya and hope to evade recapture, or stay on board with you and hope I have a function in your activities. I do not care for either choice. If Motoya were safe, I would stay there. If I am of no use to you, I would not want to remain here. Such a dilemma tears at us. We are endangered at home and useless in what you call space. We live in danger on Motoya and as slaves elsewhere."

Amargon fell silent. At no time had she looked up. It seemed to Bailey that she was speaking mostly to herself, to clarify her life in her mind. Beside her, leaning against her, Kayana was shedding tears.

And Michael had yet to show on the bridge, or to respond in any way.

"I don't know what to say," said Bailey. Air left the cushion as she sank onto her captain's chair. The enormity of trafficking on Motoya left her depressed. Without intervention from The Commission, no solution seemed possible. She had been confronted with an evil beyond her ability to fight.

"Do not be sad," said Amargon. She now raised her eyes. "This is neither your fault nor your battle. This is simply the way of it. Some of us cope; others are taken."

"It's not right," Bailey seethed.

Kayana nodded agreement, as tears continued to streak her mauve face. "One day perhaps I will be forgiven for being involved in trafficking. Vattar and I did not deal in capturing Motics, although we did transport several. Bailey, I need to make this right. We have to do something." Turning to Amargon, she added, "I do beg your forgiveness."

"You have shown me nothing but kindness," said the Motic. "Your past is forgiven, my friend."

"This Control Consortium," said Bailey. "What exactly does it do on Motoya?"

"I do not know everything," Amargon answered. "They arrange downdocks for incoming spacecraft—"

"Including traffickers?" Vigdis interrupted.

"The Control Consortium is not concerned with the purpose of the visit. They arrange hangars for ships and small warehouses for storage. For departures, permission is perfunctory. No one cares what the cargo might be."

"Earlier you mentioned trade," said Bailey. "What does Motoya produce?"

"Smoked fish. We can them and trade them for small needs. Laser packs for the sawmills, for example. We use the lumber to build or repair the kiosks. The kiosks sell or trade fruit and nuts and other forage items. Sometimes the Control Consortium buys these things from us. But the primary sales come from mining."

Bailey raised both eyebrows. "Mining? But you would have to be out of the water for prolonged periods."

Amargon shook her head. "Ocean floor mining," she explained. "Dredging for nodules of various metals: manganese, gold, iron, and others. The miners, the dredging vessels, come and take the nodules. Motoya receives no money for this."

"How deep is this ocean?" Bailey asked.

"I do not know how you measure it." Amargon said several words in her own language, which the Universal Translator rendered phonetically.

"On average, about five hundred meters," said Vigdis.

"A shallow ocean," was Kayana's comment.

"But only where the nodules are," Amargon said. "I suppose there are nodules in deeper waters. Perhaps eventually we will be forced to go harvest them."

"Can you swim that deep?" asked Bailey.

"Oh, yes. We can go to the deeps. Our bodies have pressure equalizers."

"Like sperm whales," said Bailey.

"I-I suppose so."

Bailey sighed. "Still no Michael."

"We're on our own," concluded Vigdis. She turned toward the Videx. Her reflection was as grim as Bailey had ever seen it. "I do not know whether we can do this as a private contractor, nor do I know whether we have the funds for it. But let us see what can be done."

Vigdis raised an organization called Worldwide Security Systems, and spoke to one of the senior clerks, whose name was Nasoro. Yes, WSS manufactured Armed Security Satellites, and sold them to planetary governments, local militia, and other authorities. The cost per satellite, installed and tested and with a service agreement, was seventeen million thalers. Security satellites could not be sold to private individuals.

Vigdis ignored this last. "I want six installed," she said. "Four in synchronous orbit around the equator at ninety-degree intervals, and two polar. I want them in place and activated around Motoya three local days from now."

"Impossible!" snorted Nasoro. "Now, if you represented the local government, I would be able to do this, but as you are a private individual—"

"A private individual who is willing to pay two hundred forty million thalers—that's forty million thalers per satellite—to have this done on time, including applicable full maintenance agreements. No questions asked. Further, if you will run my name, Vigdis, through GalaxyNet, you will find that I am acting on behalf of The Commission."

A shocked silence followed, broken by, "I-I...hold, please."

"I did not want to bring The Commission into this," Vigdis asided to Bailey.

"Because of Michael?"

"He might still intervene; his silence is puzzling, and perhaps ominous."

"What are you doing?" Amargon asked.

"The first step is to protect Motoya."

Nasoro came back on. "Your terms are acceptable," he said. "Please transfer half the amount to us, and we will begin the process of deployment." His tone added that he doubted she had the funds.

Bailey passed her fundscard, and Vigdis slipped it into the slot on the instrumentation console. After Nasoro gave her the WSS account code, she completed the transfer, received a receipt, and closed communication.

"What is Step 2?" asked Bailey.

"We downdock, and have a little talk with the Control Consortium," said Vigdis. "Wear your gauntlets; you may have need of them."

012: A 6-Step Program to Freedom

A single small building housed the activities of the Control Consortium. After downdocking on open tarmac, the four from *Skygnat* made their way directly to the entrance. Half the interior was devoted to three individual offices; the other half was an open bay, with counters, desks, a communications center, and a table for refreshments. Personnel ranged from humanoid from several different worlds to two individuals with legs like the trunks of a baby elephant and tentacles for arms that extended from gray shoulderless bodies. All probably spoke in their native languages, but the Universal Translator made them intelligible. Also present were two docile-looking Motics, one at the refreshment table, ready to serve, the other with a cleaning device that was aimed at some small debris in a corner.

Vigdis, whose mission this had become, did most of the talking. Although Michael had yet to make an appearance, she spoke with the authority of The Commission, supported by the identification cards Michael had issued to her and Bailey.

"This installation is now under the authority and supervision of Amargon of Motoya," she said, in the tone of a formal announcement. "It is therefore directed that all of you evacuate these premises immediately; you will take nothing with you except personal items. You are to depart from Motoya no later than midday tomorrow. This installation is to be staffed fully by indigenous peoples."

Three individuals now emerged from the offices to learn the reason for the commotion. Others squawked protests, mostly to the effect that the Motics did not know how to manage a spaceport. Vigdis's voice overrode them. "I know how to manage all aspects of spaceport operations," she declared. "I am quite capable of training your replacements."

"There are only four of you, and fourteen of us," said a pale-skinned male with wide-set golden eyes. Evidently the two Motics did not count. "You are unarmed. You cannot order us to do anything."

A few of his associates added words of encouragement.

Bailey stepped to the fore, and held up her forearms, crossing her gauntlets. A bright yellow beam, jagged like lightning, struck the back door of the building, shattering it into fragments that spilled onto the low vegetation outside. Forearms still crossed, she turned to the golden-eyed male. "I can reduce those odds to four against thirteen with no trouble at all," she told him. "Gather up your belongings and go."

Kayana and Amargon moved to the communications center and nudged the operator out of the way, none too gently. After a brief examination of the modules, Kayana nodded her approval to Vigdis.

Some warily eyeing Bailey's gauntlets, the members of the Control Consortium left the building. Bailey followed them, and watched them disperse among the collection of bungalows that stood some fifty yards away. Satisfied with their cooperation, she eased back into the doorway where she could watch and still listen to Vigdis and the others.

"That's Step 2," said Vigdis. "Now it becomes more difficult."

"I was afraid you'd say that," Bailey called back.

"Amargon," said Vigdis, turning to her. "We need Motic personnel. The operations here are fairly simple, but some training will be necessary. It shouldn't take long. You can tell the people you approach that this is a step toward Motic freedom and independence. That should motivate them."

Amargon appeared not to know what to say. She stammered out some words. "It-it will. I-I will...oh!" Weakness took over, and she could barely stand.

Bailey was right beside her, a hand on her shoulder. "Let's get this done. We have only three days. Stay strong."

"Y-yes. Yes, of course."

104

Amargon left. Each step she took was steadier. For a few moments Bailey and Vigdis stood regarding one another, their communication silent.

"And Step 4?" whispered Kayana. "Bailey goes to the spaceport?"

"On my way."

"Are you sure this will work?" Kayana asked Vigdis, after Bailey had dashed off.

"Certainty is a strong word, my friend," replied Vigdis. "But this gives us by far the best chance of succeeding."

Tears welled in Kayana's violet eyes. "You called me friend."

Vigdis shrugged as she sat down at the communications module and desk. "Yeah. I did." She ran her fingers over several dials and components. "This apparatus is primitive, but it will suffice," she announced. "You can upgrade later." She sat back, and laced her fingers behind her neck. "Now we wait for someone to call in for permission to downdock."

"But you did not say how you would keep them all at the spaceport," Kayana pointed out.

"Didn't I? I'll do it by quarantine. Have you ever heard of Motoyanic barbiula?"

"Of...of what?"

"It's a highly contagious and infectious disease indigenous to Motoya. It is seasonal, and this is the season for it. It has only a very mild effect on Motics, because they have a natural immunity to it, but on non-indigenous life forms it can be debilitating. Primarily it affects the reproductive system, especially the male gonads."

"I've never heard of it," Kayana said doubtfully.

"I'm not surprised," said Vigdis, "as I just made it up."

Kayana punched her shoulder. "You are so wicked." But she sobered. "Do you think it will work?"

"Anyone who breaks quarantine will have to deal with the gauntlets of Bailey Belvedere. Hang about, I've one more thing to do." She flicked a couple of toggles that

105

allowed her to transmit on all frequencies. "This is Motoya Control Consortium Communications. Due to a severe outbreak of Motoyanic barbiula, which is highly contagious and infectious, and can seriously affect the reproductive system, all ships and boats are required to return to dock, and all non-indigenous personnel are to return to their craft at the spaceport. Anyone showing symptoms of being unable to mate or copulate should notify Communications, and we will see what can be done for them. We cannot allow barbiula to spread. Therefore, any ship or boat found on the seas six hours from now will be sunk, and all spacecraft are required to remain at the spaceport until quarantine is lifted. Anyone attempting to break quarantine will be killed, and their bodies cremated immediately. Repeating,..."

Vigdis finished two subsequent broadcasts, and received seventeen acknowledgements. Kayana verified the number of non-Motic vessels that were authorized to be out on the oceans; the numbers matched. Kayana breathed a sigh of relief, for another hurdle had been cleared. "You are sooo wicked," she said, unable to hide the admiration in her voice.

Waiting began. With Bailey at the spaceport to monitor arrivals and clear departures, and with the docking of sea-going vessels, there was little to do until the WSS had emplaced and tested the satellites and the Motics whom Amargon had gathered were trained in operations.

At the spaceport operations office, Bailey was fielding a few questions from concerned individuals. Most of them involved the length of the quarantine, to which she responded that she expected it to be lifted in three to four days. Two ship's captains complained that the Motics in their cargo holds would smell terribly by then, and couldn't she release the ships now.

To which Bailey said tersely, "Motoya is under new management. The Motics are to be released now. I will accompany you to your ships and see that this is done.

106

After they have been released, you will depart and never return."

"You can't do this!" declared Captain Stith of the *Tudor*. Already his round face was red, and his meaty fists balled.

Bailey fixed him with a military glare she had used before to confront insubordination. On this occasion, however, she did not bother to remind him of her rank. "How many crew are aboard the *Tudor*?"

"What? Two. Why?"

"Can they pilot the ship?"

"What? Yes, of course they can."

"Is the hatch open? The ramp extruded?

"What? Yes. Why?"

Bailey crossed her gauntlets. "Then they don't need you," she said, and sent a yellow beam through his chest. She then turned to Captain Worret, a tall spare man whose dark eyes now paled with fear. "Any questions?" she asked. Worret shook his head. "Then let's go to your ship. Now." She pointed to two other men and said, "You bring his body. I don't want it in here."

Obedience, she noted, was immediate, and for a moment she recalled her Army days. As she led them toward their ships, she resisted the urge to get the men in step and call cadence. While Worret waited below, she led the way up the ramp of the *Tudor* and made for the bridge, where the two men deposited the captain's body and were dismissed. A few quick instructions gained the release of four Motics, who wonderingly descended down the ramp and hastened toward the sea, as if fearful of being recaptured before they could reach the waves.

To the crew, Bailey said, "After I disembark, take off and do not return. The *Tudor* is now yours. Use her wisely." Glowering at them, she added, "And avoid slaving."

Bailey followed much the same routine with Worret and his *Lost Lake*. From the cargo hold emerged five Motics, in various stages of oil decomposition. Advised that they were free, they hurried down the ramp and toward the sea. After explicitly forbidding his return, she headed back to the spaceport operations office. Along the way she stopped at a bench under a spreading tree to gather herself.

Deep breaths failed to calm her completely. Effectively she and her crew had just engineered the takeover of an entire planet. The realization slugged her. She began to question the wisdom of what she was doing. As if reading her mind, Michael materialized beside her on the bench.

Startled, Bailey almost drew her sidearm. "So far, so good," said Michael, unperturbed.

"I wondered what you were thinking of all this," she said.

"I think you have a good plan," he told her. "Your intentions are good. But there will be slaver ships who will test your defenses, once they are emplaced."

Bailey turned to face him. "Do you object?"

"Not at all. In fact, The Commission is sending a team of four to assist with the training of the Motics and to help temporarily with the defenses until the Motics can defend their world on their own."

She considered this announcement for a moment. "This sounds like you have another assignment for us."

Michael grinned. "Yes, it does, doesn't it."

Bailey waited a beat. "And?" she prodded.

"How do you feel about smuggling?"

She shrugged. The subject was not something on which she had formulated an opinion. "There's a time and a place for everything. On my world, rum-running was popular in the Caribbean and elsewhere. Bootleg whiskey. Cotton and wool. And slavery, too, sadly. Of course, here in outer space, I suppose smuggling would be more difficult to control and would involve a lot of different items."

"Vigdis has your assignment," said Michael. "You leave as soon as my people are in position." He vanished before she could reply.

013: The Horror, the Horror

The team from The Commission arrived within the hour after Michael left. Bailey and Vigdis briefed them and, with nothing more to be done, they boarded the *Skygnat* and entered null-space to hold there without a course direction. They now numbered four, for Amargon had asked to accompany them, a request Bailey granted, keeping her reservations to herself. A goodly supply of Motic soap now rested in Amargon's stateroom, as did some of her clothing, personal items, and other hygienic needs. She was taken aback by the private quarters, as privacy itself was not a Motic concept.

Bailey tapped her foot in mock impatience. "Well, Vigdis?"

She leaned against a bulkhead and folded her arms across her chest, hands grasping her elbows the way she had seen Bailey do. "We are to proceed to Barnolo and there pick up a shipping conex of perishable produce that has to be delivered quickly to Winny Wept, to a settlement called Vellen."

Bailey waited. "And that's it?" she asked.

Vigdis's lips puffed out with her sigh. "That's all he gave me."

Bailey looked to Kayana. "Winny Wept?"

"I know the name," she said. "But I've never been there."

Amargon, too, shook her head.

Vigdis said, "There's very little information available. You would call it a terrestrial world, the surface divided roughly equally between land and water. Plate tectonics are known to cause seismic quakes and volcanoes, and Vellen itself is located near a volcano."

"Just like Pompeii," said Bailey.

"Vellen is a little further away, and aside from some shaking has not been affected."

Bailey's lips pursed tightly, and her brow clenched. "This is Michael. There has to be something more."

"I cannot imagine what it might be," said Amargon. "You told me Michael can be devious, but this task seems straightforward."

Kayana chuckled. "That's what makes me nervous."

"Set course for Winny Wept, Vigdis. Travel time?"

"Half an hour," she replied. "No points."

Barnolo proved to be very sparsely populated, and the primary activity centered around a commercial transfer point, where goods were shipped in and then distributed. The shipping conex, a container made of corrugated structural plastic, fit easily into the *Skygnat*'s cargo hold. A lock secured the door—someone on Winny Wept held the key—and nothing was heard to shift around as the conex was forked into the hold. Bailey signed a bill of lading for the fresh vegetable matter and dried fruit and fish, and with the hold secured and the transaction completed, she instructed Vigdis to set a course for Winny Wept.

This, thought Bailey, seated in her starboard captain's chair, was too easy. It was a task unworthy of them, and unworthy of Michael to have assigned it.

"I still don't like it," she said. She stretched out her legs and slumped in the chair. "Travel time?"

"Just over two hours," Vigdis replied.

"Winny Wept?"

"Mining and agriculture," she said. "Tedious labor, and not much equipment. Shovels and picks for the mines, hand-picking for the produce."

"Wait," said Amargon, before Bailey could ask. "Why are we shipping produce to a world that produces, er, produce?"

"That," said Kayana, "is a very good question."

Vigdis began to frown, and her purple eyebrows merged. "Something?" asked Bailey.

"I am not certain. I thought I heard a sound, but the 'skip is silent."

"Do a diagnostic," Kayana suggested.

"I don't know. It did not sound right...there it is again."

110

"Oh, no," cried Bailey, as she fairly flew from the chair. Her running footsteps echoed down the gangway as she ran to the cargo hold, as did the echoes of her muttering, "Oh, no. Oh, no."

The others followed, almost catching up to her. Bailey opened the cargo hatch and dashed to the conex. The door was locked. From inside she heard thumping against the plastic walls.

"Vigdis!" she yelled.

Vigdis yanked the lock loose and tore the door off. A smell now released blasted them. All but Vigdis choked, but none were deterred. Inside the conex they counted seven naked people of various origins, and four bodies on the floor. The living staggered toward the opening. One of them, blue-gray in the hold's overhead light but otherwise humanoid and male, stumbled against Bailey and would have fallen to the deck had she not caught him. Others also collapsed, Vigdis cradling two, but not all could be caught, and two sprawled onto the deck.

Bailey led the man to a murphy bench against the bulkhead, but he was too weak to sit, and collapsed onto the deck instead. She sat down, holding his head against her stomach, trying without success to stuff her legs under him to protect him against the deck. Tears rolled down her cheeks and onto the man's face. Bleary red eyes shifted to look at her. He lifted a hand, but was too weak to dry the tears. And all the while, Bailey Belvedere cried, "Oh, no. Oh, no."

Vigdis sat her two—a mother and a child—on another bench. After taking the woman that Kayana was holding up, she said, "Bring some water, and that jar of menthol salve for our noses," and Kayana dashed off. Amargon led her man to a bench, and went back for the two sprawled on the deck. One of them was utterly limp, having just died. The other, a young boy, reached his arms up to her, and the Motic carried him away.

Kayana returned with the water and salve. Vigdis began giving sips to the captives, while Kayana went around smearing menthol under noses. Bailey continued to sit with her man, but her muttering ceased as she

111

looked into his eyes, which had irises as yellow as marigolds. He did not blink. He gazed up at her face, and perhaps there was just the faintest touch of a smile on his lips. But his eyes slowly closed, and he did not draw breath again.

Bailey sat numb. Vigdis tried to ease the body away from her, and stopped at her scathing look. Bailey's mind refused to function, and was no longer a part of her. It had gone into an unfathomable darkness, surrounded by the strange sounds of stranger creatures. They would haunt her for long afterwards. She began to shiver, though the hold was warm. Her hand brushed the man's face, his cheek, his forehead, as if tenderness might restore him to life. Shadows drifted over her: Vigdis and Kayana and Amargon.

"See to the others," Bailey said tersely, through clenched jaws. Immediately she regretted the tone. Her hands fluttered helplessly. "Just see to them, please. Vigdis? I don't, don't know..."

Vigdis laid a hand on her shoulder. "Nobody knows," she said softly. "This is beyond experience."

She looked up. "You're so practical."

"It helps keep me from crying."

"But you're crying."

"So are you," said Vigdis.

For a long moment she fell silent. Her voice was barely audible. "He died in my arms."

"I saw."

"Vigdis...who was he? Where was he from?"

"A world called Thullia. He is...was Borangian."

"He must have family..."

"Shall I set a course?"

"Yes. Please. And see if you can identify the origin of the other five bodies." Against her will, Bailey was recovering. The nightmare in the darkness was beaten back, at least temporarily. There were things to do, people to seek out and destroy. "Find out about the others, too," she instructed. "Then plot a course that will return all of them. But first, Thullia."

"Not back to Barnolo?"

"Not just yet," she said. "Right now, I'm too..."

"Infuriated?"

"To put it mildly. And I want to be cold there, Vigdis. I want to be arctic."

"I myself plan to be in computer mode."

Bailey shifted a little. "Help me get him to one of the spare staterooms," she said. "The other five as well."

"It's six, now," Vigdis told her, with infinite sadness. "I'll take care of it. The course is set. You should be on the bridge, with the survivors."

She nodded. "Still practical?"

"But it's still not helping."

"Vigdis...he smiled a little at me as he died."

"Because he died free."

Vigdis helped Bailey to her feet, and a slow trudge brought her to the bridge. The *Skygnat* was not equipped for a multitude of passengers. Even the bridge was crowded, with five survivors and Amargon standing around and trying not to collide with one another. Bailey had no idea what to say to them. But the fearful looks in their eyes wanted reassurance. For all they knew, she and her crew were also slavers. For a moment the memory of the dying man dominated her vision. Blinking it away failed. She shut her eyes briefly, and when she opened them, she began to speak.

"We're going to take each of you home," she told them. "In the meantime, my crew and I will see to you. You'll be fed, and have more water to drink. We'll treat those with injuries as best we can, but we've no medical personnel aboard, so—"

Amargon signaled for attention. "I have had some training," she said. "I'll examine each of them. I cannot do everything, but at least I can ease some wounds."

Bailey inclined her head in gratitude. "For now, we're bound for Thullia. One of my crew will come around to ask you your home planet, and we'll plot a course that takes us to each one."

Much of the fear and concern had passed from their eyes and expressions. Bailey considered that a major accomplishment.

113

"I'll see everyone in my stateroom," Amargon announced.

Moments later, Bailey was alone on the bridge. She might then resume her tears. It was difficult, nigh impossible, to tell herself that she was doing some good in the galaxy when, no matter where she went—Earth or other worlds—the crimes were basically the same. Cruelty, injustice, slavery? How had those become fun in the galaxy? At this moment, she felt like changing the gravitational constant of the universe in order to destroy everything and start over.

She hissed at herself for being maudlin. But the emotion was far stronger. She was not a killer, but she would kill in a righteous cause. And what could be more righteous than killing slavers?

"And why does The Commission turn a blind eye to slavery?" she muttered to herself. She considered the question, and presently came to the conclusion that Michael had dropped this assignment on her to ensure the very reaction she wanted to make. It was small consolation. A man had died in her arms. Never would she unsee that; never could she.

The sudden light left her blinking. Michael had arrived, but she saw yellow spots before her eyes. A shape took form in the port captain's chair. Visual acuity gradually returned. He sat there with just the hint of a sad smile on his lips. He waited until Bailey had gathered herself before he spoke.

"I'm sorry," he began. "That was a rough way to introduce you."

The statement angered her, for it meant that he had known about the contents of the shipping conex. Her eyes felt on fire as she glared at him. "Damn you," she growled. "You could have stopped that."

"I'm no happier than you about it, Bailey Belvedere." He drew a knee up and wrapped his arms around his leg. "As powerful as we are," he went on, "we cannot know or do everything. That is why we search for, train, and deploy operatives to seek out wrongs and right them. I told you once that you could be one of the best

114

ever. You have shown me nothing that would dissuade me from that evaluation. I think your strongest point is that you are emotionally involved in what you do. That sounds contrary to operative theory, which emphasizes a cold detachment, but it is nevertheless true, Bailey, at least in the case of certain operatives. You are effective when you *feel*. Leave the cold analyses to Vigdis."

"I can be detached, Michael. I've been cold before. I'll be frozen when I get back to Barnolo."

"I understand. And that's all right."

"But?"

He nodded. "Exactly. Your emotional involvement is and should be *ad hoc*." He leaned back. "I'm glad you and Vigdis are...compatible."

Bailey arched a black eyebrow. "You know...about us?" She made a little sound of annoyance. "Well of course you would know." She glowered at him. "If you tell me we complete each other, I'm going to shoot you, you know."

Michael laughed. "I am aware of that movie."

A silent moment passed, broken by Bailey. "Why are you here, Michael?"

Now he bent forward, to look her in the eye. "Tell me what you plan to do."

"I'm going to return each surviving captive to her or his own world. I'll bury the others."

"And then?"

"Michael, just don't ask."

"I already know," he said softly. "I want to hear it from you."

Bailey got to her feet and began to pace around the bridge. Anger crossed her face, as did determination. For several steps she clenched her fists until the knuckles were bloodless. The glint in her eyes demanded silence from him.

Finally she came to a stop before him, and gazed placidly down at him. "I'll go to Barnolo first," she said without inflection. "Then to Winny Wept. I'll thank you not to give me any more assignments until I'm finished."

Michael hesitated, reluctant to pass on advice. A deep breath steadied him. "You probably will not survive Winny Wept," he said gravely.

Fury darkened her eyes to battleship gray. "I don't care."

"Bailey..."

Her breath came shallow and ragged. She spun away from him and resumed her pacing, stalking around the bridge on stiff legs. Her anger unfocused at first, it eventually came to rest on Michael. Nobody had drawn their last breath in his arms. He had not been present when Vigdis had torn the door from its hinges to reveal the deep misery in the faces of the survivors as they cowered in the shadows of the conex, fearful of what was about to happen to them. He had not seen the bodies on the floor of the conex. He had not smelled...

She slowed to a stop.

"Vigdis, for all her humanity—and yes, she is human—is bonded to you both as a woman and through her computer aspect," said Michael. "She is difficult to kill, but it can be done if enough firepower is brought to bear. You could kill her with your gauntlets. Of the four of you, she has the best chance of coming through alive. But she will be damaged by the loss of you.

"Kayana is conflicted. You killed her brother, yet she is loyal to you for several reasons. She will follow you. Amargon is painfully inexperienced in the things you do, but for your salvation of her she will follow you to the ends of the universe. Bailey, you know all this. I understand your willingness to sacrifice your life if necessary in order to avenge the captives and bring about a measure of justice. But do you want your crew to die with you, for you?"

Bailey hung her head. "No," she said, almost inaudibly. "No, of course not."

"The use of involuntary labor on Winny Wept—"

"It's called slavery, Michael," she snapped.

"Yes. Slavery. It's extensive there, and several corporations profit by it. They will go to war to protect their investment. Let The Commission deal with it."

"When?" she exploded, arms flailing. Her voice echoed throughout the bridge. "It's been going on for how long, Michael? A millennium? Several of them? What's kept you from intervening?"

Michael considered his response. "You're from Earth," he said at last. "Did you ever play Jenga?"

Her brow furrowed. Where was he going with this? "I know about it," she said. "Never played it."

"If you pull out the wrong piece…"

"The tower collapses. I under…oh."

"Just so. A collapsed economy harms billions of people. It certainly did not help Earth, you may recall."

Bailey thought about that. "Corporations have labor resource departments, don't they?"

"Most do."

"I'd like to meet the ones in charge of those departments for the corporations involved on Winny Wept."

He stood up. "It will be considered, Bailey. Meanwhile, focus on Barnolo. You and your crew can handle that."

He vanished before she could respond.

014: A Self-Solving Problem

Following the course Vigdis had laid out after Thullia, the *Skygnat* crew dropped off the other survivors in sequence. There remained for them to choose a world on which to bury the other bodies. After some consideration, Vigdis announced that she knew one such world, and Bailey bade her set course. Then, leaving the rest of the crew on the bridge, she retreated to her stateroom.

Seated at the foot of the bed, hands clasped between her knees, hunched over as if to regurgitate, Bailey Belvedere wept bitterly. The incident with the captives in the conex had diminished the thrill of traveling in outer space to an unidentifiable emotion at the bottom of a misery index. What, indeed, was she doing out here? It was not enough that she had *carte blanche* to kill bad people—or people she judged as bad—stacking their bodies like cordwood if necessary. Mathematically, she tried to tell herself, if you kill evil-doers, you must eventually exhaust the supply of them. The *reductio ad absurdum* was that eventually you might become the sole inhabitant of the galaxy. But math was of little consolation. Michael as much as had said that the problem of slavery was galaxy-wide, and that her abilities and options to deal with it were in fact extremely limited. No matter how much good you did, it would never be enough.

Small steps, she thought. Small victories. And still she wept. So immersed was she in despondence that she failed to hear the stateroom door slide open, and was only made aware of a visitor when the additional weight made the sleeping pad sink a little.

Who? she thought, and turned her head just enough to find Vigdis beside her, her pale purple body now clad only in a long ochre sleeping shirt. She was close enough to lean against. Bailey discovered that she needed just that, and laid her cheek against Vigdis's shoulder.

Together they sat seemingly for hours, not speaking, letting the physical contact do their talking.

Finally Vigdis whispered, "I am your friend and companion and confidante, as well as your lover. When you are down, I will hold you. When you are up, I will cheer you. No matter what—*no matter what*, Bailey Belvedere—I am here for you."

Sniffling, Bailey shook her head. "You don't know —." A hard hug stopped her.

"But I *do*," Vigdis told her. "Like you, I am human. I can grieve, and I am grieving now. But I also know that suns rise on most worlds, and life does go on. This is your midnight moment. I have come here to be with you in any way you want, in any way you need me, to ease you back into daylight."

Bailey thought that she had never even imagined such a strong statement of love. Tears now flooded her face.

"But do not lose sight of our purpose," Vigdis went on. "We are not here specifically to combat slavery. We are here to help people, as we have done by liberating Motoya. As we will surely do elsewhere. You gave the *Tudor* to those two crewmembers, with an admonition. Perhaps they will take that to heart and engage in general transportation. It will not always be given to us to know the effect our actions have on others."

"I know," breathed Bailey. "Oh, Vigdis..."

Vigdis stretched out on the berth and pulled Bailey down alongside her. Embracing Bailey, Vigdis pulled her close—not a beam of light shone between them. "Rest now," Vigdis said softly. "I have placed the *Skygnat* in stasis in null-space. Kayana and Amargon are resting as well. We all need this break. When you awaken, I will still be here." She kissed Bailey's forehead, and waited until Bailey closed her drying eyes before allowing herself to drift off into her own fitful slumber.

Bailey awoke blinking to darkness. With herself and Vigdis asleep, there was no need for lights, and Vigdis had shut them down. But Vigdis's sensitive hearing detected the shuttering sounds of blinking eyes, and she came awake instantly.

"I'm right here," she told Bailey. Unnecessarily. "It's all right. You're all right."

Bailey's mouth felt desiccated. Her tongue fumbled around it until it was moist. "I had a dream," she croaked, and shook her head. "A nightmare."

"I'm not surprised."

Bailey sat up and dropped her feet to the deck, and Vigdis with her. "What about you?" she asked Vigdis.

"I don't actually dream. I wish I did."

Bailey had a dry laugh. "Not like this."

"Tell me."

"People," she began and licked her lips. "People were falling, and I couldn't catch them. No matter how I tried, they were just out of reach. Oh, Vigdis..." She began to weep once more. "What if I...what if...?"

"You have three friends. We'll help you catch as many as we can."

"It's not enough," she sobbed.

Vigdis patted her shoulder. "It's not supposed to be. A missed catch only makes us try harder the next time."

Bailey found a tiny nod. "Don't...don't let Kayana and Amargon see me like this."

"What makes you think they themselves are not like this at this very moment?"

She sighed; she should have thought of that on her own. "You're right. I should see to them." A long breath dispelled her reluctance. "I'm going to freshen up," she said. "I'll meet you on the bridge."

Vigdis stood up. "Are we going to Barnolo?"

Bailey considered that. "Not just yet. I'm not...I don't know. But I'm not."

"You have a talent for clarity."

Bailey punched her arm. It was like striking concrete. "Off you go, then. Be with you in ten."

It was fifteen. Listless, Bailey went through a mechanical and desultory freshening, a light splash of water over her face, a brush dragged through her shaggy black locks, a change of clothes to a lemon yellow outsuit

120

that did not coordinate well with her hair or eyes. Leaving the stateroom, however, she managed to take a deep breath, pull herself erect, and stride to the bridge, where the other three were waiting for her. Kayana handed Bailey a mug of coffee, and she sat down in the starboard captain's chair, her customary seat, and gazed up at the others as if expecting some sort of report. In return, they regarded her as having made a decision and was about to announce it.

Bailey dragged fingers through her hair, undoing the meager repairs she had performed with the brush. Words began to fail her; she had to say something.

"I think we all need to recover from what has transpired with us during the last several days," she said, feeling her way in the dark. "It has been emotionally draining for all of us," here she glanced at Vigdis. "I'm open to suggestions."

At first, no one spoke. But Amargon cleared her throat. "I suggest we return to Motoya," she said.

A sound of surprise escaped Vigdis. "Why?"

"With the slavers gone, it will gradually become a peaceful world," the Motic explained. "We need not think of anything...well..."

"Negative?" Bailey supplied.

Amargon nodded. "Just so."

Kayana spoke up. "We need to find a problem to deal with," she said. "One that does not involve slavery."

"Something to take our minds off it," said Bailey. "I think I agree. Vigdis, you must have some ideas."

Vigdis nodded, thoughtful. "There is a world called Zanga," she said slowly. "It has but one landmass worthy of continental status, and in the translation from the UT it is called North Vyella and South Vyella. All the other landforms are islands of various sizes. The two Vyellas are connected by a narrow isthmus."

"Like Panama," said Bailey.

"I suppose so. This isthmus lies at the equator, with the northern and southern halves of the landmass angled across it. Both halves, then, lie in the tropical zones, north

121

and south. We can expect to be hot and sweaty. We can find relief at the beaches."

"So what's the problem?" Bailey asked.

"North Vyella is inhabited mostly by an indigenous people known as the Valians. They are humanoid, rather like Kayana in appearance if Kayana had deep ochre hair and eyes and pale ochre skin. They are relatively primitive; they do not have space travel, although they have access to it.

"South Vyella has been settled by peoples from other worlds. They came seeking their fortunes, and some have found these in timber, fruit, and some minerals, including phosphates. They also grow faffa, which is an excellent fodder for bovine analogs, and is in demand on other worlds."

"So what's the problem?" Bailey asked again.

"North Vyella has better soil for agriculture," Vigdis answered. "Some of the peoples of the south covet it for their crops. As I said, the Valians are primitive. Those of the south, while not armed, are able to import weaponry if needed. There are some who have already declared that it is needed, and have begun to smuggle in arms."

Bailey sighed. "And you want to drop us in the middle of this disagreement."

"Pondar Ocnorb is a charismatic entrepreneur from Ogodda who is attempting to unite the peoples of South Vyella under the promise of more agricultural land," said Vigdis. "If he should succeed..." She left the possibility hanging.

"Bailey?" Amargon said cautiously. "I know someone on South Vyella. She may be able to help us."

"A Motic like yourself?" asked Kayana.

"She is wanted by some authorities," Amargon told them. "She was a slave who killed her owner and managed to escape. She is known to us on Motoya, but we would never betray her. She is regarded as a danger to other owners because of the example she set, and because so far she has gotten away with it."

"I don't understand how she can help us," said Bailey.

122

"She is Ocnorb's groundskeeper, though he is not or pretends not to be aware of her past."

Bailey considered this. "So our task would be to dissuade this Ocnorb to avoid violence, or in the extreme, to...I don't know that he should be killed, but perhaps removed to a distant world."

"Any of the three solutions would be satisfactory, I think," said Amargon. "Perhaps we should try the simplest one first. Vigdis, you said he was an entrepreneur. What is his business?"

"Primarily it is nitrates for fertilizer."

Bailey sighed. "Which can also be used in explosives. Wonderful." She turned to Vigdis. "All right, let's opt for some peace and quiet. Set course for Zanga and get us going."

015: Zanga

Disembarking the *Skygnat* at the South Vyella Spaceport, the crew found the climate rather more than advertised. With the temperature at 317K and the humidity near sixty percent, all of them broke out in sweat before they reached the bottom of the ramp. This worried Amargon more than the other three, for it meant that she would be compelled to bathe more frequently than usual. She cast a jealous eye at Vigdis, who was in total control of her perspiration and at the moment was desert-dry.

At the Terminal, Bailey let an airfoil and, following directions from both Amargon and Vigdis, they soon arrived at a ramshackle cottage on the northeast shore of the ocean. A roof of terracotta tiles kept the rain out, but the outer walls needed patchwork or repair. The overhang above the front door appeared on the verge of collapse. The single front window was cracked. A flower bed stretched across the front of the cottage, and a few plants with pale yellow flowers had made it through the year; the others were dry husks.

"Tighimra lives here?" asked an incredulous Kayana. "Surely Ocnorb pays her better than this."

"She prefers it this way," Amargon explained. "A place no one wants is a place no one bothers." The front door was slightly ajar; she knocked at the doorjamb, which rattled the frame.

"One moment." Presently Tighimra drew the door open. Over a simple aqua shift that fell to just above her knees, she was fronted by a white apron festooned with bits of flour. "I know you. Amargon, what are you doing here?"

Amargon laughed. "You, baking?"

"I'm breading fish cakes."

Amargon introduced the others. "May we come in?" she asked. "We would rather no one was aware of our visit just yet."

Bailey raised an eyebrow. "You're Ocnorb's groundskeeper?"

Tighimra showed no expression. "As unlikely as that appears at the moment," she said without rancor. She widened the doorway. "Please, come in."

The interior failed to match the exterior. Fresh, pale blue paint glistened off the walls of the front room; off-white shone in the light from the kitchen. A hallway led to the bedroom and the hygiene alcove, and Bailey caught a whiff of the special soap that Motics used when salt water was not readily available. The furnishings were, however, Spartan: a settee, a low wooden table, a few unmatched straightback chairs, all on a wine and cream carpet. It was not clear what, if anything, Tighimra did for entertainment, but two potted plants in the window in the east side of the cottage suggested care not rendered to the front garden.

The kitchen was simple, ideal for one: an electric stove with oven; a cooler; white counters with brown speckles; a few cupboards with doors of dark hardwood. Dishes of hard green plastic and aluminum cookware were washed by hand, and left to dry in a strainer by the sink. A window above the sink gave onto a view of the beach fifty meters away and the ocean beyond.

"I apologize for my earlier remark," said Bailey. "I like your place. It's comfortable."

"Amargon said you were human," said Tighimra. "I'm not familiar with your species."

"I come from Earth." Bailey made a face. "That's not quite accurate. I escaped from Earth."

"A world unknown to me." She began to address the breading of fish cakes, with a yellow batter and a coarse, granular flour, and laying them in a freezer container. "And Kayana is?"

"I come from Harlange," she said.

"The outlaw world. I have heard of it." Tighimra glanced over her shoulder. "And you are Vigdis...I am unable to place you."

Vigdis laughed. "I'm complicated. But I too am human. Is this important?"

Tighimra nodded thoughtfully. "It may be. From what I know so far, none of you have any vested interest in what occurs here on Zanga. Not that I am displeased to see another Motic, Amargon, but you did not tell me why you have come here."

Without hesitation, Bailey said, "We're here to stop a slaughter, if we can."

Tighimra barked a laugh. "Four of you. I don't think so."

"We don't have to stop an army," she said. "Just one person."

The Motic groundskeeper nodded. "Pondar Ocnorb." She tilted her head, considering. "Possible. But it would be success or death. The latter including mine. Were you an army, I might risk it."

"All we need from you is an introduction," Bailey pressed.

"And should you fail, Ocnorb will know who introduced you." She shook some breading off a fish cake. "No, I will not risk it."

"People will die," said Kayana.

"Perhaps so. But it will not be I who kills them." She turned to look at them. "If you will excuse me, I do have work pending."

Bailey gathered the others, and after gestures of departure they left the cottage for the airfoil. Once aboard, Vigdis said, "So we're leaving?"

Bailey shook her head. "Of course not. We failed to enlist her help. But there must be other means of access; we simply have to find it." With that, she had Vigdis pilot the airfoil back to the city of Vellam, where they meant to seek accommodations.

Just outside the city they noticed a fenced compound of buildings, and a courtyard with several large piles of whitish powder. Soon enough they passed a sign that read OCNORB NITRATE WORKS. A few transport airfoils awaited loading, while others flew off for places unknown, their loads covered by tied-down tarps to prevent the loss of powder to the air that flowed over them.

"Don't slow down," said Bailey, as they passed by the compound. At the entrance stood a security shack with one uniformed guard inside and another, clearly armed, standing at the gate. Both eyed the airfoil as it went by.

"From what Tighimra told me, this is but one of several such compounds," said Amargon.

"Ocnorb is wealthy," said Kayana. "There's no doubt of that. But his influence seems to operate beyond that wealth. He is favored by the local population."

Bailey nodded agreement. "Which means our next step after we arrange lodging is to go out and listen to what others have to say."

"In a tavern?" asked Amargon.

"Is that a problem?" Bailey asked.

"I may not be welcome. I would attract unwanted attention to you. In fact, with me around, you might find it difficult to obtain a room."

"It never ends," Bailey muttered. "All right, then. Vigdis, we want a place that needs our custom, and is not picky about the members of our entourage. Something like a bed and breakfast."

"A what?" said Kayana.

Bailey explained. Vigdis said, "I'm searching local accommodations now and...I've located a place that might do."

"Take us there."

The structure in question proved to be a large house that had been remodeled to include several sleeping quarters on the second level and a small restaurant on the first. Only two airfoils were docked in the courtyard out front, and Bailey guessed that one belonged to whoever managed the house. A few bits of debris littered the courtyard, and the few shrubs along the front of the house needed attention, for they had grown leggy. The ground around them looked parched, with only a few clumps of sad grass interspersed at the base of the shrubs. Nothing bloomed.

The house itself had been maintained well enough, although the exterior walls of structural plastic could have

127

benefitted from a fresh coat of white paint. The eaves and edging had been replaced recently, and painted a deep green. Panes of acetate in the three upper-level dormer windows were intact and clean, and drawn dark curtains hung alongside. The tiles on the gabled roof were older but still in good condition.

A set of three wooden steps led up to the porch and the entrance. A Welcome sign poised just above a black button, which Bailey pushed. Answering the summons was an older female humanoid in a simple full-length dress and a white apron. Her name tag bore oddly-formed lettering which the Universal Translator, when requested, rendered as Hoillre. Her black hair was tied back above her side eyes and secured under netting. Her front eyes were dark and deepset; in the light from behind her, they appeared to be pale emerald. Her skin had just the hint of pale green. They dominated an oval face in the center of which was a flattish nose with a single nostril from which a few stray hairs protruded. She had a generous mouth with unadorned pale pink lips. Her smile of greeting exposed the ivory incisors of an omnivorous mouth.

"We'd like a room and meals," said Bailey.

"And you are welcome to them," said Hoillre, opening the door for them. "However, there are only two beds to a room."

"That won't be a problem." Bailey led the others inside to an informal counter for registration. There she completed a Palmetto template and displayed her fundscard to the sensor. "Two days and two nights," she said. "With the option for us to stay longer if necessary."

Obviously pleased to have guests, Hoillre assigned them to the middle front room upstairs. "The key is in the door," she said. "We take the evening meal an hour before sunset. And there is no cooking allowed in the rooms."

"Out of curiosity," said Vigdis, "how many other guests are here?"

Hoillre eyes saddened. "So far today, you are the only ones."

"This is a nice place," Bailey said gallantly. "I'm sure we'll be comfortable here." With a parting gesture, she led the others upstairs.

The room was appointed as expected: two beds, a table and two chairs, a desk with a chair in the desk well, thick curtains at the sides of the dormer window, charcoal carpeting on the floor. The hygiene alcove was stocked with toiletries, and the water from the sink faucet came out clear.

Kayana flopped down on the bed nearest the window, staking a claim. But her brow furrowed with concern. "The lack of attention to the front yard makes no sense," she said. "The building itself and this room appear to be in good shape. Why the difference?"

"There's no gardener," Amargon suggested. "And we saw only the woman."

"I think we can assume at least one and maybe two more staff," said Bailey. "Two, I think. One as a room attendant, the other as a cook with other assigned duties with the attendant." She frowned at Kayana. "What's on your mind?" she asked.

"It's almost as if they are trying to dissuade people from staying here."

Vigdis shook her head. "Yet Hoillre seemed happy to have us. But I agree with Kayana: something here is just a bit off." She looked at the key in Bailey's hand. "Better lock the door."

"Paranoia, Vigdis?" Bailey asked. But she complied with the suggestion.

"Just until we think this through." Arms braced behind her, Vigdis leaned back on the bed. "On the one hand, we have Tighimra, who declined to become involved with us, not because of what we wanted to do, but because she thought there were not enough of us to do it. On the other hand, we have an older building that has been kept up, but the condition is scarcely noticeable due to the trash and debris in front."

"All of which means what?" Amargon asked. "I don't see how the two hands are even related."

Vigdis shrugged. "They don't have to be related," she said. "Right now, they're observations. Added to them is Pondar Ocnorb's plan to forcibly acquire territory in North Vyella. To do that, he needs a military force capable of taking and holding that territory. That costs money and takes training." She made a face. "We need more observations, information. And we're not going to get them sitting in here."

"Amargon, is Tighimra the only other Motic on Zanga?" asked Kayana.

The Motic shrugged. "Probably there are several, even many. But I do not know them. If you wish to find one, you'll have to look for them."

"They most likely would work in the service industries," said Vigdis, with an apologetic look for Amargon.

Amargon responded sadly. "I have to agree."

Bailey was shaking her head. "No, we're missing something. Two things. First, the plants at Tighimra's dwelling were poorly maintained, as was the front of it. The same is true of this house. This is not accidental; the two factors are connected in some way."

"And second?" pressed Vigdis.

"It's only tentative. But Hoillre showed neither prejudice nor animosity toward Amargon. I don't know what it means, if anything. But it is an observation worth bearing in mind."

"How long before sunset?" asked Kayana. "Vigdis?"

"Two hours. Why?"

Kayana shook her head. "Not enough time. I was thinking of a walk in Vellam, to get a feel for the town. But there's just enough time for a nap before dinner." She looked to Bailey. "Who sleeps where? Or do we sleep in shifts?"

"Bailey and Vigdis are lovers," said Amargon. "And I would not mind sleeping with you, Kayana. I am... comfortable with you."

"I suspect we'll all be too busy sleeping to make much noise," said Bailey.

"Delicately put," said Vigdis.

A knock at their door stopped Bailey's reply before it began. She raised her gauntlets, prepared to cross them, and Vigdis moved to the side of the door. "Come in," said Bailey.

A Motic female entered, dressed in a maid's black outfit, fronted by a white apron. "Is everything to your satisfaction?" she inquired.

Her mouth somewhat agape, Bailey lowered her arms. "Yes, it is," she said, and did not know what else to say.

The maid stared at Amargon. "I-I did not realize..."

Amargon introduced herself, and learned that the maid was Pachola.

"Motoya," sighed Pachola. "It's been years..."

Kayana patted the mattress. "Please, sit down."

"Oh, I can't! I'd get in trouble." She looked forlorn. "Oh, I wish..."

"Do they let you sleep?" asked Amargon.

"Yes, of course. Hoillre is not a bad mistress. I am treated...as well as can be expected, under the circumstances."

"When do you go off duty?" Bailey asked her.

"After dinner, when the dishes have been cleaned."

"And where is your room?" Amargon wanted to know.

"In...in the attic. There are three of us..."

"All Motics?" This from Vigdis.

Pachola nodded. "I do not understand these questions..."

"We're going into Vellam after dinner," said Bailey. "We're strangers here. We'd like to hire you, through Hoillre, of course, as our guide."

That stunned the maid. "I-I will ask, ask her, but..."

"Please ask. And you can report that we are happy with the room."

Pachola backed toward the door. "Yes. Yes, of course."

"A break?" asked Vigdis, after the door closed.

Bailey considered for a moment, and shrugged. "It could be. But for now, I believe a nap was mentioned."

016: Manumission

Although closely associated with the Spaceport, Vellam was a town, and not the principal city of South Vyella. While there were places of interest, especially for sojourners, and several industrial sites, few buildings featured government or administrative functions. Vellam was, as Vigdis declared, a boring little town, a place where newcomers either shopped, celebrated, or departed for major settlements.

But there was no doubt that Pondar Ocnorb ran Vellam. Posters with his face appeared on the walls of most structures, even those in residential areas. Words on such posters included prosperity, security, and liberty. In contrast, outlying dwellings and buildings had the appearance of not having been kept up, including Tighimra's house and Hoillre's B&B, as if they were places no official would bother with. Bailey looked worried as she and her entourage of four—now including Pachola—sat down at a picnic table in a park across the way from several taverns and other places of entertainment.

"I've seen this before," Bailey said, so softly that the others could barely hear her. "On my own world. Dictators and would-be dictators professed themselves in favor of these things, but delivered the opposite. My world collapsed under their weight. The Commission has declared it unsalvageable."

"Are you saying it could happen here?" asked Pachola.

Bailey's sigh puffed out her lips. "I don't know. But it is certainly possible."

"Uh-oh," said Vigdis, looking past her shoulder.

Bailey turned around on the bench. Four armed men in uniforms were headed their way. They carried black truncheons.

"Local police," whispered Pachola.

"Yeah, I got that." Bailey's lips pursed.

As she and the others stood up, one of the men aimed his truncheon at her, and motioned for her to stand aside. She marked him as the leader by his demeanor and the black arm stripes on his uniform blouse. But she did not step aside.

Seen from almost within arm's reach, the man was taller than Bailey, and more massive. Like Hoillre, he had the pale green skin, emerald front eyes, and flattish nose with a single nostril. Bailey had not seen Hoillre's side eyes, and wondered what color this man's were.

He did not smile as he identified himself. "I am Constable Tuinne, and these slaves are under detention for violation of the mixed company law. Stand aside, or be detained for obstruction of official security actions."

"They are from another world," Pachola protested, stepping forward. "I am the only one here subject to Vyellan law."

"Stand," ordered Tuinne, ignoring Pachola, "aside."

With a faintly mocking smile on her face, Bailey stood her ground.

Pachola tried again. "I *said* they're—"

One of the other policemen raised his truncheon and prepared to club Pachola into silence. Even as the weapon poised to begin its arc downward, Bailey said quietly, "Vigdis."

Faster than the eye could follow, Vigdis interposed herself between the Motic and the truncheon. The blow landed on Vigdis's forehead, with no discernible effect on her. The truncheon, however, cracked audibly, and left the policeman staring at it and her in wonder.

"We don't want any trouble." Bailey spoke calmly into the stunned silence that followed. "We did not know the law here. We will return these two Motics to their places of employment after we have issued their orders." Forearms crossed, she sent a thin and jagged beam of light into the grass before Tuinne's jackboots. A trickle of pungent smoke began to arise from the spot. "Surely that is a satisfactory resolution to a difficulty that was unintended." She tilted her head at him. "Wouldn't you say, Constable?"

Tuinne stared at her, and at his feet, and back at her. His thick green lips writhed as he sought a response.

Already the other three with him were easing away, hands on the sidearms in their clips, ready to receive orders. Bailey's gauntlets remained crossed. Finally he said, with as much authority as he could muster, "See that this is done forthwith," he snarled. He then spun on his heel and walked away.

"We had better leave," said Pachola. "This was not a good idea."

Bailey touched her arm. "I'm sorry. I did not know..."

Anguished, she led the others back to the airfoil. There, she asked Vigdis to pilot it, not trusting herself at the moment. She moved aft and sat down beside Pachola, but found words difficult to summon. Finally the Motic broke the uneasy silence between them.

"You meant well," she said. "But this is the way it is here."

"Mixed company?"

"We Motics are not to be associated with by others, unless it is in the course of our duties," she explained. "We got away with it because they did not know what to do with you. And how did you do that, anyway? That spark you sent down."

Bailey kept her answer simple. "It's...a gift I have, to defend myself and others."

The boarding house loomed ahead. Vigdis docked the airfoil in front, and they returned to their room, with Pachola invited along. At first she hesitated, but encouragement from Amargon swayed her. They entered and all but Bailey found seats on the two beds. Bailey wandered around the room, not quite pacing, not quite trudging. Hands stuffed into pockets, head lowered, she finally came to a halt at the dormer window. Vigdis rose from the bed to join her.

"I'm lost," said Bailey. "I'm treading water here, trying not to sink."

"I think I actually understand that metaphor." She slipped an arm around Bailey's waist. "We need to see this Ocnorb. The subtle approach has been unsuccessful so far. Perhaps we should approach him directly, as visitors

134

from another world who are interested in acquiring phosphates for our agricultural lands. Perhaps the topic of agriculture will encourage him to tell us something of his plans for North Vyella."

After a glance over her shoulder, Bailey nodded. "Tomorrow morning," she decided. "Just you and I and Kayana."

"That would be prudent," Vigdis agreed.

"I hate doing it that way, though."

"You would not be you if you did it without conscience."

"So well you know me." She turned around and leaned against the window sill. "Amargon, you'll remain behind in the room tomorrow. Pachola...do you like working here?"

The Motic shrugged. "It is a job," she said. "The treatment is better than I have had before." With a subtle emphasis she added, "And sometimes I meet interesting people."

"Do you miss Motoya?" asked Vigdis.

"Dreadfully. So many of us are scattered. I haven't seen my shores for...for more years than I can count."

"Diaspora," muttered Bailey. "It happens everywhere, it seems, to peoples who are different." To Pachola, she added, "Would you return to Motoya if you could?"

Pachola frowned, uncertain where this was going. "Gladly. But that will never—"

"Would you please summon Hoillre to the room?"

Still puzzled, Pachola left the room. Within a couple of minutes she returned with a stern-faced Hoillre in tow.

"It's after hours," said Hoillre, confronting Bailey. "What is the meaning of this?"

Pachola's ears perked up, anxious to hear the response.

Bailey said, "It happens we require another slave for our activities here. Pachola has shown herself to be adequate. How much for her?"

"This is most irregular," said Hoillre, her tone controlled.

135

"I apologize," said Bailey. "I suppose I can buy one elsewhere."

"Well...wait. I paid..." Her brow formed a single green line as she considered her words. "Never mind. Fifty thousand thalers."

Bailey suspected this was at least twice as much as Hoillre paid, but she decided not to challenge the amount or to negotiate downward. Better, she thought, to indicate extensive funds by accepting the price. "Very well, I accept. Vigdis, give her your fundscard, please, and see to the transaction. Hoillre, please add Pachola to the list of occupants of this room. We'll work out the sleeping arrangements."

"Yes, of course." Hoillre keyed the financial data into her Palmetto, and verified the result while Vigdis watched. Finished, she said, "She's all yours. Now to find a replacement," she added grumpily.

Bailey waited until the door had shut behind Hoillre. Pachola was aghast. "What have you done?"

"You'd better sit down," said Bailey. After Pachola did so, next to Amargon, she continued. "As of this moment, I am manumitting you, Pachola. You are free. If you will stay with us while we conclude our mission here, I promise you, you will see your shores again, probably in a few more days."

Pachola gazed up at her with wet sapphire eyes. Her voice was hoarse with emotion. Even the UT staggered to translate. "What you say? What you say to me?"

"As soon as we can manage it, Pachola, you're going home to Motoya."

Immediately Pachola broke down. Amargon embraced her, and passed a comforting hand over her back. The sight caused tears to form in Bailey's eyes, though they did not fall. Vigdis took her aside. "Do-gooder," she whispered.

"That's 'armed do-gooder' to you, my friend," Bailey replied gently. "In this case, the weapon was Michael's money." This was jaded by the realization that Hoillre would simply go out and buy another Motic. Perhaps two of them.

136

As if reading her thoughts, Vigdis touched fingertips to Bailey cheek. "You do what you can," she said softly. "Already you've done more than most."

"I'm with a good group of people."

"And what works," said Vigdis, "is that you think of us all as 'people.' That...out here, that's unusual."

"Baby steps. Let's get some sleep."

Vigdis demurred. "Um..."

Bailey's eyes widened. "Oh, you can't be serious."

"Don't you want to?"

"Well, yeah, I do, but—"

"Then we'll keep it hushed."

"Oh, yeah, right. No, Vigdis. Wait till we're back aboard the *Skygnat*. Better yet, let's wait till we're on the grass by the shores of Motoya. We'll have all night then." She raised her voice. "Lights out in ten minutes, people."

017: How to Prevent a War

In the morning, after ablutions and breakfast, Bailey, Vigdis, and Kayana climbed aboard their rented airfoil. Vigdis performed a Palmetto search for Pondar Ocnorb and learned that he had an office in southern Vellam, although the search did not indicate whether he was present in his office at the moment. Following directions, Vigdis piloted the airfoil to the Ocnorb Company Office. This turned out to be a cube of a building, with a framework of steel-gray structural plastic that held in place great panes of acetate windows. To Bailey, who had seen fast-food restaurants on Earth become showers of glass shrapnel when struck by bombs, the OCO gave her pause, enough for her to wonder whether her face had grown pale.

In front of the OCO was a docksite with several airfoils already in marked spaces. At regular intervals along the sides of the site, tall and slender trees stood guard. Both sides of the building itself had been planted in grass, with a narrow flower bed separating the grass from the wall. All the plants looked well-tended.

A uniformed guard inside the lobby eyed the airfoil as Vigdis docked it. Through the great window his round face was impassive as he watched them enter and approach his desk. His emerald eyes narrowed as they drew up to his table.

"We're here to see *Seele* Ocnorb," said Bailey, having gotten the proper honorific from Vigdis. "We understand we can purchase phosphates for our farmlands."

The guard seemed to find this reasonable enough. He did not speak, but directed them with a wave of his hand to a counter along the back wall of the lobby, where a young female stood in anticipation of their arrival.

At the counter, Bailey repeated the purpose of their visit. The woman, whose name tag read Gallre, asked the perfunctory question. "Do you have an appointment with *Seele* Ocnorb?"

"Sadly, no," replied Bailey. "We've only just arrived on Zanga. Our information was that North Vyella might have the fertilizers we required, but we might receive a better deal from Ocnorb Company, particularly if we negotiate directly with *Seele* Ocnorb."

Gallre raised a hand. "One moment, while I check with the Orders Department." She tokked a Palmetto behind the counter and spoke into it and listened.

Vigdis shook her head at Bailey, a sign that she could not quite make out what was being said.

Finally Gallre looked up. "This is rather unusual," she said, almost apologetically.

"It's a rather large order," cued Bailey.

Another conversation on the Palmetto followed. After Gallre closed out, she said, to Bailey. "*Seele* Dolmen is in charge of the Orders Department. He is on his way down. You may speak with him."

Bailey sighed. "My orders are to negotiate with *Seele* Ocnorb."

"As may be," said Gallre, now with a trace of impatience. "But *Seele* Dolmen has his orders as well."

Resigned, Bailey drew the others aside to wait for Dolmen. He arrived within the minute, attired in an expensive pastel green outsuit, his black hair glistening with the cream that held it in place. He spotted them and approached, introducing himself as Seff Dolmen. His eyes were pale gray, which Bailey attributed to colored lenses, though she was puzzled by the affectation.

"As I informed your receptionist," said Bailey, "my orders are to negotiate with *Seele* Ocnorb. I do not know why this is so difficult to arrange, unless in fact he is not in his office at present."

"We have strict procedures here, *Saala* Bailey," he said, his voice gravelly and his tone slightly condescending. "I can take you and your party to my office, where you may broach your requirements. If I might ask," he did not care whether she would allow the question, "which world is this purchase for?"

"Earth," Bailey said tersely.

"I do not know this world."

"I do, *Seele* Dolmen." The UT translated her requirements. "We wish to purchase five hundred metric tons of phosphate fertilizer."

Dolmen looked around, as if to learn whether anyone had overheard.

"That is a considerable shipment," he said, more quietly now.

"Funds are not the problem. Timeliness of delivery, is."

"We should speak in my office," he said, and turned to lead the way.

Bailey cleared her throat for attention. "*Seele* Dolmen, my instructions are that if we cannot deal with *Seele* Ocnorb, we are to search for the same deal in North Vyella."

Dolmen spun back around, and pulled himself fully erect, so that he was almost as tall as Bailey's six-two. "I do not think you grasp the reality of the situation here on Zanga. North Vyella will use the money to buy weapons with which to attack—"

"*Seele* Dolmen," Bailey snapped, her tone now severe, "it is of no interest to me what North Vyella does with the money we pay them. What is—"

"*Seele* Bailey, you—"

Undaunted, Bailey overrode him. "*What is of interest to me* is that Earth obtains the fertilizer, the phosphates it wants, toward agricultural production." She gave him her Palmetto code, and noted with quiet but smug satisfaction that he was flustered. "Go confer with *Seele* Ocnorb, or whatever it is that you do," she continued dismissively. "If you decide you want to revisit this issue within the next two days, you know how to reach me. Vigdis, Kayana, let's go."

As they departed the building, Bailey's glance back noted a sheen beginning to form on Dolmen's pale green skin.

Bailey had a prickly feeling in her spine from the time they left the building to the time that Vigdis had

140

flown the airfoil out of sight. She relaxed a little, and blew a sigh of relief.

"Yeah," said Vigdis, commiserating. "I suppose there's no accounting for character, but that Dolmen put a lot of money at risk. In theory, of course."

This last was a reference to the fact that Bailey had no intention of placing an order, but wanted to talk with Ocnorb about not attacking North Vyella. Grimacing, she shook her head, and clung to the taffrail as Vigdis made a sharp left turn onto the mail glideway. She wondered whether she had blown the mission. There was no telling how badly Ocnorb wanted or needed the funds for soldiers' pay and for arms and equipment. Thus far, she had seen nothing of a military nature in Vellam, but a mobilization for attack would probably occur elsewhere, out of sight. That thought turned her to face Vigdis on the bridge of the airfoil.

"We should have done this before," she said. "But start monitoring all transmissions that might involve the military."

Vigdis nodded. "On it."

Bailey turned around. "Kayana, you don't seem to have much to say about our little encounter."

The purple woman shook her head. "I saw what you saw. But I do think Dolmen is frightened. He's worried that he might have jeopardized the deal you offered the company. But he's powerless to do otherwise."

"That's how I read it, too."

"I think you'll hear from him soon," Kayana went on. "If I might suggest?"

Bailey made a little gesture. "Of course, Kayana. You needn't ask permission."

"If it were me, I'd let his first attempt to contact you go into messaging."

"Stall him, you mean?" She considered this briefly. "That's not a bad idea," she decided. "But no more than twice, I think. We wouldn't want him to give up."

Vigdis docked at the house, and they went inside to their room. Amargon and Pachola were sitting on the bed by the window, snacking on bits of smoked fish. The

141

aroma permeated the room. They listened attentively while Kayana related what had transpired at Ocnorb Company. Neither Motic had any suggestions to make, but Pachola had a question.

"Does Dolmen know where we are staying?"

Bailey shook her head. "We didn't tell him. But if Ocnorb has a decent intelligence service, he can probably find out."

"She has a point," said Vigdis. "I'd better stand guard tonight." With a grin she added, "That should clear up some bed space."

Amargon stood up, and Pachola with her. "It's time for our showers," she announced, and they each held bars of their special soap when they went to the hygiene alcove.

"Vigdis?" said Bailey, now that they were alone with Kayana.

"I've been monitoring communications," she said, tension in her tone. "Ocnorb would like us to be found."

Pevely's lips tightened. "I was wondering about that. But there's not much we can do to prevent him from eventually learning our whereabouts. Just...stay with it, Vigdis. Patch into house commo and ask Hoillre to send up some local fare for all five of us. We'll all stay here until something develops."

Bailey, who had expected to receive unsavory food from Hoillre, was pleasantly surprised to find instead five meals of soft curly noodles with a spicy brown sauce, green and red vegetables, and a fruity beverage, all of which everyone found palatable, a comment happily relayed to Hoillre. By the time the dishes were taken away, dusk had fallen. Outside along the glideway several people ambled about under fusion globes on tall poles of gray structural plastic. Vigdis, who had the best vision, identified most of them as locals, while two or three were clearly from other worlds, as these had tentacles and no true shoulders. Most seemed to be sightseeing or shopping, but Vigdis was watchful for anyone who showed more than a casual interest in the house, or who was standing in the shadows.

Bailey, meanwhile, had other security concerns. Leaving the room, she went down to the main floor and asked Hoillre about a back door and other entrances to the house. There was only one, used to receive deliveries. Hoillre showed it to Bailey; it was locked from the inside, and the lock looked secure enough that anyone who tried to force the door would awaken everyone in the house. Nevertheless, Bailey asked for the door to be opened. A rough glideway had been cleared in back for delivery vehicles, and a few small fruit trees offered minimal cover. Beyond that stretched open meadow, and an assailant might be spotted a few hundred meters away. Bailey sighed. It was not the fence she had hoped for, but at least the enemy had no concealed approaches to the house.

Back inside the room, Bailey drew Vigdis aside and told her of potential security concerns. "I'm good," replied Vigdis. "But not even I can watch both the front and the back approaches."

"It looks like we're both staying up all night."

"That should free up even more bed space."

Bailey sighed. "I'll watch out one of the back windows. It's all right. In the Army we sometimes pulled twenty-four hour watches."

"I pull them all the time."

"I hate you," said Bailey. But she punched Vigdis's shoulder and smiled when she said it.

Bailey chose the back window that gave her the best view, and pulled up a castered chair for her vigil. She was unable to put a finger on what she expected to happen. It was quite possible that Ocnorb or Dolmen would take no action during the night. Having left her Palmetto code with Dolmen, she saw no reason for either of them to do anything but make contact with her in the morning.

As the night dragged on, Bailey found herself wishing they had stayed aboard the *Skygnat* in null-space, where they would be totally safe. But if Ocnorb made a move against them in the night, it would reflect on his attitude toward them. She wanted to know whether he was belligerent or merely vexed. Or whether he even cared that she had berated his second-in-command.

Tree branches moved in the dark shadows; a crosswind had begun to flow. Now she also watched for any plant movement against the wind, for that might well indicate a stealthy approach. But nothing untoward happened. She fought against dozing off. She got up from the chair and walked around to stay awake.

Finally Vigdis joined her there. "I think you can go to bed," she said. "Ocnorb and Dolmen both posted wake-ups on their Palmettos."

"What about you?" worried Bailey.

"I'll keep watch, just in case."

"You're sure about this?"

Vigdis kissed her. "Off you go. Try not to nudge Pachola out of bed."

"I thought she would be sleeping with Amargon."

"There's no accounting for attractions, Bailey Belvedere. As well you and I know."

"Wake me when the sun comes up."

The quiet night began fitfully for Bailey, who was unaccustomed to the routine sounds of the house. A board creaked; a mild thump; the breeze against a window. All conspired to make her keep one eye open. Pachola, beside her, seemed unaware that she was no longer alone in bed. Bailey, on the other hand, was well aware of Pachola, whose body temperature was a good five degrees higher than her own. But when Pachola rolled over and snuggled against Bailey's back, Bailey found it easy to rest, doze, and sleep.

In the morning, when Vigdis awoke her, the Motic was still clinging to her back, and was already wide awake, as if she had been watching over her sleeping companion. Gently Bailey extricated herself from Pachola's embrace and sat up. Her throat was dry; she accepted a mug of water from Vigdis, sipped from it, and passed it to Pachola.

"Quiet night?" Bailey asked, her throat still a little parched.

144

"Ocnorb has directed Dolmen to reach you, and to invite you for a consultation."

Bailey got up. "How do you read it?"

"I think he wants to talk, but on his terms."

Amargon and Kayana began to stir. Bailey waited until they were fully awake before she explained to them the plan for the day. Neither Motic was pleased at being left behind again.

"You bought me," said Pachola. "I should be with you."

"I freed you."

Bailey turned away, but Pachola caught her arm and tugged her back around. "You will be searched for weapons before you see Ocnorb," she said. "They will not search me. I am a slave in their eyes."

"She has a point," Vigdis agreed.

Pachola's voice grew tender. "Yes, you freed me, Bailey. It is for that reason that I *choose* to serve you, in whatever capacity you will have me."

Closing her eyes, Bailey took a deep breath. Unaccustomed to such servitude though she was, she knew a rejection would hurt Pachola's feelings, but would not stop her from following her choice. Eyes open now, she slowly nodded.

"All right, Pachola. I accept the choice you have made."

Joy radiated from Pachola's blue face. "I shall need the weapons."

Amargon spoke up reluctantly. "I'll stay here with Kayana and guard the room."

Bailey shook her head, and completed the assignments. "No. You and Kayana stay with the airfoil while we go inside. I'll let you know what floor we're on. If it becomes dicey, crash the airfoil through the window and rescue us. Vigdis, inform Dolmen that we will arrive in twenty minutes."

In fact it was nineteen. Kayana and Amargon kept the airfoil on idle in the docksite while the others entered the Ocnorb Company headquarters. A different uniformed guard was on duty just inside the door, but he made no move to stop them as they passed by. Apparently word had gotten to him of their anticipated arrival. Dolmen was waiting for them in front of the counter, behind which a subdued Gallre stood by. Bailey approached him directly. His eyes were still gray.

"*Seele* Dolmen, good morning," she said. "I apologize for the short notice, but I had heard that you and *Seele* Ocnorb had wanted to speak with me further on the matter of fertilizer. As we intended to depart for the north at midday, I thought this would be the most opportune time for that discussion."

Dolmen's expression grew stern. "May I ask where you heard this?"

Bailey played it to the hilt. "My sources of information are and must be confidential," she replied. "As your sources are, *Seele*."

"Yes, of course." He made a quarter turn, as if inviting them to follow. "*Seele* Ocnorb's receiving office is this way."

Even as he spoke, he motioned to the guard, who approached them with a scanning device, which he passed over Bailey and Vigdis. Satisfied that they were unarmed, he nodded curtly to Dolmen and returned to his post.

"Standard precautions," said Dolmen, although his tone was not apologetic.

"Understandable," said Bailey, struggling to keep a straight face.

The receiving office was on the first floor, around to the side, where there was a better view through the great windows of the plants and flowers. Dolmen held the door for them; two paces inside, they stopped.

The office was sparingly appointed. A desk and a chair. Speakers in each corner of the ceiling, from which wafted soft music at the threshold level. Nowhere for visitors to sit down. A finely woven carpet depicting scenes from some legend on the floor leading to the desk. The view from the desk was that of the garden outside. Bailey found the overall presentation relaxing, although she knew that everything had been arranged to emphasize the power of the individual behind the desk.

Pondar Ocnorb rose from his castered swivel chair to greet them.

Easily as tall as Bailey and Vigdis, he was a good half-body wider. Belatedly Bailey recalled that he was native to another world, Ogodda. Ocnorb's pale white skin glistened in the sunlight. He was wearing a sepia business outsuit one size too small, an affectation that drew attention to his sheer bulk. The unusual shape of his head drew Bailey's attention, for it was broad at the jaw level, and tapered upward almost to a point, where a tuft of black hair covered the pyramid thus formed. His nose was broad and flat; tinted lenses protected his eyes, as if they were sensitive to sunlight, a factor supported by his overall pale complexion.

He gestured them forward with a bulky arm, and came round the desk to greet them. His voice was gravelly, as if he were chewing the words first, and he did not smile as he and Bailey's party exchanged introductions. True to her role, Pachola kept silent and stood behind her companions.

Formalities completed, Ocnorb said to Bailey, "I'm told you are very direct and to the point, so I will be as well. Five hundred metric tons of phosphate fertilizer is a large quantity even for us, and I should not like to miss the opportunity to provide it. However, it must arrive in discrete packets, so to speak. Perhaps as large as fifty metric tons at a time."

"That is unsatisfactory," said Bailey. "I do not understand why you cannot provide the entire tonnage. What else can you use phosphates for, that you should have available such limited quantities?"

"Ours is a complex business, *Seele* Bailey. Ocnorb Company has, let us say, fingers in many cakes. Providing fertilizer is but one cake."

"Perhaps North Vyella is not so diverse," she said. "As I told *Seele* Dolmen yesterday, I have other options."

Ocnorb gave her a hard look. "It is inadvisable for you even to consider them."

Bailey frowned. "Why is that? Is there an enmity between you and the north?"

For just an instant the question startled him. His tone lowered by a full octave. "What have you heard?"

"As I told *Seele* Dolmen a few moments ago, my sources are confidential."

Ocnorb moved to his desk, opened a drawer, and pulled out an energy weapon, aiming it in Bailey's general direction.

"Vigdis," Bailey said softly, but she was already on the move, interposing herself between Bailey and Ocnorb.

As Vigdis began walking toward him, he fired a blue beam at her. It deflected off to one side, and scorched the wall. Ocnorb's jaw dropped.

Vigdis drew up to him. Her left hand grasped his right elbow, and squeezed the nerve there. Her right hand caught the weapon as it spilled from his numbed fingers.

"Let's be careful with that," she said amiably. "I'm ticklish."

Pachola, in the meantime, took an energy weapon from her pocket and handed it to Bailey. She in turn aimed it at Dolmen, who raised his hands and eased back.

Bailey spoke with calculated uninterest. "I'm assuming you do not wish to do business with me. Am I wrong?"

Ocnorb glared at her.

"Apparently not. Vigdis, render him transportable. Amargon, do you see us?"

The response came over the Palmetto. "We have you in sight."

"Come get us. Don't worry about the breakage."

The airfoil rammed through the elastic acetate window and docked on the showcase carpet. While Bailey covered their departure, Vigdis slung the massive body of Pondar Ocnorb over her shoulder as if he were an empty burlap bag and leaped onto the airfoil, followed by Pachola, who climbed aboard. While Dolmen watched helplessly, Bailey backed away until she touched the airfoil, then slung herself aboard.

"To the *Skygnat*," she told Amargon. "With speed, if you please."

The Motic pilot eased the airfoil from the window frame and aimed it toward the Spaceport. No one said much. A gesture and a word from Bailey got Amargon to make an adjustment in the flight path. Vigdis, unbidden, opened the *Skygnat*'s hatch and extruded the ramp in preparation for their arrival.

"What do I do with the airfoil?" asked Amargon.

"Leave it where we dock it," Bailey instructed. "Disposition is someone else's problem. Pachola, Amargon: thank you both. You did well. Kayana, after we get aboard, search the medical supplies for some sort of sedative and give Ocnorb a dose that will last at least four hours."

"I'll use a long, sharp needle," she said.

"A simple pill or syrup should do nicely," said Bailey, smothering a laugh. "But I applaud your enthusiasm."

"What *are* we going to do with him?" asked Vigdis.

"I'll think of some—"

A vibrant and shrill sound filled the air behind them. It rose to a crescendo, and started over again. A blue beam hissed past them and reflected off the tarmac before dissipating. Vigdis needed no orders to accelerate. Bailey glanced over her shoulder at the pursuing airfoil, its flashing red lights conveying authority. The beam was meant as a shot over the bow. Someone standing in the airfoil now aimed the laserifle more carefully.

Instantly three things occurred. Pachola cried out in pain. A blue beam seared Bailey's arm and blood began to flow. And Vigdis took charge.

"Retract ramp and seal hatch," she yelled, though it was unnecessary for her to speak the orders aloud. "Open cargo hatch."

"Bailey's hurt," cried Kayana. "Pachola is bleeding."

"Try to stop the bleeding while I get us aboard."

Bailey scarcely heard Vigdis's last instruction. She collapsed onto the console, smearing her blood there, and slipped into the footwell.

018: Double Duty

Drifting: passing through a cloud into the sunlight and back into another cloud. Something clamped around her left upper arm. Slippery.

A light crunch of structural plastic, and some jostling. She knew they had just docked the airfoil in the cargo hold. Clamp around her arm. Head nodding. Lights in and out. She had the sensation of flight, and wondered whether this was it, the journey to the next stage, whatever it was. Feebly she struggled. She did not want to meet her Maker with this thing clamped onto her arm.

A shout, or a cry in the dark. Vigdis's voice, barely recognizable. "Michael, you bastard, where are you when we need you?"

No response came.

"Pachola," she whispered, her throat tight and dry. At least, it sounded to her like a name. She had no idea what came out of her mouth.

She opened her eyes. She was not floating, but being carried. Fingers tight around her left upper arm. Lots of red there. There should be pain, but she felt nothing. Arm numb below the clamp.

Words. Vigdis. Something about a medical bay.

Need a morgue. I'm dying.

"No, you're not," said Vigdis. "I won't let you die."

Well, that was clear, then. It must be some other problem that I have.

Hours or years later. Bright light in her face. The Afterlife, it was, then. And it had a full moon.

Blinked. No, a moon-shaped face, complete with Mare Imbrium. Or was that an oculus for peering at her.

"I'm Doctor Steeb. Can you tell me your name, please?"

Huh?

She mumbled something. It sounded to her like, "Vig."

Steeb understood. "She's right here," he said, and drew her towards him.

A familiar face. There should be others. Pachola?

Her lips made a P sound.

"Pachola is in the next room," said Vigdis. "She is recovering. Tell the doctor your name so he can complete his chart."

"Blee Beved."

Steeb smiled. "Close enough," he decided, and noted something on his Palmetto. "Bailey, can you understand me?"

Duh!

She simply nodded.

Steeb laid the Palmetto on the foot of the bed. "I'm Doctor Steeb," he said again. "Some people call me a doctor, and some call me other things, but I'm what you've got. You're on a world called Arbuth. It is the closest world to Zanga that asks no questions. I won't give you my background, except to say that I was considered a good general practitioner before...well, before.

"You lost a lot of blood. You might have bled out without Vigdis holding onto you. And onto this Pachola, for that matter. She saved both your lives. We do not stock human blood here," he almost laughed, "but we have a good facility for developing what we need. We do have Motic plasma, which helped your friend. About half of your blood now is...replicated. It is fully functional, and over time your body will replace it with your own blood. The loss of the quantity of blood you suffered can be detrimental to other functions—brain, muscles, and so forth—but our scans show no signs of deterioration. You will make a full recovery. That's my prognosis."

"Pachola?" There; she got the whole word out.

"She is in roughly the same condition as you, and will make a full recovery." He picked up the Palmetto. "Your task now is to become ambulatory, which should take no more than another day here. Vigdis will remain with you. To be accurate, she cannot be moved from you without the aid of a small army. If you need something, she will send for a nurse or myself."

151

"Eat?"

"I'll have some gelatin sent to you. And leave that bandage alone on your arm. If it itches, scratch someplace else. It's almost healed."

"So quickly?" said Vigdis.

"We may not look modern, but I assure you this clinic is as advanced as any."

Steeb departed; Vigdis sat down on the edge of the bed.

"How long?" croaked Bailey.

"The better part of three days. You were comatose."

"Was close."

"It was my fault," said Vigdis. "I should have seen them coming."

"Love you."

"I don't deserve it."

"Tough." A quiet moment later, she said, "Orbit?"

"Ocnorb? Kayana had to bring him out of sedation. We assumed you did not want him dead. He's half-sedated and half-conscious, and bound with nylon in the cargo hold. We feed him once a day. He can stand to lose a few pounds. When he has to wee, Amargon places a tub at his feet and opens his outsuit. She, ah, is not gentle. I think she enjoys it. I like her; she's feisty."

Bailey laughed, and coughed. "Wee?"

"I had to look it up. Apparently the word had some currency in that context on Earth."

A nurse entered the room and handed Vigdis a dish of yellow shimmery stuff and a spoon, checked the vitals register on the monitor, delicately removed Bailey's catheter, and exited without a word.

"Ready?" asked Vigdis.

"You're feeding me?"

"Unless you can sit up."

"I'll sit up! I'm not helpless."

A few minutes later the dish was empty, and Vigdis set it aside on a table. "Better?" she asked.

Bailey nodded, still sitting up. "Pachola?"

"On the other side of the curtain. Shall I open it?"

"If she is awake; otherwise, let her sleep."

152

After checking, Vigdis opened the curtain. Pachola had sapphire eyes only for Bailey. On a human, Bailey thought her expression would have been one of adoration. She supposed it might be similar for Motics.

"All right there?" she asked Pachola.

"Better now." She turned her attention to Vigdis. "Thank you. Again."

"Any news from Michael?" asked Bailey.

Vigdis shook her head. "I'd guess we're on our own now, except for the occasional special request. We've won our wheels, as they say. Bailey Belvedere, he was not there when we needed him most."

"Next time he shows up, introduce him to our one-way airlock."

"Directive noted."

Another silence followed. "So I just lie here and recover," said Bailey.

"That's the plan."

"Where are my clothes?"

"The ones you and Pachola had on? In the recyke aboard the *Skygnat*. They should be clean now." Vigdis opened a door to display a pair of blue outsuits and two pairs of black boots. "When you're ready."

Struggling, Bailey managed to get her feet on the floor. After extracting the air tubes from her nose, she motioned for Vigdis to assist her toward the hygiene alcove. "I need to wee."

"Thank you for sharing."

"You can wait outside."

The ablution finished, Bailey emerged, a little more balanced on her feet. Still, the expression on her face was that of effort. She made it to the bed and sat down.

"Bailey?" worried Vigdis.

"Just..." She drew a breath. "Just recovering."

"Don't try to do too much."

"I have to deal with Ocnorb," she said, shaking her head. "That problem won't keep." Her grin chilled the room. "Search your database. Find me a planet with a low population density, rugged terrain outside the settlements, cold weather, and hard work. A mining colony with

153

workers who do not want to be found. That will be Ocnorb's port of call."

"I know of several ideal worlds."

"I rather thought you might. Have Kayana re-sedate him tonight; leave him in the cargo hold. Then pick out one of those worlds."

"Already ahead of you. Now, lie back and rest for an hour. Then we'll walk you around to get your legs back. And Bailey..."

"I know," she said tenderly. "Thank you for saving my life and Kayana's."

Vigdis selected for Ocnorb's destination a world further out the spiral arm, orbiting one of the old stars in the Vellax Cluster. The five habitable worlds were not officially listed by name in the GalaxyNet or on the star charts. If you knew your way around the cluster, you knew what to call them. If you were ignorant, you didn't need to know. Vigdis based her selection on a composite of reports that, added together, gave the name of the world as Kholoda and its location in orbit around a red dwarf known locally as Miser, because of the insufficient light it gave out. She also gleaned enough general information for them to pass, not as locals, but as previous visitors, thus disinviting too many questions.

All this she explained to Bailey in the latter's stateroom as they sipped hot cocoa and sat on the berth.

"Average high temperature during what passes for summer is 283° Kelvin," said Bailey. "What's that in Fahrenheit? Around fifty?"

Vigdis nodded. "In winter, the highs approach the freezing point of water."

"We'll let him keep his clothes. No communications devices, though. If he wants one, he'll have to work for it, and the people in charge are not all that generous with the pay scale."

"I estimate that he will have to labor in the scheelite mines for more than a month before he can get his hands on a Palmetto," said Vigdis. "They'll probably put him through a wringer. First he gets the device; then, a month

154

later, he gets the power pack that goes with it. And funds will be hard-earned. He'll need to pay for food and lodging and extra clothing before he can begin to save enough for the Palmetto." She eyed Bailey's cocoa mug. "Are you done with that?"

"Why?"

"Pachola has asked to see you."

Bailey frowned. "About?"

"She wouldn't say." Vigdis raised a hand. "Before you ask, no, I don't want to speculate."

She sighed. "I was hoping to get a nap in. All right, send her in."

Vigdis got up. "I'll be on the bridge."

A timorous Motic entered the stateroom after knocking and being invited in. She approached the berth tentatively; her sapphire eyes uncertain as she avoided looking directly at Bailey. Arriving at the berth, she seemed not to know what to do.

Bailey patted the spot beside her vacated by Vigdis. "I won't bite," she said.

A little bark of laughter, almost as an afterthought, erupted from Pachola as she sat down and folded her hands in her lap. But she did not speak.

At first Bailey allowed the Motic to get at what she had come to say in her own way. But the silence between them lengthened, and Bailey was beginning to miss her nap. Finally she gave Pachola a gentle nudge with a, "You wanted to see me?"

Pachola nodded, but continued looking down at her hands. The tip of her blue tongue swept between her lips. "I...I do not wish to return to Motoya on a permanent basis."

"All right." Obtuse, Bailey asked, "Where would you like to go?"

Pachola's eyes flicked toward Bailey and back to her hands. Her chest rose and fell with a long breath.

Intuition finally kicked in for Bailey. "Oh," she said quietly. "I see."

155

Now Pachola twisted to face her, a plea radiating from her face. Words rushed from her. "I won't get in the way. I'll do whatever you say."

"I'm a magnet for strays," Bailey said under her breath.

"I helped when you confronted Ocnorb," she put in, defensive.

Bailey nodded. "That was a good suggestion. But we are going back to Motoya."

Pachola's face fell. "Oh."

"Not that," Bailey said quickly. "I want us all to take a couple days off and enjoy the weather and the beach. Then we'll head back out to find more trouble to get into."

"You said 'we'."

"I noticed that, too."

Pachola threw her arms around Bailey for a couple seconds, before realizing the hug might be a breach of protocol. Bailey solved that question by hugging her back.

"The second stateroom aft on this side is yours, Pachola," she said as they drew apart. "Make a list of things you'd like to have, and we'll go shopping."

"I-I'll need...some soap."

"See Amargon for a bar until we can get you supplied. And now, if you don't mind, I'd like to get into my nap."

"I...could stay."

Bailey gently demurred. "I really do want a nap."

"But you, you don't have to nap alone."

Whether Pachola was offering from a sense of indebtedness or from her inner self, Bailey had no idea. But it did not matter. She stretched out on the berth and motioned for Pachola to do the same.

"Draw that quilt up over us," said Bailey. "Vigdis will awaken us when we're half an hour out. I'll try not to snore."

"And I will try not to do this," said Pachola, and trilled her nostril flaps at Bailey.

Three hours later, Bailey and the crew were gathered on the bridge of the *Skygnat*, with a view of the

156

matte black of null-space in the Videx. Pachola was staring at it as if she expected at any moment that it would change. As a slave, she explained, she had only traveled in shipping containers and cargo holds. The remark brought Bailey's ire to the fore.

"There has to be a way for those Motics who want to be free and back on Motoya to do so," she said heatedly.

Amargon was not so sure. "Half a million of us scattered all over the spiral arm, Bailey. I don't see how…"

"Nor do I. Yet."

"I have not received anything from Michael regarding Ocnorb or the Motics," Vigdis put in. "It seems he is…what is the phrase? Enough rope?"

"We're five people," said Kayana, her purple hair glistening and moist from a recent shower. "We're good together, but we're just five people."

Bailey almost laughed. "We've one more free stateroom left. As a team we're rather limited in size. What we need is the help of someone who…" Her voice trailed off as her gaze poked a tunnel through the Videx and well into the rest of the null-Universe beyond.

"Bailey?" worried Pachola, moving to her, dropping to one knee on the deck beside her captain's chair.

A quick shake of Bailey's head stilled Pachola. The others on the bridge remained silent. Presently Bailey spoke, slowly, gathering strength.

"This would be a project for someone ruthless enough to complete it, yet not so fierce that it gets in the way of the work," she mused out loud. "Someone with funding, and with an organization to carry out orders without delay or bickering. Someone with time to dedicate to the task, however long it takes."

"It sounds like you want an altruistic bully," said Vigdis.

Bailey flashed a grin. "Yeah, it does, doesn't it? Vigdis, take Kayana to the cargo hold, bring Ocnorb around, and let's have a negotiation here on the bridge."

By the time Kayana and Vigdis brought Ocnorb to the bridge, the *Skygnat* was poised a hundred thousand

157

kilometers from Kholoda, with the dark and forbidding world in the Videx. Ocnorb was not bound as he sat, or was seated, on a murphy bench, but Vigdis hovered nearby, a severe scowl on her face. Bailey rather imagined that she had told him in specific detail what would happen to him if he did anything other than sit, answer questions, and otherwise keep his mouth shut.

Ocnorb sat in sullen silence. His massive body now seemed shrunken, and his arms and legs now appeared enfeebled as he sprawled on the bench. Unable to summon the will or the courage to glare at Bailey, he gazed instead at the Videx and at the strange world far below.

"The planet below is called Kholoda," said Bailey. "Ah, I see you've heard of it. Kholoda is one possible destination for you. You have to earn your way. I estimate that it will take a minimum of two months of hard labor for you to afford a new Palmetto and send for a rescue."

At the suggestion of another possible destination, Ocnorb perked up a little. He was all attention when Bailey resumed speaking.

"On Zanga you manage a business," she went on. "You have an obedient staff and work force, and your organizational skills are beyond question, I should think. My sources have told me that you're planning to invade North Vyella and capture some agricultural territory. I had rather pump you out the airlock than allow you to do this."

Ocnorb found his voice. "This was not about fertilizer, then."

"It never was," Bailey told him. "At first, it was about stopping an invasion, stopping a war. If you want to live, and you don't want an exile to Kholoda, I have another proposition for you." She paused for effect.

"You do have my attention, *Saala*," he said.

"I hope you understand that if you deviate even a millimeter from what I want you to do, I will kill you outright. You've seen and felt the effects of just a little effort from Vigdis. Compared to me, she is kind."

Ocnorb licked his lips, moistening them. "Go on, please."

The "please" satisfied Bailey. She softened her tone. "There is one other factor that is relevant here, *Seele* Ocnorb. I and my companions are representatives of The Commission. Does that register with you?"

He swallowed hard. "What do you want of me?"

"A significant portion of the population of Motoya—the Motics—has been enslaved to work for various corporate entities, stores, shops, and so forth. They are to be asked if they wish to return to Motoya and freedom. Those that do wish this are to be transported home. Harm of any kind is not to befall them. Some of them will require a special soap; you will maintain a supply of this for them to use until they can be escorted back to Motoya. I will leave the logistics to you and your staff. Find the Motics. Those who wish to return to Motoya are to be taken there. They are not to be harmed."

"That...that could take years."

"You have enough stocks of fertilizer to keep you in business for about two years, maybe more," said Bailey. "You can remain in business by not allocating all your staff to this project. I will also issue you personally a fundscard for project expenses. A periodic accounting of those expenses is mandatory. You will also report progress to me every ten days. Failure to comply in any way with these conditions will almost surely result in your death, and in the deaths of those associated with you on this project."

Bailey sat back in her captain's chair. She gave him a minute to mull it over. "Well, *Seele*?"

"I...have a question. Some of these Motics were purchased. Will their owners require compensation?"

"They may apply to The Commission for it."

"Then will I have identification to show that I am working for the benefit of The Commission?"

"A temporary card identifying you as an auxiliary representative of The Commission will be issued to you."

"The sooner I am returned to Zanga," said Ocnorb, "the sooner I can get started."

"You've made a wise decision, *Seele* Ocnorb. But do bear in mind the conditions of your work. I will countenance no deviation whatsoever. One more item, *Seele*: if you carry this off successfully, I will recommend you to The Commission." She did not wait for a response, but addressed Vigdis. "Set course for Zanga, and...hmm. We need a verb here."

"Jump?" said Vigdis.

"Jump?"

"It is effectively what we do," Vigdis explained. "We jump from one point to another through a controlled wormhole."

Bailey nodded. "Let's Jump."

019: Resuscitation

After dropping off Ocnorb, there followed a Jump to Motoya for a few days of rest and relaxation. Motoya Control, now managing spaceport arrivals and departures, welcomed the return of the *Skygnat*. Pachola was overjoyed to see her home world again, a sight she had abandoned hope of ever seeing again. The weather remained warm, and the skies clear and azure, for the cooler rainy season had yet to arrive. On the beach, she accompanied Bailey, identifying for her the sources of the various detritus they encountered—shells and remnants, various forms of algae, and some small creatures that scuttled here and there in search of food or safety.

Bailey for her part felt slightly uncomfortable in Pachola's company. The Motic rather reminded her of a limpet in search of something to attach to. Never before had Bailey experienced being the object of hero worship. In this instance, all she had done was purchase Pachola, manumit her, and get her shot. It hardly seemed worth all the attention she was receiving.

Complicating the relationship was the fact that Pachola was an adult. Under the circumstances, a child might have been expected to behave in this manner. But Pachola was an adult female, at the moment wearing nothing more than a simple hipwrap of tanned fish skin, and she...

Bailey stopped, a sudden question in her gray eyes. Pachola stopped with her, curious as to the reason.

"Motics don't suckle their young," said Bailey. "But you have breasts."

"Not really," said Pachola. "These are implants, and the nipples are the result of altered DNA."

Bailey was aghast. "What? Why?"

"Some males like to have something to hold onto while they..."

Pachola turned to gaze out over the ocean, obviously distraught from some memory. Questions fled

Bailey, for now she understood more than she cared to. She laid a hand on Pachola's bare shoulder.

"The implants can be removed," she said, her voice just audible over the wash of the waves ashore. "And DNA alterations can be reversed. I'll pay the cost."

For a long moment Pachola did not respond. Gradually her shoulders slumped, and her face reflected inner sadness. "No," she whispered at last. "No, I think not. For one, I want to remember what was done to me, what was done to many of us."

Bailey grimaced. "Like tattooed numbers on a Jew's wrist," she said absently. "I think I understand that. Never forget."

Pachola nodded. "Never forget. And never again."

They resumed walking the beach, just out of reach of the lapping waters. Presently Bailey realized she had missed something in what Pachola had told her.

"You said that was one reason," she said. "Was there another?"

For several steps Pachola did not reply. She came to a stop, and Bailey turned back to her. The Motic did not meet her eyes, but instead scuffed bare toes at the sand. "You and Vigdis are..."

"Lovers and friends, yes, Pachola. As well as colleagues."

"She has breasts, yet she cannot suckle young. She cannot even have children."

Bailey shrugged. "I'm not so sure that's true. But what is your point?"

"Her breasts are an affectation to please you," said Pachola, and turned away toward the ocean.

Realization stunned Bailey. She had no idea how to respond to that. Yet she could not leave this alone; she had to do something.

A step brought her within reach of Pachola. Slowly and tenderly she reached for the Motic's hand—two fingers sandwiched between two opposable thumbs—and fitted her own fingers to it. Together they strolled the beach once more. Ahead and further inland on a low hillock grew a shade tree surrounded by lush-looking ground cover. Bailey pointed to it.

"Let's go up there and talk," she said.

"T-talk?"

"We can start there, and see what happens."

One by one the brightest stars appeared in the overhead purple sky of Motoya. The color reminded Bailey of Kayana's hair and skin, but sapphire and pale blue were the colors on her mind at the moment. The lovemaking—she could hardly call it coupling—had left her puzzled by the lack of ecstasy from Pachola. After three completions, Bailey had to pause, not only for breath, but for reflection. She had assumed that all sentient species were capable of orgasm. Her interactions had pleased Pachola, as much was clear from the little soothing sounds she made. The Motic derived pleasantness and perhaps even a bit of pleasure from the physical contact, but nothing more—at least, nothing more that Bailey was able to distinguish.

"You are distressed with me," whispered Pachola, lying beside her on the verdant groundcover.

"God, no." Bailey rolled onto her side to face her. "But I was not able to...to return the favor."

"Of course you did. I felt loved, I felt pleasure, and I felt safe."

"Safe?"

"I knew you would not hurt me." Pachola sat up, drew her feet under, and gazed fondly down at Bailey. "I have been...used by more species of males than I care to remember. Some of them used me and left. Others kept after me, trying to elicit a response I did not understand, not until this evening, when I listened to you."

Bailey laughed. "I think I'm almost embarrassed," she said.

"I am not capable of such a response," Pachola went on. "But now I understand that you are. You are concerned that you did not please me. I say this in all honesty—I have never known a touch like yours.

163

"Bailey, we Motics have a short season of reproduction. We are fertile only during this period. Motic females who wish to reproduce may do so. Others may choose to abstain. That is how it is here, for us.

"We do know love, I think as you know it. I may take a partner or two—a companion or two—but it is mostly to build a life together. Obviously, we may choose to reproduce, to raise what you call a family. And I tell you true: I had given up on such a life. On such a relationship. I am grateful to you, yes, but more than that, Bailey Belvedere, more than that, I love you for who you are."

Bailey flicked away a tear she had not realized she had shed. Her voice was tight when she spoke. "Pachola, you said 'or two.' An inter-relationship of three individuals. A triad."

The Motic broke in quickly. "Yes, I know about you and Vigdis, and I promise you I will not interfere. I will be happy with this evening—"

Bailey's hand covered her mouth, smothering any words. "I will not speak for Vigdis, but I will point out that she saved your life as well as mine. Computer that she is, she also has feelings, emotions. When she says she loves me, she means it, and she knows exactly what she is saying. Pachola...I want you both in my life."

"We are of one mind, then. And we will speak with Vigdis." She looked away. "Now that this has come to be, there is one other matter..."

"I think I know what you are about to say, but I do not see how it can be done."

"A simple DNA splice would enable reproduction between us. I think it best that I carry the child to birth."

Bailey searched her face. "You're serious."

"I am," Pachola said solemnly.

"I-I had never considered having children. The world I come from...it was no longer a world in which to raise a family."

"That is not a 'no,' Bailey."

"It most definitely is not a 'no.' But can this be done here on Motoya?"

164

Pachola shook her head. "The nearest world with the necessary facilities is Yolonya. That is where I was taken for my implants."

"Perhaps we should choose another world."

"No. Aside from being taken there for the implants, I have no bad memories of this place. I was treated well."

A silence ensued, like that in the night sky. Looking up, Bailey saw nothing but her own image in a constellation—eyes, ears, nose, mouth, and a dust cloud for hair, a dust cloud in which stars were constantly being born. Being born. Two words that now had special meaning. She was soon to be a...father? No. The child would have two mothers, or three, counting Vigdis.

How extraordinary...

"Bailey?"

She could barely make out the shape of Pachola in the dark. The only detail of her were the sapphire eyes that glowed in the remote starlight. But she recognized the tone in Pachola's voice. Tugging at the Motic's arm, Bailey drew her down beside her, and once again they used their hands and mouths to speak of their love.

Talk followed after their recovery. Not the so-called pillow talk, but of matters of the near future. "Ocnorb is going to return the Motics to Motoya?" Pachola said, astounded.

"That's the plan," Bailey replied. "He had a choice: it was that or death. He chose wisely, I think."

"But...the Motics are coming home? Oh, Bailey!"

"It is a large undertaking.," she cautioned. "I doubt everyone will be found, and I doubt all of them will want to return here. But all those who do want to return will be able to."

"I can't believe The Commission would involve itself," said Pachola after a moment of thought. "They haven't shown any sign that they care about our fate."

"But Michael has not interfered," she pointed out. "This tells me that the project has his tacit approval."

"Oh, I hope." A frown curled down the corners of her mouth and lined her forehead. "Who is Michael?"

The question made Bailey wonder how much to tell her. An uneasy silence settled in as Pachola began to worry. Bailey cleared her throat to prepare herself, then told Pachola everything. If she could not trust the Motic after all they had been through and done, then what was the point of the relationship?

Finished, Bailey sat back and watched Pachola digest this new information. Her response was unexpected.

"I think it is time to show you where I live," the Motic said slowly, carefully. "Or where I used to live before I was abducted. Leave your clothes here; no one will bother them." Pachola got to her feet and held out her hand. "Come with me."

Bailey took her hand unquestioningly, and held on even as it became obvious that Pachola was leading her toward the waves. Surf foam gathered around their feet as they stepped into the water. When they reached a point where they were up to their necks, Pachola said, still holding Bailey's hand, "Take a deep breath, exhale, and take another deep breath. Then let half of it out."

The instruction left Bailey guessing, but trust strengthened her, and she did as she was told. Pachola ducked under the waves, dragging Bailey with her. Still their hands remained joined. Within a few seconds Bailey began to worry about breathing. She still had air, but Pachola was leading her deeper and deeper. When the air ran out, how could they reach the surface without taking in water? Further and further they swam out into the ocean, half a minute, then a minute, and Bailey's lungs demanded fresh air. She fought against the panic that she was on the verge of drowning. Air, she needed air, and she needed it now. Bubbles began to burble from her mouth, escaping upwards.

Pausing, Pachola abruptly turned on Bailey and kissed her hard, lips pressing lips so that they blossomed. The Motic blew air into Bailey's throat and lungs. The ache in Bailey's ribs was relieved. Now she understood.

The underwater swim resumed, and deeper and deeper into the ocean they swam. Another minute passed, and Pachola gave her more air. Finally they reached a rugged and irregular wall of rock mostly covered with coral. Sunlight was so dim here that Bailey was unable to determine the coral's exact color, but she did see an opening in the rock. Still holding Bailey's hand, Pachola led her to the opening and swam inside.

Now they began to ascend in the water. Most unexpectedly for Bailey, they broke the surface. She found herself inside a cavern. Pachola climbed out onto a great rock ledge first, then helped Bailey out of the water. Dripping, Bailey staggered toward a smaller ledge that extended from the side wall of the cavern, and sat down there, gasping for breath. A moment later, Pachola joined her there, breathing normally the air that was as warm as that on the surface of Motoya.

Recovering, Bailey looked around, first for the source of light. Though dim, it was enough to read by. It issued from the luminescent rock ceiling, higher than Bailey could reach. An opening in the other side wall led to places unknown. But it was the furniture, made from cut and polished slabs of coral that was pink in the luminescent light that snagged Bailey's full attention.

Standing against the back wall, and easily recognizable, was a bed and a stack of storage drawers. The bed was covered with fabric that had been stuffed with some soft material. "Leaves from the land," explained Pachola, unasked. "Likely they are rotted by now. I shall have to replace them."

"Clothing in the drawers?" asked Bailey, and made a face as she realized the silliness of the question.

With a tolerant smile Pachola shook her head. "Waterproof pouches with a few—you would think of them as books. They are produced on the surface. We sometimes read them during our leisure time down here, and exchange them with each other when we have finished." She gazed ruefully at the stack. "I doubt they are still there," she added. "They are common property, and I have been gone from here for many years."

"But now you are back home."

167

A plaintive look crossed her blue face. She spoke tightly, with a courage implicit in her tone. "No. At least, I hope not. This is my native world, yes, and I hope to visit it often in the years to come. But my home is with you, Bailey Belvedere, if you will have me."

"I will have you, Pachola," Bailey said solemnly.

Relief washed across the Motic's pale blue face, and made her sapphire eyes glisten. Her tone grew more conversational. "There are other items in the drawers," she went on. "Tools for prying shells from rocks, and implements for preparing the flesh for eating."

"Raw?" asked Bailey. "Like sushi?"

"What is sushi? Something raw, I suppose. Ah, no, we cook our food on a heating pad that operates from a solar battery. I shall have to take mine to the surface to recharge it. Other tools and implements. We bring the bedding and the fabric down in waterproof containers, but we assemble it here." She stopped and looked thoughtful. "And there is the art, of course."

Bailey lofted an eyebrow at her.

Pachola got up and opened the top drawer of the stack. A cry of pleasure escaped her as she said, "Oh, they're still here." Reaching into the drawer, she withdrew an object wrapped in fish leather and brought it to Bailey. "Go ahead and unwrap it," she said. "But be delicate with your grip."

It was much heavier than Bailey anticipated. Carefully she peeled the wrapping free and found herself holding an *objet d'art* in gold. Fine wires had been bent into shape to create the illusion, rather than the form, of a young woman riding a sea creature. The intricate design must have taken weeks to complete, tediously tugging each component this way and that until it matched the vision of its creator—Pachola. Long ago Bailey had seen similar objects in museums before they were ransacked; but she had never seen anything like this.

With a light touch she turned it over and examined more of the exquisite detail. The fine golden hair on the woman's head; the open mouth and tiny teeth on the beast. Even thinner wire as eyeliner. Pachola must have

168

used a magnifying glass to do some of this. Soon she wondered about the inspiration. Had Pachola seen something like this? Or did it come from her own mind, as most great art stemmed from the unique vision of the artist?

"It is based on an ancient Motic legend," Pachola said softly.

Bailey nodded, without taking her eyes off the sculpture. "You created this." It was not a question.

"And a few others, yes. Bailey...nobody knows that some of us are able to sculpt these. Those on other worlds do not know that the ocean bottoms are littered with nuggets of gold, manganese, and other metals. If ever they found out, it would be the end of the Motics and Motoya."

"They will not hear it from me, Pachola."

"I know." Tenderly she accepted the return of the sculpture, and rose to replace it in the drawer. There, she turned back around. "We have some six hours before the sun rises above the horizon, Bailey Belvedere. Already we have loved, and if you wish, we will love again. But the truth is that I would like to lie with you and sleep. It is safe here to sleep, and to dream." Following a brief pause, she finished, "If that is your wish as well."

Bailey drew a little breath and nodded. "It is my wish as well."

020: Pro-Choice

Drifting awake, Bailey had no way of knowing whether morning had arrived. Given her rested state, she felt as if it had. She remained motionless to avoid disturbing the still-slumbering Pachola. Eyes now on the light from above, she began to wonder at the emotions running through her. For five terrible TFA years on Earth she had abandoned all hope of ever living a normal life, of having someone in her life to love. Of tenderness for the sake of tenderness. Yet now she had not one but two lovers. Moreover, here she was, in love with someone who was a DNA splice away from carrying their child. And what would the child look like? Elements of both parents, surely, but which ones? Gray eyes or sapphire? Black hair or ultramarine? Female, it seemed likely. Nose flaps, to prevent sea water from getting in? And what about the body oil? Worries all, yet solvable all.

"You are concerned," whispered Pachola, startling Bailey. The Motic's respiration had not altered during her awakening, nor had Bailey felt her eyelids flutter.

"I can think of nothing that would cause you questions here," Pachola went on. "Therefore, the concern must be of something between us, between you and me. It is not of the love that we feel for one another, or of your safety so far under water, for those are declared and assured. Therefore, it must be of the child I have offered to create with you."

Bailey laughed lightly. "Reasoned like Mister Spock."

The hair of Pachola's indigo brows brushed against Bailey's bare shoulder as she frowned. "Spock? Is this one of your philosophers?"

Another laugh. "In a way, he was, I suppose. No, Pachola, I meant that you have grasped the matter that I was considering."

"Considering," she repeated. "Again, that is not a no."

In that precise moment, Bailey's answer went from abstract to concrete. "It is a yes, Pachola. I would love to make and care for a child with you."

"This is good, for I am fertile now."

In the embrace of joy that they shared, not one shaft of light from the luminescent ceiling made its way between them. Bailey's only thought, tenderly whispered into Pachola's ear, was, "How extraordinary."

For a long time they held each other, neither moving except to breathe. A part of Bailey wanted to remain here in this cave forever, though of course that was impossible. Still, they might stay here another moment or two, another moment or two. "Another moment or two," she whispered, as if uttering the words would make it so.

At last they untangled, and found the strength to sit up. A brief silence reigned, during which they leaned against one another, content in the warm contact of skin against skin. Finally Pachola said, "The others will wonder where we are."

"Well, we can't have that. Deep breath, let out half of it?"

"So well you know me."

Emerging from the waves, and after letting the morning air dry their bodies, Bailey and Pachola gathered up their clothing and dressed. By the time Bailey had laced her boots, Vigdis had reached them. "Kayana and Amargon are already aboard the *Skygnat*," she announced. "I tried to raise you, but you left your Palmetto here." She said this last hurriedly, as if she had had some concern.

"I should have told you," Bailey said, contrite. "I'm sorry." Then: "Was there something from Michael?"

"A missive on my Palmetto," Vigdis replied. "He wants you to make best speed to Yolonya."

That stunned Bailey. The tip of her tongue flicked nervously over her lips. "Did he say why?"

"He did not."

He knows, thought Bailey. *Implicitly he approves. But what does it mean?*

"Is *Skygnat* sealed for travel?" she asked Vigdis. A nod sufficed. "Jump the skip here, and let's board up."

With the course set, and null-space showing in the Videx, Bailey briefed the others on the bridge. Kayana and Amargon were pleased by the announcement, but Vigdis looked uncertain. Bailey raised an eyebrow, the question obvious.

"It is," responded Vigdis, "a private matter."

A look from Bailey dismissed the other three, leaving her alone with Vigdis on the bridge. She bade Vigdis sit down in the port captain's chair, and waited for an explanation.

"As captain of the ship," Vigdis began slowly, somberly, "it is advisable for you to be in active condition."

"Pachola will carry the child," Bailey said quickly.

"No, you...misunderstand me. I-I...Bailey, I..."

The hesitation and uncertainty puzzled Bailey and left her more than troubled. Was something amiss with *Skygnat*'s computer functions? She did not quite know how to address that question, but as the ship's captain she had to find the words.

Before she could speak, Vigdis continued. "We—you and I—are lovers as well as friends and colleagues."

A smile found its way to Bailey's worried lips. "Yes."

"I-I had thought that one day..."

Now she frowned. "Vigdis, what is it?"

"That one day you and I would..."

Realization burst forth from Bailey. "Oh, God, Vigdis! I should have known..."

"You could not know, for we have not discussed it. But...it should be I who carries the child to term."

A sardonic laugh fled Bailey. "I'm right popular. But Pachola and I—"

Vigdis shook her head. "Again you misunderstand, Bailey Belvedere. I *too* wish to be impregnated by you."

For a long moment Bailey was stunned into silence. While it was true that Vigdis was fully human, she was also virtually invulnerable. Beams from energy weapons

172

reflected off her as if they had struck a metal mirror. How...?

As if reading her mind, Vigdis said, "I can enable myself to be implanted. I would wish this in preference to the process of in vitro. I wish to become a mother, in the full sense of the word."

"I never thought of in vitro development," Bailey said, hushed. "Of course science out here would have advanced to that level and beyond." Her eyes narrowed. "But you and Pachola wish to give actual birth."

"That is the way it is done, is it not?"

"It's one way. Vigdis, are you—"

"Yes. I am sure. I am a self-created human female. Becoming a mother is as human as I can possibly get. If," she hesitated. "If that is what you wish."

There was no way Bailey could turn her down, not now. "It is what I wish, Vigdis," she said soberly. "Time to Volonya?"

"Two hours forty-two minutes. There are some seconds involved as well."

Bailey got up. "We'd better tell the others."

"There is now...one other matter."

"Well of course there is." But she was smiling when she said it.

"As you know, I monitor the skip, including conversations. Now Amargon and Kayana..."

Bailey rolled her eyes. "We're going to turn *Skygnat* into a nursery."

"Is that a bad thing?" worried Vigdis, as they made their way aft toward the galley.

Bailey slipped her arm around Vigdis's waist. "It's the way of life, my love," she said. "It is the way of life."

Volonya was a smaller world, with a surface gravity of just seventy-seven percent that of Earth. While there was no danger of anyone inadvertently launching themselves into outer space, walking did require caution until acclimated sufficiently to maintain equilibrium. Several times as Bailey and her crew trod from the

173

docksite to the clinic one of them stumbled and had to be supported and steadied.

The Volonya Adjustment Clinic itself was smaller than Bailey had anticipated. Of beige structural plastic with transparent acetate windows, it was scarcely larger than convenience store. In appearance, however, it rivaled the best clinics she had seen on Earth. The front door opened automatically at their approach. Bailey expected to catch a whiff of antiseptic but instead the air was cool and fresh. Inside the lobby, a young gray-skinned woman greeted them and beckoned them to the counter behind which she sat on a stool. A Palmetto lay flat before her on the countertop. Her name tag was translated by the UT as Willow; the appellation fairly described her physical form. She flashed two solid rows of ivory at them, and asked how she might be of assistance.

"We were told to ask for Doctor Jonger," said Bailey, and gave her name. "Is he here today?"

"Yes, he is. Let me see." Willow tokked her Palmetto and read the result. "He has just finished with his last patient of the day, and is free now for consultation." A casual wave of her hand indicated a door that led deeper into the clinic. "His office is the first door on your right. I have already informed him that you are on your way."

"It does not sound as if he is very busy," Bailey said pleasantly.

"Of late, no," replied Willow, now eyeing both Pachola and Amargon. She leaned a little closer and whispered conspiratorially, "I very much fear we shall have to reduce our services. Well, in you go."

Bailey located the room without difficulty, for the door was inscribed with the occupant's name. She knocked on the door and waited for the invitation to enter, which came almost immediately. The room was crowded for five, but it was Doctor Jonger who took up the most space. Half a head taller than Bailey, he was also half again as wide, with a body of decent muscles overridden by a layer of fat. Still, he looked to be in good shape, and the dark eyes that dominated his pale round face seemed to twinkle as he greeted them one by one. After Bailey introduced them, he sat down at his desk, folded his hands together, apologized for the single visitor's chair in the office, and asked how he might be able to help such a disparate group of people.

"I don't recall seeing in my office a group consisting of Motics, a Harlangian, and...forgive me, but I do not know your worlds of origin."

"Same worlds," Bailey told him. "Earth. You probably don't know it. Doctor Jonger, we are here because we are interested in undergoing one of your DNA splice procedures."

Immediately Jonger raised a hand, cutting her off. "With regard to Motics," he said the name without rancor, "we are greatly reducing our outpatient list."

Bailey frowned. "I don't understand. I was given to believe that the VAC was one of the finest, if not the finest, such clinic in the Spiral Arm."

Jonger's smile revealed two solid rows of ivory that, as those of his receptionist, replaced individual teeth. "We have worked hard to make it so," he conceded. "But recent events indicate that many of our services will no longer be needed."

"But I don't understand," Bailey said again. "Why should this be?"

He settled back in his chair. "Well over half our work is performed on Motics," he began, and squinted at Pachola. "In fact, you look familiar. Breast implants? I think I recall assigning one of our techs to you years ago."

Pachola did not smile. "Against my will, although that was not your fault."

"Yes, well." He sighed. "I do not see what more I can do for you or for...Amargon, was it? For either of you."

"You have not heard what we want done," said Kayana.

Bailey waved her off. "What's happened, Doctor? You seem distressed by the reduction in services."

He hesitated, then shrugged, as if to say the subject matter was not something he should not talk about. "Motics who would need our services, particularly breast implants, are going back to Motoya," he said slowly. "The

175

interstellar trade in them has decreased significantly, and soon will cease altogether." He peered up at Bailey. "I take it you have not heard of this."

Bailey managed to keep a look of smug satisfaction from her face. Apparently Ocnorb's activities were already having an effect. "I've been out of the loop, so to speak. Doctor Jonger..." After a deep breath, she broached her requirements.

This gained her a long speculative look from him. "Interesting. And unexpected. Yes, we can do this quite easily. But it will be costly."

"How costly?" Bailey asked.

He smiled. "There is an old saying that if you have to ask how much, you probably can't afford it."

"They have that saying on my world, Doctor. And you have no idea what I can afford."

"Very well. Roughly two million thalers per pregnancy; the exact amount depends on any needed variations in the overall process. This includes the actual splice and special requirements, as well as delivery at the end of gestation. By special requirements is meant...oh, say, a post-operative adjustment in skin color, or eye or hair color, that sort of thing. Perhaps instead of a hand with two middle fingers and two opposable thumbs, you would prefer the offspring to have hands with five digits, like yours, or four like...Kayana, was it? And there are many other options."

"You mentioned gestation, Doctor," said Amargon. "Can you tell us what to expect?"

"The Motic gestation for a Motic child is twenty-two standard days," he said carefully. "With the splice from another species, that could well vary. Moreover, and forgive me for telling you something you already know, Motic children spend their first years in the water, and obtain oxygen through gills which atrophy in favor of lungs as they develop. A DNA splice can eliminate this gilled period, if desired, but the result will be a faster initial development of the child. The child may begin to walk at just a few days old, and reach half the adult height within, say fifty days. Those are estimates, of course, as we have performed only a very few operations similar to the one you want."

Bailey extracted her Palmetto, asked for and received Jonger's code, and transmitted to him the prepared and precise list of desired characteristics. She hoped it was satisfactory and could be done; the list was the result of three hours of consideration among the five of them on the bridge of the *Skygnat*, and all concerned were happy with it. Jonger read it over twice, and gazed up at the ceiling. Without looking at them, he said, "Do you truly want the children to oil as Motics do? Except for the child of Bailey and Vigdis, was it?"

"It is part of half of their heritage," said Pachola. "With the soap, or access to bodies of salt water, there is no difficulty. We do not wish to lose our identities, but to combine those identities."

"And the nose flaps?" he asked her.

"Those are essential for underwater swimming. Doctor Jonger, we have gone over our list thoroughly. We know what we want, and what we do not want."

"Yes, of course. But I must counsel you that in the event a characteristic should prove undesirable, changing or eliminating it is also costly."

"A million down," said Bailey. "The other million upon completion of the process." An extended hand offered him the fundscard bankrolled by Michael.

"In fact, that should go to our accountant." He nodded to himself. "Very well. You'll remain in the clinic overnight, and in the morning we will begin with a more detailed description of what will be done. The entire process, not including gestation, will take no more than a day." He pushed a button on a panel on his desk. At the voice of acknowledgement, he said, "Prepare five adjoining rooms for our patients, and arrange an evening meal for them."

"As simple as that," said Bailey to Pachola. They smiled at one another.

021: Mothers

Somewhat apprehensive at first, Bailey accepted the details of the procedure. Her part in it merely required the removal of two ova, while Kayana needed to donate but one. For the two Motics and Vigdis, far more was needed: a full analysis of their DNA, and identifying sections that were to be altered or adjusted, based on the donated DNA. It was not a process that Bailey understood. While she sat on the edge of her bed, Vigdis tried to explain it to her, and lost her after three or four sentences.

"It will work," Vigdis finally assured her, having abandoned her detailed explanation. "It will be all right. You will see."

"I know. I'm just...but yeah, I know." Bailey gave her a sidelong glance. "What did Doctor Jonger say about your DNA."

"There is nothing wrong with my DNA."

"Vigdis...," pressed Bailey.

She averted her eyes for a moment, before fixing her with a penetrating stare. "In point of fact, my name is not Vigdis, but a Harlangian name you could not pronounce. In addressing me the first time, Michael called me Vigdis, and I have grown accustomed to it. Are you familiar with the name?"

"A Norse goddess," said Bailey. "Of war, I think."

"I would like our daughter to follow in that tradition. Will you allow me to choose her name?"

"I was hoping we would both name her."

Immediately Vigdis was contrite. "Yes, of course. I am sorry, Bailey Belvedere. I meant no...I'm sorry." She drew a breath. "What name would you choose?"

"My middle name," Bailey answered after a moment. "It was also my mother's name. Mia. Your turn."

"In keeping with the origin of Vigdis, I have selected Idun."

"A Norse goddess?"

Vigdis nodded. "Of spring, new life, and youth."

Bailey eased the names from her lips, tasting them. "Mia Idun," she said to herself, testing. "No. Idun Mia?" She brightened. "Yeah, that flows nicely. And it's most appropriate."

Vigdis hesitated. "There is something else to discuss. With two minor adjustments in the DNA, which I may make without assistance, and neither of which will have any effect on what Doctor Jonger and his staff are doing, Idun Mia can, like myself, have direct access to the *Skygnat*'s computer, which is to say, to me."

Bailey's initial reaction was to say, "I don't know." Vigdis's face fell with disappointment. That hurt Bailey. It was all too obvious that Vigdis wanted this connection. It came down to a matter of trust: Vigdis would do nothing to jeopardize Idun Mia. Therefore…

"You'll want to monitor her closely," said Bailey.

Vigdis brightened. "Yes, of course. I will be one of her mothers."

Tears welled in Bailey's eyes, but did not spill down her cheeks. "Mothers," she whispered. "We're going to be mothers. All five of us."

"You wanted this."

"More than I ever realized. I had given up…oh, Vigdis."

"I have to go," she said reluctantly. "I have a meeting with his staff. If that goes well, and I know it will, the implant will follow. I will see you as soon as I can afterwards."

"Vigdis…"

"I love you, too," she said, and slowly stepped from the room, closing the door behind her.

Having nothing to do other than wait, Bailey closed her eyes and waited. Two eggs from her were necessary, two ova. She to donate, the medical people to accept and prepare them to fertilize two other eggs. To create two new lives.

How extraordinary.

She dozed off with that thought. Not long after, two med techs entered, administered anesthetic, extracted two ova, helped her recover, and left.

179

That's it, she thought hazily, her eyes half-lidded? That's all? The anesthetic slowly wore off, but was not replaced by pain anywhere. Modern medicine—no recovery necessary. At this, she gave a light laugh.

The door opened; a female med tech entered. Sallow-skinned and dark-eyed, she was wearing medical greens and non-skip slipons. Asked how Bailey was feeling.

"Groggy."

"That will pass. What do you want for dinner?"

Bailey started. "Din-dinner?"

"It's just under an hour for dinner. You can have what—"

Her eyes ached, so wide they were. "I've been asleep for...for what, seven hours? What has...how are my companions?"

The tech's face saddened. "You haven't been told? Well of course you haven't been told."

Horror filled her face as she sat bolt upright. An arm swept the top sheet aside. Her hoarse scream echoed in the room. "*Who? What happened?*"

The tech sat down on the edge of the bed, and touched Bailey's arm. "It's Doctor Jonger who should tell you."

"Tell me!"

"She's gone. Believe me, it's better this way. Her cells...the DNA..." She swallowed hard. "He'll explain. The doctor will explain. The other three are just fine, and in recovery. Their procedures were successful."

"Who, damn it?"

"The one called Vigdis. She..."

Fighting a storm of dizziness, Bailey tried to gain her feet. She would have spilled to the floor had the tech not caught her. Even so, she struggled. "Let me go!"

A buzzer sounded; the tech had summoned help. Almost immediately two male techs dashed into the room and clutched at Bailey, trying to get her back onto the bed. Military training kicked in. Four knuckles paralyzed the solar plexus of one of the new techs; an arm bar sent the other into the wall, and his head rocked against

180

structural plastic. The female tech managed to inject Bailey's arm. Even so, Bailey staggered toward the door, opened it, and fell into the hallway. Crawling she knew not where, she got another few meters before the injection finally took effect.

Bailey awoke to tears. She had been crying in her dream, for reasons unknown. With wakefulness came remembrance.

Vigdis.

How was that possible? She, who could not be killed, had died.

Bailey tried to move, and found her wrists and ankles restrained to the bed frame. Not to keep her there, so much, but to prevent her from hurting herself. Then the fear kicked in: if they could kill Vigdis, they could kill her companions. And they could kill her.

But why? What mistake had she made? This was a high-technology medical facility with a top reputation. Did it have something to do with the Motics? If so, then why kill Vigdis?

She turned her head from one side to the other. Nylon restrained her: unbreakable...but Vigdis could break it. If she were here. Which she wasn't.

Bailey wept.

Through bleary eyes she spotted monitor leads attached to her hands. Oxygenation. Blood pressure. Pulse. If they were monitoring her, they would know she was awake.

"Hallo!" she yelled.

Echo of footsteps. Hiss of opening door. Sight of the same female green-clad medical tech. For a moment she observed Bailey. Then turned to leave.

"Wait."

But she left.

At least they knew she was awake. Now maybe they would tell her something.

More echoes. Doctor Jonger entered the room. He did not close the door, but beckoned to someone in the

181

hallway. Waiting for that person's arrival, he approached Bailey's bed.

"I apologize for the restraints," he said in his professional bedside voice. "You might have hurt yourself. The tech will release you so that you can sit up."

"Vigdis *can't* be dead."

"I'm sorry. Truly I am."

Bailey's neck hurt as she shook her head, rocking it back and forth on the pillow hard enough to negate his claim. "You don't understand. She *cannot* die."

The female tech came in and released Bailey's bonds. She sat up. Hands to the side of her head fought light-headedness. Her vision blurred momentarily; then Jonger came back into focus. She transfixed him with a stare that could melt rock, and waited for an explanation.

It was not immediately forthcoming.

Doctor Jonger sat down in a visitor's straight chair and crossed his legs. "First, the ova transfers from you and Kayana, is it? They have successfully fertilized the ova of Pachola and Amargon. They will deliver healthy babies after a gestation period whose length we estimate at ten to fifteen days. All four of you will receive lists of characteristics as well as instructions for post-natal care. We would hope that the Motics will deliver here, but of course any facility with the staff and equipment can assist you."

"Vigdis," growled Bailey.

Jonger crossed his legs the other way. "I can give you the specific scientific details. In fact, they will be uploaded to your Palmetto."

"*Now!*"

"Yes, of course. In summary, the implant of your ovum nucleus was not merely incompatible with the ovum of Vigdis. The RNA failed to transfer the DNA information correctly. Once that information reached Vigdis's ovum, it began to spread throughout her body, a chain reaction that killed every cell that it came in contact with. This is not a phenomenon we have ever seen or predicted before, and of course we had no way to deal with it once it began.

I can tell you that she...passed without waking up, and that it was very quick."

Bailey licked her dry lips. "How...how quick?"

"It was called six minutes and twenty-two seconds after the two ova made contact."

"It? *It?*"

"Her passing."

"Death."

"Yes. Her death."

"I want to see her body."

Jonger looked down at his feet. "That is no longer possible," he said, his voice barely audible. "She was cremated."

Rage billowed inside Bailey and exploded in her words. "An inexplicable death occurs and instead of thoroughly investigating it you destroy the body within an hour or two of death? You're lying!"

"I assure you—"

"No. No." Bailey's eyes tightened. "Where are her ashes?"

"They...they have not yet been disposed of," he told her. "I can...give them to you. We have no urns here, however. A leather pouch will have to serve temporarily."

"You've never had a patient die before?"

"In point of fact, Bailey, no, we have not. Frankly, I don't understand it."

"Then why cremate the body?" Bailey shouted. She felt anger boil into her face, and knew it was red and apoplectic. Saliva filled her mouth. "You should have conducted more tests!"

"We did everything—"

"Did you?"

"I'm sorry." Ponderously he rose to his feet. "You and the others will remain here overnight for observation. A tech will give you a sedative to help you relax and sleep."

"I don't want a sedative! I want Vigdis!" She began to sob. Presently she slumped onto the bed, her entire body trembling. "I want Vigdis," she moaned, over and over.

A nod from Jonger to the tech ordered the sedative. It took effect within seconds.

The room was dark when Bailey awoke to the sound of the door opening. Dim hallway light rushed in, backlighting a female med tech armed with a syringe. The time had come for another sedative. Bailey waited until the tech had drawn within reach. Then, in a lightning move, she seized the tech's arm with one hand while she drove her other hand into the nerve center just below the sternum. With the tech now temporarily immobilized, Bailey drove the needle into her shoulder and emptied the syringe. Seconds later, she slipped the unconscious body onto the bed and covered her with the top sheet, bunching the sheet around the face so that a casual glance might inform anyone else that she, Bailey, was still under sedation.

Yet something was wrong. On a terrible suspicion, Bailey checked the tech's pulse—and detected none. Pressed her head to the tech's chest to listen for a heartbeat, and heard none.

Bailey's own heart stuttered. Every second now was vital. She did not bother with her clothes, but dashed to the door and listened for sounds in the hallway. The clinic was quiet. A silent mantra formed for her: please no, please no. She peered around the corner. The hallway was empty for the moment. Silently she hurried to the adjoining room, the open-backed white gown swirling around her knees, and managed to open the door without a sound.

Kayana lay in bed. Sleeping? Bailey's heart now thundered as she crept toward the bed, hoping against hope. Kayana opened her eyes, answering that hope.

"Bai—"

Bailey's hand covered Kayana's mouth. She bent down and whispered, "No noise. We're in danger. Come with me."

Under the hand, Kayana nodded. Together they headed for the next room, with Kayana covering the rear. Bailey nudged the door open. Pachola was sitting up in bed. A dark frown formed on her face, followed by a smile of greeting. Kayana closed the door behind her.

"Are you all right?" whispered Bailey.

"Yes. Why wouldn't I be?"

"They told me Vigdis had died."

"No! Oh, no!"

"Shh. A med tech tried to kill me with an injection."

"What's going on?" Kayana asked.

"I don't know," Bailey replied. "I cannot fathom it. Nothing is making sense right now."

Kayana cracked the door and peered around the jamb. "It's still clear."

"Next room," said Bailey. "Amargon."

The room proved empty. The bedding was in disarray, but the bed itself was unoccupied. Vertical racks supported various tubes and cannulas. A monitor screen had frozen with the last recorded vitals: a pulse rate of fifty-two, oxygenation at ninety-eight percent, and a respiration rate of eighteen breaths a minute. Dangling from another rack, a blood pressure tag was starting to contract. The monitor had frozen at one ten over seventy-two. But the tag was not now connected to anything.

"This is insane," cried Bailey.

"I'll check the next room," said Kayana.

Bailey's despondent tone fell an octave. "Why bother?" she said dully. "Only four of us are left." She glanced around the room. "Three, now."

"Best be sure," said Pachola. Two seconds later, following a soft sound, she said, "What was that?"

"Closet!" said Bailey. "Amargon." She rushed to the door and yanked it open.

Vigdis spilled out.

022: Malpractice

In Bailey's arms, Vigdis managed to hold herself upright. "I'm okay," she whispered shakily. "I'm recovering." She looked over Bailey's shoulder at Kayana and Pachola. "Amargon. Next room. Bring her."

Bailey sat her down on the edge of the bed. "Vigdis, what...?"

"It is a bit of a story, and one that can be told later, after we are in null-space."

Bailey shook her head. "Jonger lied to me about you."

"I thought as much. For what it is worth, he did what you paid him to do. Amargon and Pachola are pregnant...as am I, Bailey Belvedere. There are no worries on that, but I would kill Jonger before I would allow him or his staff under his orders to deliver Idun Mia." Vigdis stared at the wall for a moment. "I may kill him anyway for what he did."

"Take a number," snarled Bailey. "Get in line."

Amargon rushed into the room, followed by her two rescuers. "We have to get out of here," she said breathlessly. "I overheard...Jonger ordered them to inject us."

"That will not be necessary," said Vigdis. She got to her feet. "I am now me. I am recovered. I am no longer a human being who has made herself vulnerable by the need to be implanted. Although still fully human, I am in fact invulnerable again. Jonger is in his office awaiting word about us from his techs. He does not want me dead. Quite the contrary."

"But we have no weapons," Pachola worried.

"We will have no need of them," Vigdis said grimly. She tugged at Bailey. "Let's go."

An alarm sounded before they were halfway to Jonger's office. Bailey guessed that the tech she had inadvertently killed with the lethal injection had been found under the sheet of her bed. But the activity was confined to another hallway; Bailey's group was headed further into the bowels of the clinic. To Room 117.

Almost as if he expected to be the object of a hostile search, Jonger was emerging furtively from his office when Bailey arrived. The doctor's face paled immediately, and his eyes emitted sparks of fear. A none-too-gentle shove from Vigdis sent him reeling back into his office. Once the group was inside, Vigdis secured the door.

Another shove, this from Bailey, forced Jonger into his desk chair, which spun around once and almost once more. Bailey stepped around his desk so that she might engage him face to face. She spat one word at him, a demand that was impossible to ignore. "Why?"

Words failed to coalesce in his mouth. His lips writhed. He croaked a sound filled with terror. Bailey had no sympathy for him. An insolent gesture drew his attention to Vigdis. "Does she look dead to you? Is that your diagnosis, *Doctor*?"

"Y-you don't—"

"Understand?" Fists on hips, she leaned her upper body toward him, every muscle clenched with fury. "I'm in better health than you thought. I came out of the sedative too soon. Had I not, your tech would have injected me with a lethal dose of something. I know, because instead I injected her. The same order from you included Pachola, Amargon, and Kayana. *That* is what I understand. Talking, an explanation, can keep you alive, Doctor. But not for much longer. Vigdis's fingers hunger for your throat." She straightened. "Well?"

Jonger cleared his throat twice. It remained constricted with fear. "She...her DNA. It contained silicon and silicon compounds. She...she is not human. Or she is more than human. The arrangement of the atoms..." He paused to lick his lips. "May I have some water?"

Bailey glared at him. "No." She prodded him. "Atoms?"

"Y-yes."

He coughed, but whether from a dry throat or for sympathy, Bailey did not know or care.

"Yes, atoms," he continued. "In arrangements commonly found in computers. As far as we were able to test, the arrangements do not affect her humanity. But she definitely has computer aspects in her DNA, and these are able to replicate. The child she is carrying will also possess these aspects, these attributes. Manifestly, Vigdis and her child are impossible. Yet they exist. If we could..." His lips tightened, as he realized he was about to say too much.

Bailey gave a weary nod. "If you could control this, you could make money beyond your wildest aspirations. But the secret had to remain within the clinic. Maybe your techs don't even know. But they do follow orders. Perhaps they knew what they had been ordered to administer, even if they did not know why. Perhaps not.

"Money helped to destroy my world, Doctor. Now you would have it wreck life in the spiral arm, in the galaxy. Maybe it wouldn't go that far; I don't know."

"What..." He licked his lips and tried again. "What are you going to do?"

Bailey turned away. "*Michael! Now, damn you!*"

The flash of light failed to catch anyone off-guard but Jonger, who cried out, blinking rapidly. Michael stood beside Bailey at the corner of the desk, hands shoved into pockets, an expectant look on his face.

"I have been monitoring," he said.

"You might have intervened," she snarled. "This was close, too close."

"You and yours would not have been harmed," he said indifferently. "You've done something interesting, however. I want to see how it plays out."

She parked a hip on Jonger's desk. "That is not why I summoned you."

"I know. But tell me anyway."

"I want you to use your powers to fix Jonger," she said, before she could stop herself. "Not that I mind killing him; his actions warrant it. But he and his staff are highly advanced in the field of genetic adjustment. It would be a shame for the spiral arm to lose that. But he fell prey to greed; a latent flaw within him. Maybe not everyone has a price. I doubt you do. I'd like to think I do not. But he saw his price reached and exceeded. He also issued the kill orders. Before this, I am sure he was pleased with himself for the work he was doing. So was his staff. So that latent attraction to wealth and the willingness to kill patients to protect that attraction need to be deleted from his personality.

"For the staff, it is a different problem. Right now, I do not know whether any of them were aware that they were about to commit murder by lethal injection, at Jonger's order. If they were, then they need adjustments. I don't know what they would be, exactly, but I'm sure The Commission does."

Jonger's eyes widened. "The...The Commission?"

Bailey turned to him and gave him her best superior smile. "I am an operative of The Commission," she told him. "And this is my team you wanted to murder."

He slumped in his chair in abject surrender, knowing his was now a lost cause.

"If the staff was unaware of what they had been ordered to do," Bailey went on, "perhaps no adjustment is needed. I leave that to you." Now she challenged Michael. "What is your decision?"

"An interesting bit of reasoning, Bailey Belvedere," he said, after a brief massage of his chin. "You're showing mercy."

"Conditionally," she reminded him.

"Yes, that is understood. Very well: it shall be as you have stipulated." Bailey started to signal the others to leave, but his raised hand stopped her. "There is one more matter to discuss: the pregnancies of Vigdis, Pachola, and Amargon."

"They will not be terminated," she grated. "Got that?"

"That, too, is understood," he assured her. "No, I simply propose that I assign a...you would call him a gynecologist or obstetrician, with additional expertise in pediatrics. I have also taken the liberty of informing him of the nature and circumstances of the pregnancies with which he is to deal. In whatever way you wish, he will assist with the deliveries and the post-natal care."

Bailey felt doubtful. Worse, she found Michael's interest to be suspicious. Yet she was unable to see the harm having an ob-gyn available might do. "Motics have been giving birth for several millennia now, Michael," she said. "And without medical assistance except from what I would call midwives. And Vigdis is…well, Vigdis."

"I will not make it an order, Bailey."

"Wisely avoided."

"Would Averwell be acceptable instead as an observer who will assist if called upon to do so?"

"It can't hurt," Vigdis threw in.

"Averwell," Bailey repeated. Slowly she nodded. "All right, Michael."

For a couple of seconds Michael closed his eyes. When he opened them again, he said, "He is now aboard the *Skygnat*, and is waiting for you on the bridge. And now, if you please, I have some work to attend to."

At Bailey's signal, the five left the office, Bailey closing the door softly behind her.

023: The Impossible Child

Averwell arched a dark brown eyebrow at Bailey as she instructed Vigdis to set the course for Motoya. Michael had informed the ob-gyn of Vigdis's special status, and he did not question Bailey as she spoke to the computer rather than to Vigdis. But he did wonder why they were headed directly for the Motic home world, and said so.

Averwell was half a hand taller than Bailey, and seemed fit under the pale brown outsuit. He hovered nearby, watching the action and the Videx. He looked almost human, thought Bailey. Only the burnished-gold irises surrounded by a dull yellow, set him apart from her species—unless, she thought, he had seen Jonger earlier for adjustments. His off-white skin suggested a career indoors, which might be expected of someone in his profession. Once she got past the eyes, the lower half of his face would have escaped notice in a mall crowd.

Averwell carried himself confidently, which increased Bailey's interest in him, for otherwise his overall appearance might be regarded in some circles back on Earth as effeminate. His hands told a different story; his grip was firm when he and she clasped elbows in greeting.

With null-space in the Videx, Averwell looked around for the proper place to seat himself. Vigdis aimed him toward a murphy bench, and herself sat down in the port captain's chair, her reserved spot. Amargon dropped down beside him, but kept her eyes on Bailey, as though awaiting instructions.

"It's two hours and more to Motoya," Bailey told him, in her friendly but captain's tone. "I'm fairly certain no one here will give birth before then. You might check out your stateroom; if there's something you need, let Amargon know. Amargon?"

The Motic got up. "If you'll follow me," she said to him.

"I could use a cup of tea," he said.

"We'll stop by the galley."

Alone on the bridge with Vigdis, Bailey regarded her briefly from head to toe. "How do you feel?" she asked.

"Already Idun Mia is growing inside me." She raised an eyebrow. "Bailey, you were...businesslike with Averwell. And a little abrupt. He is a member of the crew now."

"Temporarily."

Bailey looked away. Already she was aware of her tone in addressing him, as she was aware of the reason for it. Not since Vattar had there been a man aboard the *Skygnat*—if Vattar could be referred to as a man. And Averwell was...was...

"He's not grotesquely ugly," said Vigdis, her eyebrow still arched. "And he is intelligent, knowledgeable, and educated, and with a useful and helpful skill."

Bailey barked a nervous laugh. Vigdis had come very close to her own thoughts. "You're on the verge of being out of line," she told Vigdis. But a faint smile traced her mouth as she said it.

"You know I'm right."

"Yeah." She looked at her hands, not knowing what to do with them. Finally she leaned back in the captain's chair and laced her fingers behind her neck. "I spent the last five years avoiding men whenever possible, and shooting them if I had to. It's been...oh, wow, a long time since I..." A look of distress came over her. "Oh, God, Vigdis, I didn't mean..."

Vigdis got up and walked to her, and took her hand. "I did not take it badly, Bailey Belvedere. You and I and Pachola will keep what we have. But your heart—and our hearts—have more room in them, should you or we want to fill it. We've just been through a very emotional time; someone we thought we could trust tried to kill us. You grieved for what you were told was my death. You, we, are vulnerable now. One step at a time, Bailey Belvedere. What is that human phrase?"

"*Que será, será?*" she tried.

"Yes, just so. But our lives are also what we make them. And lives are best when we make them together."

Bailey gazed up at her. "When did you get to be so wise?"

192

"It's the company I keep." She tugged Bailey to her feet. "Two hours and some points to Motoya. My computer aspect has the bridge. Unless you'd prefer to sit there and stare at the interesting view in the Videx."

"You know me better than that."

"Of course I do. I'm carrying our child."

Although the Motics were aquatic, on land they sometimes resided in coastal settlements, near enough to the salt water for frequent bathing. None of the huts—made of stone, wood, and thatch—belonged to any one individual. Two huts, located in the glen of a small wood and close enough to the ocean to hear the waves die, served five; Averwell found a hut near enough to the other two that he could reach them in seconds in an emergency. As Motics gave birth in the water, his primary focus was Vigdis.

The waiting game began. Seemingly with each passing hour the tummies of the pregnant grew larger. Jonger had supposed a gestation period of twenty days or so, but at the current rate of growth that would effectively immobilize both Pachola and Amargon a week before due date. The infant of Bailey and Vigdis, however, seemed to be developing even faster, and Averhill was compelled to revise Jonger's estimate to roughly ten days. Vigdis's preternatural physical strength made her burden easily manageable.

Driven by nervous energy, Bailey and Kayana often took walks along the shore, scuffing at shells and clumps of seaweed, watching sea birds—rather, bird analogs—dive into the water for edibles, and passing the time quietly, each with her own thoughts. On occasion, Averwell joined them. Not normally talkative, he sometimes found himself carrying the burden of the conversation.

"It's just a shell," Bailey said to him on one such walk.

"Yes, but what kind?" he replied. "Does it have any uses?"

Bailey gave a dry chuckle. "What use would it have? The creature eats whatever comes into its mouth when it's

193

in the water. It takes in air through gills. Afterwards, it excretes waste material and releases used air."

He cast the shell aside. "On some worlds, the linings of shelled sea creatures contain glands whose secretions are useful in making dyes."

"Averwell, it's a shell," Bailey said, with a touch of impatience. "The creature who inhabited it became some other creature's dinner. The shell itself is interesting in shape and in coloration. Maybe you should regard it according to those qualities."

Kayana touched her arm. "It's all right," she soothed. "He doesn't mean anything by his questions. Motoya is a new world for him."

"For you and me as well," said Bailey, calmer. "Sorry, Averwell. Although as often as you walk with us, perhaps we should change your name to Hoverwell."

He stopped on the dry sand. "Would you like me to leave?"

"I talk too much," Bailey muttered, contrite.

"In fact," he told her, "this is the most you've said on any of our walks."

"I'm just...I-I can't wait to hold our daughters. Idun Mia and Talilla."

He studied her face. "You've never had children of your own?"

"Certainly I have. Idun Mia and Talilla."

"No, I meant—"

"I know what you meant, Hoverwell. And, no. I just never met the right..." She looked away, blushing furiously.

"Would you like me to leave?" Kayana asked.

"No," said Bailey. "I think I'll take a dip in the ocean. It's as cold a shower as I'll get."

"I don't understand," said Averwell.

Bailey grinned. "That's probably just as well."

But Kayana had already stopped to look back at the huts. "It's Pachola, waving," she said, hushed. "She wants us. I think—"

"Oh, my God," cried Bailey. "It's time. It's *time*. Averwell—"

He ran off. "I'll just get my things," he threw over his shoulder, and almost stumbled over a low embankment.

With Kayana alongside her, Bailey dashed to her hut. She did not know what to expect to see. Did Vigdis's water break? Were there contractions, and how far apart? What she did not anticipate was the sight of a naked Vigdis squatting on the wood floor, several folded blankets and a pillow directly underneath her, all still dry, her hand poised to catch the newborn. The joyful smile on Vigdis's face gave Bailey an additional shock. No pain? How was that possible? This was *childbirth*.

Bailey and Pachola knelt down before her. "Vigdis?"

"Any moment now," she said.

Averwell rushed into the hut, carrying a black medical bag from which he was already extracting two clamps and a scalpel in order to cut the umbilical cord.

"No need," Vigdis told him. "It has already dissolved..."

Idun Mia's head appeared, followed by the slippery rest of her, deftly caught by Vigdis and laid gently on the pillow. There was no blood, and Bailey suspected that the placenta had also dissolved inside Vigdis.

On the pillow, Idun Mia rolled over and pushed herself up to hands and knees. Ever so slowly, she found a smile for each of them. Averwell dropped his medical bag and gaped at her.

"That's impossible," he gasped.

Bailey held out her hands, and Idun Mia crawled into them. Sobbing now, Bailey picked her up and cradled her in her arms. Tears added to the slippery and warm body. Bailey made little incoherent sounds. Pachola caressed the infant. To her and Bailey, Idun Mia said, "Mom." She then turned to Vigdis and repeated the word.

Still astounded, Averwell gently took the infant and wiped her completely with a medicated towel for newborns. Then he passed her to Vigdis.

"She has teeth," said Vigdis.

Kayana rummaged the supplies in the corner for a package of protein grains. This she mixed in a bowl with

195

water from a sun-warmed bottle, and passed it to Vigdis, who began to feed the infant. Idun Mia was patient with the rate of feeding, but still ravenous. When the bowl was empty, she said, "More?"

There was more.

No longer needed, Averwell quietly took his leave of them, with instructions to summon him immediately should a problem arise. After preparing a third bowl of gruel, Kayana departed as well. She was not dry-eyed.

"Oh, my God," breathed Bailey. "Vigdis, she's beautiful."

Idun Mia had been born with a full head of marigold hair and with eyes that at the moment were pale violet. Bailey wondered whether they would eventually darken. She saw very little baby fat on their daughter. Her skin was a uniform violet, two shades lighter than her eyes. Aside from that, her features were human.

Even as Vigdis fed her, she seemed to be growing. When the bowl was half-empty, Idun Mia took the spoon from Vigdis and began to feed herself. At first she held the spoon handle in a power grip, but soon shifted to the customary precision grip. The bowl scraped empty, she handed it to Vigdis.

Bailey had yet to dry her eyes. Still holding Idun Mia, Vigdis got up, took a moment to stretch, and nodded to Bailey and Pachola to follow her. The four of them made their way toward the ocean. After crossing the embankment, Vigdis set the child on the sand. For a few moments, Idun Mia stood very still. Then, carefully, she took a step, and another, and another, leaving little footprints in the sand as she gradually built up to walking speed. Bailey took a picture of them with her Palmetto, and filmed the child as she headed toward the froth left by the fading waves.

"Bailey," sighed Vigdis.

"Yeah."

Standing between Vigdis and Pachola, Bailey took their hands, and together they followed Idun Mia to where the froth hissed into the sand. There they watched Idun

Mia splashing and laughing. Tears of joy and hope continued to stream down Bailey's cheeks. She drew a long breath, exhaled slowly, and regained a modicum of control of her emotions.

"I never thought to see...," she began. She did not have to complete the thought.

"She's beautiful," said Pachola.

Bailey smiled. "You're next."

"A few more days. I wonder how long it will be before Talilla will be able to play with her."

Bailey did not respond. She hoped the blending of human and Motic DNA in Pachola would produce a child much like Idun Mia, able to crawl almost right away. The sonogram Averwell had administered to Pachola had been inconclusive regarding physical development. The limbs were present, and terminated in four digits, but whether the legs were strong enough for walking, or even for crawling, Averwell could not determine. But the vague musculature of the body overall suggested that Talilla would at least be able to swim and, perhaps, to crawl.

"Furniture," Bailey said abruptly. "We'd better arrange it. I don't mind sleeping on a stack of blankets, but Idun Mia..."

"I'll see to it," Pachola offered, and turned to leave them. "I know some places."

"How long before we go back into space?" asked Vigdis.

Briefly Bailey considered her answer. "I think we're at a good anchorage right here on Motoya."

"No more do-gooding?"

"Not for a while. We have children to rear."

"Michael—"

"Can wait," Bailey said shortly. She sighed, remembering. "When I first came out here, I don't know what I had in mind. I just fell into situations. I never, ever, expected to be a mommy. I'd abandoned that notion years ago. But now...now I have two women that I love, and two children—one still on the way—to raise and educate." She laughed lightly. "Of course, given the rate of development, that may take only a year or two."

"She's swimming," Vigdis pointed out. "Stay close to shore," she called.

"Is she invulnerable like you?" Bailey asked.

"Yes. But that doesn't mean she can't get into trouble." She looked toward the horizon. "Storm clouds. We should go back to the hut." She stepped further into the water. "Let's go home, Idun Mia."

The child took her hand.

A bed for Idun Mia had already arrived and been set up by the time they returned to the hut. The wind had picked up, swaying the trees. Their rhythmic movement gained the child's attention, but she asked no questions. Behind them billowed dark gray clouds, and already a mist of drizzle was visible out over the waves. More furniture soon came, transported on motor carts by two males whose bodies bore enough sawdust to confirm that they were carpenters. They delivered their cargo and departed just before the rains struck.

Wind rattled the two oceanside windows and the door, and whistled past the hut, but Idun Mia showed no sign of fear as she gazed out the window. "Storm," she said. And, "Rain." Lightning struck at the water's edge, and she flinched, backing away as thunder rattled the hut.

Bailey had a puzzled frown. "Where is she getting those words?"

"She is connected to me," Vigdis explained. "I am teaching her."

Bailey dropped to one knee beside Idun Mia. Not to be outdone in the matter of the child's education, she said, "That sound was thunder."

"Thunder. From the storm?"

"That's right. But not all storms have thunder and lightning."

"I am not afraid."

Bailey straightened. "Next thing you know, she'll be working quadratic equations. Vigdis...yes, she is developing at an accelerated rate, but I would hope she'll have a childhood."

"I will, Mom," said Idun Mia. She stood up straight; the top of her head reached halfway up Bailey's thigh. Her intensely yellow hair was a little longer now, and dry. Contentedly she looked up at Bailey with eyes that were still pale violet. The look on her face said that she was who she was.

"You," said Bailey, tousling the child's hair, "are going to take a lot of getting used to."

"And I am hungry."

Vigdis laughed. Bailey said, "I'll just put a whole cow on the rotisserie."

024: Abduction

Talilla and Marula were born at a depth of one meter in the ocean. While Averwell fretted, unable to be of much assistance with the delivery, the two infants went through the motions of swimming, but with little success. From time to time they totally immersed themselves, and came up sputtering, spitting water. Though they had no gills, they had the genetic memory of them. But Pachola and Amargon kept close watch over them.

As planned, both infants had the physical appearance of the Motic, with two middle fingers between two opposable thumbs on each hand, pale blue skin and indigo hair, sapphire eyes, and nose flaps whose use they gradually mastered. Yet there were differences between the two. The blue skin and hair of Marula was tinted with a pale purple, a contribution from Kayana. The blue skin of Talilla was much paler, and the angle of the sunlight sometimes made her appear tanned. Her hair, like Bailey's, was black. Finally, Talilla was visibly the taller of the two.

By evening on the second day of their birth, both children had learned to walk, hold their breath underwater, and make several sounds that were distinguishable as words. Their acceptance of Idun Mia was total, even to splashing her and being splashed by her while they cavorted in the waves. The five parents gathered on the beach to watch over them, and Averwell usually hovered nearby, ready to render aid if necessary.

"You are still incredulous," Vigdis observed, as Bailey stood shaking her head.

"The children are more than human or Motic," she replied. "I can explain their growth that way. But the truth is that they defy explanation. And I have no wish to dwell on that. Idun Mia and Talilla are our daughters, Vigdis, and just as they have aunts in Amargon and Kayana, so too are you and Pachola and I aunts to Marula."

"But we are mothers first," said Kayana.

Bailey sighed happily. "Oh, yeah."

Still, she kept her worries private. The spiral arm was a dangerous place. She had no idea what Michael's plans were regarding what he probably considered as hybrids. The suspicion she had felt earlier regarding his motives had not diminished over time. After all, Michael himself had dispatched them to Volonya, even though he had to know they had already decided to go there for the DNA implants. But what did he want? What did he expect of her and her crew? Or was his focus the children, the offspring of combined species? If that was his focus, what did it portend for her daughters...for their daughters?

"Michael," she growled softly, the warning of a feral creature.

Vigdis just looked at her, without question or comment. A dismissive gesture from Bailey returned her attention to the splashing children. In that moment, Motoya had become an idyllic world where one could have relationships and raise a family without fear of violence. Ocnorb was doing his job, returning as many Motics as he could to their home world. She felt at peace.

A dark side of her feared that peace would not endure.

"You're somber," observed Vigdis.

"When something is too good to be true," she said, leaving the sentence unfinished.

"At the risk of spouting a cliché, one day at a time."

Bailey drew a long breath that straightened her shoulders and brought her erect. Thus strengthened, she exhaled slowly. Her life seemed to have reached a point of stability. After five post-apocalyptic years and half a year of armed do-gooding, the time had come to settle in. The storms on the horizon could wait. Even now, one had begun to gather in the distance. She gave Vigdis a gentle nudge, and together with Pachola they gathered up Idun Mia and Talilla and led them back to the hut. Kayana and Amargon followed with Marula. Another day was approaching its end.

Inside the hut, the five adults settled around a table onto chairs befitting their respective sizes. Talilla, not quite as advanced in growth as Idun Mia, had trouble

201

wielding the spoon in her protein gruel, but she resisted all attempts by Pachola to assist her. Idun Mia did not so much eat as devour her dish of grains, processed meat, and a small pile of fresh local greens that vaguely resembled chopped spinach. Zenille, Pachola called the recipe, and declared it healthy, though Bailey, after sticking her finger into the mass and then touching it to her tongue, had reservations regarding its taste.

While they finished up their repast, the storm struck. Winds rattled the sides and the door, and tree branches swept over the roof. Already the three children were accustomed to the sounds, even to those of thunder, and showed no sign of fear. Talilla struggled to form words, and finally said, "Loud."

Rain spattered the roofing tile with a sound that reminded Bailey of military drumming. The rhythm of it began to make her drowsy. After assisting with the post-meal clean-up, she stretched out on one of the extended sleeping pads along the back wall, snuggled up to her pillow, and closed her eyes. After a moment or two she was jostled. A quick peek revealed that Idun Mia and Talilla had joined her. Growing children though they were, they continued to show what Bailey thought of as their toddler side, as they sought safety and security with their mothers. Soon enough, Vigdis and Pachola were added, forming a mass of bodies with the adults surrounding the children. Bailey drifted off to sleep.

Bailey awoke to the breaking dawn, and to Talilla curled up against her. A hand on the child's back brought a contented sound from her but did not awaken her. On the other side, Pachola had already awakened and was watching Bailey.

"Another day," whispered the Motic.

Bailey lifted her head to look around. On the other side of Pachola slept Idun Mia and Vigdis. The latter did not require sleep, but had shut herself down to set an example for Idun Mia. Bailey wondered whether she too would be able to shut herself down, and whether she was now feigning sleep because she did not know what else to do.

I'm the mother of a child computer, thought Bailey, and laughed lightly. Idun Mia opened one eye to look at her, but said nothing, and soon returned to whatever state she had been in. Bailey's ruminations continued. Despite her military training and subsequent survival on a ruined Earth, she retained what she considered her maternal instincts. Two daughters, she now had, and with her lovers nurtured them. Most unexpected. And what was expected of her as a mother? She had not been trained for this. Motherhood was learn-by-doing. That frightened her. She had entered a vast and unknown territory that until now she had not even realized existed.

Dawn continued to break, but suddenly there came additional light. Michael had arrived, and he had moved Bailey outside toward the shore, well away from the others.

Bailey's heart thudded. What did he want of her? Of more concern, what did he have to say that the others could not hear?

He was sitting on the damp grass with one leg extended and the other drawn up into the embrace of his arms. He was gazing out at the sea, not looking at Bailey. She made herself as comfortable as possible on the water-chilled grass, her attention alternately on him and on the waves.

"If you've nothing more," she said, "I'd rather be with my family."

"Most unusual offspring."

She did not care for the tone of his voice. "Michael," she said, her tone a warning.

"Doctor Jonger has previously enabled births between two races, but they were very closely compatible in terms of DNA. The equivalent to which you will perhaps relate would be a joining between a Neandertal and a Homo sapiens. Which did in fact occur repeatedly on the Earth of, say, 50,000 years ago."

"I don't think I like where this is going, Michael."

He shrugged, and still would not look at her.

"I would like to run—"

She whirled to glare at him. "No."

"...some tests."

"No! No fucking way, Michael."

"Especially on Idun Mia," he went on, as if she had not objected. "She is unique. In fact, the relationship that birthed her was unique. In all the history of the galaxy there has never been a being like her."

"She's not a being, Michael," Bailey hissed. "She is a child, a little girl, and my daughter with Vigdis. She is not a lab rat."

"Nor would she be treated as one."

"What the fuck are you, Michael?" she yelled. "At first I thought you were some sort of godlike being, with unimaginable powers. But you're not, are you." It was not a question. "You're just a higher level of creature with some higher powers, who views all the lower levels of people as your laboratory, where you can move people around to deal with certain situations." She paused, a harsh and hard expression on her face. "Go back to your history of Earth, and look up Doctor Mengele. That's who you are, Michael. Mengele experimented on children and to hell with their parents."

"She and the other two would not be harmed—"

"Now where have I heard that lie before? No, Michael Mengele. The answer is no. Now, if you don't have a special project for us—and you shouldn't, because right now we're all on maternity leave, and you can look up that term on Earth as well—I'm going back to the hut and try to raise my daughters without having to think about you."

Bailey stood up and stalked back to the hut. At the open door, a quick glance over her shoulder revealed that Michael had vanished.

She looked inside. So had Idun Mia.

Bailey's initial reaction was to rush back to the grass and curse Michael with everything she knew and some she made up. But fear and rage eventually exhausted themselves, and she was left with an arctic calm and a grim, foreboding determination. She thought,

204

as she slowly trod back to the hut, her knees shaking, that Michael needed to be taught the lesson of mother bears and cubs. She would be the teacher.

Vigdis met her in the doorway. "I know," she said quietly. "Michael, of course."

"Very computerly analytic of you," groused Bailey, brushing past her.

Vigdis caught Bailey's shoulder and spun her around. "Not so. I am in *mother* mode now. Idun Mia is *my* daughter, too. She is *our* daughter. Anticipating your request, I have already begun searching for every scrap of information I can find regarding The Commission. Unless I am very much mistaken about you, Bailey Belvedere, you are now at war. Bailey Belvedere, so am I."

"And I," each of the other three declared.

Vigdis nodded with satisfaction. "And what is our goal?" she asked.

"Get Idun Mia back," Bailey stated with utter finality. "Kill the others."

"So it is writ," Vigdis said solemnly. "So it shall be done."

025: Radio Silence

With the decision made, the five adults and two children boarded the *Skygnat* and went into null-space. Not that they would be secure there from Michael, but Vigdis had a plan that she refused to disclose to anyone, not for lack of trust, but because Michael and the other members of The Commission were unable to read her thoughts. All she would tell the others was that she was upgrading.

The two children grew restless, as children do, and began playing with a ball in the gangway. The echoes of bouncing rubber soon reverberated onto the bridge, as did their cries of glee or disappointment. Whatever the game they were playing, it was incomprehensible to the adults. With nothing to do, Pachola and Amargon retired to their stateroom and, with one ear each open for the children, began to snooze. All the while, Vigdis sprawled in her port captain's chair, eyes closed, and shut herself off from the rest of the universe. Which left Bailey to commiserate with Kayana.

"We've come a long way since you ransacked my jeep," she told the Harlanger, but she smiled while she spoke.

Still, the words saddened Kayana on the murphy bench, and Bailey quickly apologized. Without words, they both knew that she was thinking of her twin brother Vattar.

Kayana dismissed the apology with a shake of her head. "You did what you had to do. And I am no longer the person I was. I keep the memories I wish to keep, the pleasant ones." She shot a look at Vigdis. "What do you suppose she is doing?"

Deflection was needed, thought Bailey. The question might alert the ears of The Commission. "She's probably trying to find a language The Commission doesn't speak."

"I guess that makes sense. I wonder—"

"Stop wondering."

"Yes, of course." For a moment she considered. "I think I would like to eat a waffle at Gerrell's restaurant on Lanna Lost. I hope he's doing well."

"Yeah. And he's a lot safer than he was on Earth."

"We've done some good, Bailey Belvedere."

"We're not done yet, my friend."

Vigdis abruptly sat up straight. "I have to go into the computer," she said, and vanished without another word.

The action went almost unnoticed, and elicited a simple "Hmm" from Bailey, as if this sort of thing happened often. At the same time, she tensed, for the transfer meant that Vigdis was onto something. Immediately she cleared her mind of that, lest The Commission detect the hope in her heart.

"We promised him real maple syrup," said Kayana, with light-hearted irrelevance. She continued the banter in support of Bailey's concern that The Commission would overhear. "We made one trip, and it might be time for another. And maybe some real butter, if we can find it."

"Two minutes," she said. She did not have to explain what she was timing.

Kayana got up. "The girls are quiet," she said. "I'd better go check on them."

"Parenting 101."

The Harlanger gave a light and puzzled laugh. "What's that?"

"Class at university. Never mind. Go, go."

Alone, Bailey shut her eyes and employed a meditative breathing technique to shut her mind down. It was a simple enough measure. She saw before her a black circle. Slowly it grew larger, engulfing her to enclose her in darkness and in sleep. But the circle was unable to complete the envelopment. A part of her resisted. A worry about...but she withheld the name from her lips and from her mind. Despite the failure of the black circle, she felt a little more relaxed.

"Eight minutes," she muttered. Since Vigdis had emerged from the *Skygnat*'s computer, she had never returned into it for so long a time. What was she doing in there? Bailey longed to ask her, but was afraid of disrupting whatever process now involved Vigdis.

Kayana returned with Talilla in tow. "Marula is asleep with Amargon and Pachola," she said.

Talilla climbed onto Bailey's lap, and cuddled there contentedly.

"No sign?" asked Kayana, this a reference to Vigdis.

"Not a peep. Eleven minutes now."

Kayana put a hand to her head. "I feel funny."

Bailey's brow bunched. "So do I...but it's passing. I wonder..." But she dared not complete the thought.

At the fourteen-minute mark Vigdis appeared in the port captain's chair. Her lips puffed out with her sigh. "We're safe," she breathed.

Relieved, Bailey nevertheless said, "From?"

"Give me a moment. That was exhausting."

"I'll get coffee," said Kayana.

"Are you all right?" Bailey worried.

Vigdis nodded hesitantly, but made no sound other than a second sigh. Kayana returned with three mugs, which she distributed before returning to the murphy bench. Bailey was crawling with curiosity now, but held her peace, uncertain whether it was safe now to think.

Vigdis's lips fumbled for words. Finally she said in a rusty voice, "I'll have to go back in."

Exasperated by the lack of information, Bailey said, "Vigdis, *what* did you *do* in there?"

She swallowed some coffee before answering. "The entire hull of *Skygnat* is enveloped in a gravitomagnetic deflection field," she explained. "Do you want the math?"

"Is it more complex than differential equations?" said Bailey, impatient now. "Never mind. No, I don't want the math."

"We can refer to it as a GMD for point of reference," Vigdis went on. "In simple terms, nothing gets past the field. Weapons fire, supernovas, telepathic projections, nothing."

"Supernovas?" said Bailey, eyebrows raised.

"Not even black holes. You see, as long as the GMD is activated, whether in null-space or realtime, *Skygnat* and her contents are no longer a part of existence." She looked apologetic. "It was the only way to block Michael."

Bailey stood up, and deposited Talilla on the deck. "*That*'s what I wanted to hear," she broke in.

"The rest is mostly side-effect. There is a drawback: in order to leave the ship once we downdock, we have to shut off the GMD." Quickly she raised a hand. "Before you ask, we shut it off, go outside, and reactivate the field by Palmetto."

"I was just about to say," said Bailey.

"I know." She drained half her mug. "So we are safe from Michael, as long as this field envelops us. The task now is to make Michael and the others unsafe from us. That is why I have to go back in."

"Something in your tone tells me you don't want to do this."

Vigdis nodded. "It's not dangerous so much as it is exhausting. The number of calculations per second that I must perform to create the device is...I'm trying not to think about it. I had to create upgrades just to do them. Bailey, this is a new generation of technology, and we are the only ones to possess it." Now she was downcast. "With one exception."

Breath left Bailey with the implication. She wanted to cry. "Idun Mia eventually could develop it as well," she said somberly. "Oh, God, not Idun Mia."

"I am sorry, Bailey Belvedere, but we cannot allow her to be used that way."

Bailey's eyes rounded with horror. "Wait. Are you suggesting that we...?"

"Not at all," Vigdis said quickly. "But we do have to get her away from The Commission. And to do that, I have to go back inside."

"When?" asked Bailey, resigned.

She smiled. "After some time in your stateroom."

The implication in her words chilled Bailey. "You're saying goodbye," she gasped.

Vigdis inclined her head. "There is some chance that I will become dissociated, to the point that I can no longer function in my computer or human capacity, ever."

"I won't allow it," cried Bailey. She grabbed Vigdis by the shoulders and shook her. Vigdis did not resist. "You can't do this. I order you not to. I *order* you—"

Gently Vigdis disengaged from her. "There is no other way," she said softly. "If I do not do this, we may all die, and hopefully there will be enough of the human left in me to meet you on the Far Shore." She turned to Kayana. "Will you watch Talilla while we are away?"

"Of course," said Kayana, wiping her eyes.

In the event, there was no physical expression of love, only an unceasing veil of tears that Vigdis in her human mode shed as well. Bailey's no's and why's elicited no comfort for her grief. Vigdis tried to reassure her. "It probably won't come to this," she told Bailey. "But there is the risk. I love you too much, Bailey Belvedere, to leave you to the rest of what light is left, wandering and wondering."

"H-how long?" Bailey sobbed.

"I think...if I do not have a weapon by this time tomorrow...I won't make it back. If I do not return to my port captain's chair by then... Bailey, if you cannot save Idun Mia..."

"We will die together. Build a bonfire on that beach, so we know where to find you."

Vigdis wiped her face; it failed to dry her tears. "I will. Bailey Belvedere..."

"And I you, Vigdis."

Vigdis vanished.

026: Vigil

Desolation followed the departure of Vigdis. Bailey lay sprawled on her berth, eyes dry at the moment, for she had exhausted her supply of tears. A line from Kipling found its way from her memory bank back into her consciousness. It was a reference to the bond between humans and dogs, but she adapted it to the present grief. "...it is hardly fair to risk your heart for a woman to tear." Fair, no. But Bailey had not a single regret, and never mind that the "woman" in question was computer-generated, yet human for all that. Such a short time they had known one another. Lines from Longfellow came next, bursting through her defenses uninvited. "On the ocean of life we pass and speak one another, only a look and a voice, then darkness again and a silence."

"Oh, God," she moaned, and the tears flowed once more.

Sometime later—she knew not how long—a soft knock sounded at her stateroom door. When she did not respond, Pachola slid the door open and stepped into the room. Shutting it behind her, she made directly for Bailey. There she sat down hard, jostling her.

"And just what is wrong with you?" the Motic demanded.

Bailey spun on her. "Don't you talk to me like that!" She thumbed tears from her eyes; it did not help.

"You are my love and my mentor," Pachola said quietly. "I am one of the mothers of our child. You are the other. So I speak the truth. This you know."

"Pachola, don't. Just...don't."

"I love you too much not to. I tell you that Vigdis the computer continues to monitor everything aboard *Skygnat.* Including your murmurings a moment ago of what she tells me is poetry. Poetry? At a time like this? But you know the answer to that. In our talks, you have given me an appreciation of many subjects, one of which is poetry. How it can calm the heart. How it can give focus to what you have to do. This you taught me. I did not

211

know of *Invictus*, but Vigdis assures me that a line or so is relevant to you. So I tell it to you now."

Bailey turned away. "I know the poem. I know what you are about to say."

"Do you? I told it to myself as well, for I, too, love Vigdis. This is not what she would want of me. Is it what she would want of you?"

"Pachola," moaned Bailey. Her voice shook. She swallowed hard the lump of words caught in her throat.

"Under the bludgeonings of chance—"

"My head is bloody, but unbowed. I know, Pachola," she said wearily. "I know."

"There's another line," Pachola went on. "The line, the declaration, that ends it. 'I am the captain of my soul.' You are the captain of *Skygnat*, Bailey Belvedere. Should you now confine yourself to solitude, abandoning your ship? I tell you there is a little girl in my stateroom, calling for her mommies. Are you too far gone to answer?"

Tears continued to trickle down Bailey's cheeks, but this time when she wiped them away, they ceased flowing. Hands clenched to stones against grief and worry, she took a few breaths in her struggle to regain herself. Tenderly, Pachola took her hand and helped Bailey to her feet.

"No more poetry for you," said Bailey, with mock severity, as they made for the door.

Talilla brightened when they entered. The sight of her was all that Bailey needed. The girl's pale blue skin fairly glowed with joy. She ran to Bailey and clutched at her legs until she was lifted up and hugged. The three of them moved to the berth and sat down. No words were spoken now, for none were needed. There was only the waiting.

Presently Amargon and Marula came to join them. Five now, they crowded one another on the berth. But none of them had to wait alone.

Eventually, as in all vigils, a break was needed. Talilla and Marula did not have the words; they knew only that something was not right. Inquiring after Vigdis, they

212

were told that she was working. This seemed to satisfy them. Mugs of tofu miso were allowed to cool before distribution to the children. They stared at the matte-black in the Videx and sipped slowly. More at ease now, Bailey reclined in her captain's chair and collected herself for the coming tasks.

"We need a target," she said. "Where does The Commission hold conferences, and is it the same location where they are holding Idun Mia?" She glanced at the computer speaker and for a moment hesitated before asking, "Vigdis, have you answers for us?"

"The Commission is known to gather in three locations. The most likely is Bedlinge in the Fullu System. The only known laboratory associated with The Commission is located there as well. With Idun Mia undergoing analyses and experimentation, it is most likely that The Commission in its entirety will be present there. It is of course possible that one or two members may have other tasks elsewhere. Shall I set course for Bedlinge?"

"Not yet," said Bailey. "Our location here is secure while we wait for Vigdis to return. If she does not..." She steadied herself with a deep breath. "If she does not, then we go. Travel time to Bedlinge?"

"One hour fifty-two minutes. I shall skip the points."

"Wisely avoided. Vigdis, if...if necessary, can we acquire a thermonuclear device?"

"Oppenheimer's Mushroom Emporium should have some in stock."

Bailey laughed. "Why, Vigdis. A sense of humor?"

"Part of my mission is the morale of the crew."

"Yes, of course. So can we acquire one?"

"I believe so. But it would be easier to steal one from the Emporium."

Bailey frowned. "Is that possible?"

"I believe I can manage a quick in and out, if necessary."

"In and out, Vigdis?"

"I materialize us in the warehouse, we grab one or two devices and take them aboard, and we leave. Half a minute, once I determine the precise location."

213

Amargon spoke up. "Will we be able to activate the devices?"

"That is unknown. They may be security locked. But I believe I can override that."

"All right, Vigdis, that is your assignment," Bailey ordered. "Obtain one and if possible two thermonuclear devices and learn how to detonate them simultaneously. Update me on progress."

Bailey leaned back in her chair, pondering. She had just given the initial instructions for crossing the Rubicon. How apt the metaphor! Caesar had decided to challenge the authority of Rome. The authority she had begun to challenge was far more powerful and far more vengeful. Not that it mattered. If Vigdis proved unable to develop a Commission-killing weapon, they would have to take their chances on a massive thermonuclear explosion. An explosion she did not intend to survive.

The confidence in and loyalty to herself left her unable even to consider whether to involve the others—friends and children—in the explosion. She needed, therefore, a place to drop them off, where they would be safe even if the explosion did not succeed. Lanna Lost, then. Perhaps Gerrell would help them find work and a place to live...to hide. At least they would have waffles to eat.

Bailey discovered that she was unable to fall asleep. When the children started yawning, she dismissed them all to their staterooms. The vigil was now hers. A death watch? On Earth, during TFA, she had prayed not at all, being too busy trying to stay alive. Now she recognized the incongruity—when under attack, the *first* thing one should do is pray. But what to pray for? In Gethsemane, she recalled, Jesus had prayed that a cup might pass from him—meaning his imminent torture and death. But he was obedient; he had been sent to die. How could she do any less?

Still...

She spoke in soft, reverent tones, just in case she still had a voice for the ear of the almighty.

"I would rather not have to do this. You threw the money-changers from the temple. I would throw The Commission out of power. And there is only one way to do that. I would rather not have to do what I may be about to do. If there is another way, please reveal it to me."

There was, as she had expected, no response. But that meant nothing. If it were not the will of the almighty, then she would be stopped.

She wondered what the resolution would be. She marveled that she had begun to believe again, as she had as a child. *Now I lay me down to sleep.* She recalled the beginning of that nightly prayer. She recalled the rest of the words.

If I should die before I wake.

Perhaps it would not come to that...

Two hours had passed. Bailey's mind had been nothing more than an empty book, waiting for someone to inscribe words on the paper. Having dozed off, she blinked herself awake. How much more time, Vigdis? She checked: seven more hours and some points. This time, the points were significant. She thought Vigdis would laugh at her.

Hunger reminded Bailey that she was still alive. She padded to the galley and prepared a sandwich. It might have been a BLT, with a sort of leafy thing, a slice of some red and juicy fruit, and surely that could not be bacon. Only the mayo was real. She cut the sandwich in half, and began to gnaw at it. Only after she had devoured both halves did it occur to her that she ought to have lightly toasted the bread.

A trip to her stateroom was indicated. When she emerged from the alcove, a light blinded her, and left her blinking away the phosphorescent spots. Michael, sitting on her berth, came into focus. And she was unarmed.

He actually smiled. The fiend actually smiled!

She licked her dried lips. "How did you get in here?"

"I never left. Bailey..."

"If you stand up, it is to leave. Otherwise, I will fight you."

"I would rather sit with you," he said.

215

"That'll happen," she snorted derisively.

"Please."

Bailey was unable to resist that tone. She sat down, but at the head of the berth, leaving him in control of the foot. There was no point in speaking, for she had nothing to say to him. She waited. Six more hours and points. Then he and perhaps she would be silent forever.

He said nothing.

Time passed. She resisted the urge to reach out and throttle him. He seemed lost in contemplation. Oblivious of her temptation? Or was he too powerful to consider her even the slightest threat?

He sighed, long and brokenly, as if in a series of exhalations.

"Idun Mia is perfectly all right, aside from—"

Her hands clenched to stones. "Say one more word, damn you!"

He made a little gesture; her hands unclenched. "Please hear me out, Bailey Belvedere. You cannot harm me, but in the attempt you may well harm yourself. Please hear me out."

"I don't appear to have much choice," she growled, staring down at her open hands. "But I promise you I will find a way—"

"You'll try. I know. And your present plan to kill us all will succeed if attempted. We have powers, but we are in no way gods. We are simply advanced beings. But that is not why I am here. May I speak?"

"You seem to be doing so."

"Aside from separation from you," he went on, as if there had been no interlude. "No experiments or tests have been conducted on her, except that she has developed a fondness for chocolate ice cream."

Despite her outrage, Bailey managed a tight laugh.

"Earlier in your new career I told you two things of significance. The first is that The Commission cannot be everywhere at once. That lies well outside our powers. Further, we are not always aware of difficulties in the galaxy. Sometimes we learn about them too late for resolution. That is why we have you. People like you. Not

216

many, to be sure. It takes a special kind of person to help us govern. Govern, Bailey Belvedere, not rule.

"The second is that I said you have the potential to become one of the best, if not *the* best, operatives ever for The Commission. That has proven out, as you would say, in spades." He chuckled. "Or better yet, no-trump. The bridge reference is apt. The Commission is proud of you and most pleased with your work. As am I."

Eyes hot now, she whirled on him. "What?" she gasped.

"Although I must say the decision to impregnate your computer was most unexpected. For this reason, more than any other, we increased our surveillance on you, to learn where this was leading. Contrary to what you think, we would never harm Idun Mia."

"What?" she said, softer now.

"A moment, then." He made another little gesture. She wondered whether it was necessary for him to do so. Perhaps it was like the Jedis gestured, for show in the films, signifying nothing, for the command had already been transmitted.

Another bright light filled the stateroom. Emerging from it was Idun Mia.

She was now about the size and shape of a human adolescent. A good five feet tall, at least. Her marigold hair was long enough to cascade over her shoulders, and her eyes were now a rich violet. She was wearing a simple lilac shift that swirled around her knees as she dashed for Bailey.

"Mommy!" she cried, and as Bailey shot to her feet Idun Mia collided with her, wrapped her arms and legs around her, and together they fell back onto the berth.

Repeatedly Bailey kissed the girl's neck, and murmured lovingly to her, though later she could not remember the soft words she had spoken. She clung tightly to Idun Mia, savoring the reality of her. And all the while, Michael sat in utter silence.

Eventually they separated, with Idun Mia swinging around to sit between Bailey and Michael—further proof to

Bailey that the girl was unafraid of him. She slipped an arm around Idun Mia's shoulders and drew her closer.

"Michael tells me you like ice cream."

She nodded vigorously. "Especially chocolate."

There wasn't, Bailey reflected, a child in the universe who did not care for chocolate. "We don't have any on board," she said. "But I'm sure we can find some. Meanwhile...I'd like to talk with Michael. Why don't you go to Pachola's stateroom and play with Talilla?"

"All right, Mommy," said Idun Mia. She slid off the berth and strode to the door.

Bailey said one word after the door closed. "Vigdis?" In the tone behind the word lurked a danger that even Michael could not ignore.

"I have spoken with her," he said quickly. "She has agreed, albeit reluctantly, to put a hold on her efforts until you and I have had a chance to talk. I will concede you this, Bailey Belvedere: what she wants to do, will work on us. You need not resort to thermonuclear devices. The question is: do you still want her to develop the wave generator, as she calls it? Before you answer, please know that The Commission is terrified of her efforts. She, and you, went far beyond what they had anticipated."

Bailey lifted a hand, stopping him, as realization set in. "You bastard! This was all a test, wasn't it? You never intended to run tests on Idun Mia. You wanted to do the worst thing in the world to Vigdis and myself, to see how we would react. I should kill you for that alone."

"Yes, Bailey, it was all a test. You performed beyond our wildest expectations. Before we go further, I ask that the wave generator program be terminated permanently. This is not something we want loose in the galaxy."

"If I trusted you, Michael, I might agree."

"There will be no more tests," he said solemnly. "If you feel you have reason to suspect otherwise, then proceed as you were. We will not stop you."

"It still comes down to trust, Michael."

"I know. And time. It also comes down to time."

"Where will you be?"

"Busy," he said. "We are limited in personnel and maxed out in matters that require our attention. However, if you need my kind of help, you already have it on board."

She thought about that. Not Vigdis, and not yet Idun Mia. "Hoverwell?"

"And before you ask, yes, he will report to us not only about the progress and growth of Idun Mia, but also of Talilla and Maruna. Just report, no tests. You can understand our curiosity, our interest in three unique lives."

"A spy on board." Frowning, she shook her head. "Do I have a choice?"

"You do."

"Oh." Bailey fell silent for a moment, then spoke incisively. "His life depends on no tests. There will be no second chance. Our children are too precious for experiments."

"I think you'll find him to be solicitous and of help when, if, the time comes." He stood up. "Bailey...travel well, you and yours."

He vanished in a burst of light. When the light faded, Vigdis was standing there.

027: Vigilantes

The collision of Vigdis and Bailey was audible. The silence of relief between them was broken only by expulsions of breath in their tight embrace. By the time they drew apart from each other, the shoulder top of Vigdis's green pullover was darkened with tears. More relief made Bailey tremble.

"I thought I'd never see you again," Bailey said hoarsely. "Are you all right?"

"Oh, yes. I knew I would be, an hour into the process. But I couldn't break out temporarily to let you know."

Bailey's eyes narrowed. "And the wave generator? Did you cache all your progress and notes?"

"Of course. You always keep a weapon around until the adversary proves that you don't need to—unlikely, in this case."

She reached for Bailey's hand. Anticipating a move to the berth, she turned in that direction. Vigdis stopped her. "As much as I would like to," she said, "and with Pachola as well, I think we should go and bring the others up to date."

A light chuckle trickled out of Bailey. "Of course. What *was* I thinking?"

They found the rest of the crew—which included the children—in Pachola's stateroom. The children were playing a game comprehensible only to themselves, consisting of tapping each other's fists in an obscure sequence. Pachola, Amargon, and Kayana perched on the berth, watching them with befuddled amusement. Averwell was standing in a corner, anxious for his reception and his acceptance. They looked expectantly at Bailey when she and Vigdis entered.

Gazing at them all, Bailey found herself unable to stop moisture from gathering in her eyes. Her thoughts went back to the previous four years, when all hope of a normal life, with a career, a husband, and children had dissipated like so much dandelion fluff in the wind.

During those four years she had fought for her life, fought hard and held her own against the darkness that meant to envelop all those still alive on the planet. An event totally unforeseen had saved her. With the help of others—yes, including Michael, bastard though he was—she had found herself.

Had found herself.

Defined as a woman, a career U.S. Army Intelligence Officer, a desperate survivor, a spaceship's captain, and an armed do-gooder, she was now able to dismiss all those in favor of a composite title: Bailey Belvedere. And now she had a purpose.

"Details later," she told them. "For now, we are and will remain in The Commission's good graces. Sometimes we will receive assignments; otherwise, we will find them ourselves. We're going to stick our noses into adverse situations and bring them aright. As for you, Hoverwell—"

"Do you *have* to call me that?" he protested.

"Averwell...there are some things—"

He held up a hand. "I know, I know. Intimate relationships must be consensual."

Bailey gasped. "What? No! Well, yeah, but... Hoverwell, what the hell were you thinking?"

He waved dismissively. "It's not important. You were saying?"

"What? Oh...your loyalty is to the ship, the crew, and myself. If you find you cannot abide that, you are expected to leave. And this is the only time I will say that. There will be no further advisory, only action."

"Understood. But I assure you I—"

"No assurances. Just do it." She included the others back into her attention. "As for what happens now, you lot, on Motoya there's this beach..."

Milton Keynes UK
Ingram Content Group UK Ltd.
UKHW020816080824
446708UK00027BA/424